THE RISING OF THE SHIELD HERO

20

Aneko Yusagi

Naofumi Iwatani

Raphtalia

R'yne

"Shield Bash!"

shouted my assailant
in the full-body armor
as he unleashed a skill
toward me with a heavy thunk.

Table of Contents

Prologue: Believing Sloth Will Save the World

"So, Naofumi, you're planning on making a trip back to the world you're responsible for, huh?" Kizuna asked me.

"That's right," I replied with a nod. "After the warning from S'yne's sister, it seems pretty prudent." We were currently in the council chamber in L'Arc's castle, holding an emergency meeting. The cause was simple—the night before, S'yne's sister had made a sudden surprise visit right here, to our main base of operations and the heart of her enemy, and had a very revealing chat with me. I was now sharing the content of my encounter with everyone else—however, I had also learned that S'yne believed in a peculiar jinx that she thought applied to her, and so she hadn't shared all of the pertinent details with us.

S'yne was a hero and the holder of the sewing kit vassal weapon, hailing from a world that had already been destroyed by the waves. She always seemed intently focused on protecting me and was a sworn enemy of her sister, who was currently fighting for the other side—the same sister who had been causing so much trouble for us recently.

"We are pushing back pretty nicely at the moment, so there is perhaps leeway for you to leave for a while," Glass pondered.

"But I would also like to just push through and end this." I could see where she was going—wanting to bring the whole world together, take down the stubborn enemy nations who continued to deny the truth, and then all work together to end the waves. She was right—those villains who sought to seize the opportunity provided by this chaos to try and take over the world using the holy and vassal weapons did need to be eradicated. When put another way, of course, we were trying to take over the world ourselves—but we weren't plotting to invade other worlds, and the holy and vassal weapons were lending us their power of their own volition. So we were objectively better than the guys forcing the weapons to comply. Those guys were also the ones who started using them for warfare in the first place. Kizuna, Glass, and L'Arc never would have used them to fight other people. Our allies were working to protect this world. They certainly weren't going around invading left and right.

"It would be nice if S'yne's sister is just making all this up. But the only way to confirm that is to go see for ourselves," I concluded.

"She is a tricky one . . ." muttered Lyno. Lyno was a resident of the world to which I'd been summoned and was a member of a special forces unit that had been operating under orders from the queen of Melromarc. Her unit was comprised of like-minded people—possessed of a deep hatred for Bitch. Lyno had been acting as a spy, pursuing Bitch's actions.

Yesterday, when the one holding the harpoon vassal weapon and one of the vanguards of the waves—or as I was now calling them, the resurrected—launched an assault on the Demon Dragon's castle, Lyno had appeared alongside Bitch. Then Lyno seized the perfect opportunity to fatally injure Bitch while also taking back the whip seven star weapon in the process. This certainly made her the MVP among my allies at the moment—even more so because Bitch had been provided with an enhanced accessory that was intended to prevent her vassal weapon from being stolen. But prior to the battle Lyno had switched it out, allowing the whip to be taken. This was a woman who got shit done.

We both also shared a common goal: to cause as much pain to Bitch as possible prior to killing her. I took a moment to consider if any of my allies had ever been quite on the same wavelength as me before. Raphtalia was willing to help out but she certainly wasn't as into the whole revenge thing as hard as I was.

Raphtalia had told me that she saw Lyno as "Ruft II." I wasn't sure what that meant.

For a moment it had looked like that goal had been achieved, but Bitch was under a protection from our enemies that allowed her to be revived so long as her soul remained intact. So actually, she still managed to get away with her life even after the physical death of her body. Based on the pattern so far, I was pretty sure she would show up again at some point.

"What can you tell us about S'yne's sister?" I asked Lyno.

"She loves the sound of her own voice. But now that I reflect on it, she never uses that voice to talk about herself. My investigation didn't turn up much useful information in that regard," Lyno admitted.

"I see . . ." I muttered. Yesterday we had also defeated the resurrected who had been using the harpoon vassal weapon, successfully recovering the ofuda and harpoon vassal weapons and the whip seven star weapon. That meant the only holy weapons remaining in the hands of the enemy in Kizuna's world were the jewels and blunt instrument, and the only vassal weapon was the ship. The issue was they were held by the sworn enemies of S'yne, who had now holed themselves up in the castle of the kingdom of the resurrected who had held the harpoon vassal weapon.

"Also, I really hate her name and so I don't want to say it ever again," Lyno said.

"She never seems to want to share it with us and I hate using people's names anyway," I replied.

"You should use people's names," Raphtalia chided, but I was happy to ignore her. I had my nickname system and it worked for me. If I said "S'yne's sister," everyone knew who I was talking about, and that's all that mattered.

"In all fairness, she was very kind to me. I can't stand her name, but she seemed to be quite a decent person. The rest of them over there are like some kind of cult, either totally obsessed with a hero and trusting them implicitly or looking for an axe to grind," Lyno reported, sounding sick of the lot of them. To me, it sounded like confirmation of another one of the resurrected and his harem.

"Like Takt and his allies?" I asked.

"Yes, you can consider them to be something like that but on a much larger scale. Regrettably, I was unable to ever meet with the one who is actually in charge . . ." Lyno's spy activities had placed her as an ally of Bitch, restricting her access to information outside of that circle. This was easier to understand when cross-referenced with the style of harem Kyo used. He and Takt were likely the first vanguards of the waves that we fought.

"Yomogi and Tsugumi, you were also responsible for managing their female allies . . . and exchanging information, right? So should we just consider this a larger version of that system?" I asked. The celebrations of our victory yesterday had brought together most of Kizuna's allies, making them available to attend this meeting today. Her allies from her adventuring days were here too and sharing their own information with Kizuna and her current party—of which Yomogi and Tsugumi were already members.

"I don't really want to talk about that . . ." Yomogi said.

"Indeed. I think we can tell what kind of organization they are running," Tsugumi concurred. With these two, it wasn't quite a case of the brainwashing coming to an end after the resurrected they were infatuated with were defeated. Yomogi had taken issue with Kyo's way of doing things from the start, and once she found out the extent of the truth about him, she had rejected him completely. Tsugumi was now on our side because the resurrected she had been infatuated with, Trash II, had foolishly attacked us and been killed. In her case, Kyo had been abusing her and almost got her killed, a death from which Kizuna had saved her. That was also a large part of it. While becoming friendly with Kizuna, Tsugumi had started to notice all the problematic things Trash II was doing. Now she had expanded her point of view enough to be able to tell when others were being as stubborn as she once had been. Their other allies had moved on to join the forces of other resurrected, and apparently in the end these two had been forced to take them out.

"Bitch was placed in a unit testing prototypes for new technology, right?" I confirmed with Lyno.

"That was definitely a large part of it," she asserted. "They were seeking successful experiments in order to enhance the overall fighting strength of their forces." That sounded like what Rat did for us back in my village. A group like that would likely be working autonomously rather than receiving directions from the big-bad resurrected who ran the whole show. That was pretty much how I ran things, after all. I didn't have the time or inclination to follow everything that Rat and her nerds got up to. I just let them do whatever they wanted and then skimmed over the reports.

Rat was managing the monsters that had invaded my village, which was something. But I honestly hadn't seen many more results from her than that. Developing the camping plant was about the only thing that came to mind.

"So what position did Bitch hold?" I asked.

"She was a newcomer to their organization, who got lucky and managed to save their world," Lyno said.

"That's pretty much what S'yne's sister said," I replied. Something about Bitch saving one of their captured holy weapon heroes during a wave.

"That was enough to get her a meeting with their boss. She spread the lies on so thick it makes me sick to think about it," Lyno said. That made sense, anyway—she'd exploited a piece of luck to make an impression on their leader and boost her own standing. I wondered how their boss would handle all her failures . . . but if she was going to keep coming, we'd just keep on sending her packing.

First and foremost, however, we needed to think about how we were going to become stronger. Now that we knew the power-up method for the whip, the true extent of the strength of S'yne's sister had been made painfully plain to us. If S'yne's sister's forces had indeed been exploiting the whip's power-up method—the ability to enhance stats by spending levels—then even at the same level they could be many times stronger than us, and that didn't even account for them being able to make full use of the abilities of the holy and vassal weapons.

"I also got this." Lyno took out multiple notebooks and accessories from her pockets and presented them to me. "I've got copies here of the plans for their various inventions and also for the accessories that bind the seven star weapons."

"I should be able to make some sense of these myself," I said, taking one of the books and casually looking through it. I quickly realized I didn't have a clue what any of it meant and so gave up on that idea.

"The accessories were rigged to destroy themselves if they fell into enemy hands, but I managed to disable that function before it was triggered," Lyno continued.

"Well done," I said with feeling. "Examining the accessories themselves might be the fastest approach, but it will still take some time." That analysis could be entrusted to a specialist in the field. Since I was a hero, it was perhaps more fitting for me to be working on raising my level in order to overcome our future battles. I could let Kizuna's people analyze them here, but it felt like it would ultimately be more efficient to do that on my world too. My hope was this analysis could lead to the creation of an accessory capable of destroying their own impervious accessories. A typical game of technological one-upmanship. During our last encounter, things had worked out because Lyno had made the switch before the fighting even started, but next time we could be sure they would be using the real deal. The only thing we had that looked like it might be effective against even their impervious state was Kizuna's Hunting Tool 0. That was a pretty special weapon, and it had high stats too. This enemy we were facing would likely wheel out some defense against that too. So the one-upmanship would continue. But it was a game worth playing, because if we could get the upper hand, then it would greatly increase our chances of taking back the holy and vassal weapons that our enemies held.

One issue to consider was S'yne's sister. The chain vassal weapon that she used had remained with her even after she broke the accessory on it. Each world had its own rules. There might well be a vassal weapon spirit who was invested in the destruction of other worlds for some reason. Working to break the accessories on weapons possessed of such a spirit would ultimately be meaningless . . . but so long as there was potential for it to work out, we had to try.

"We are getting off track. Getting all of this gear checked out is another reason why I'm thinking of going back. If it's all a bluff on their part, so be it," I said.

"Fair enough, but do you even have a way to get back?" Kizuna asked. At this question, I looked over at Rishia, who was already buried in the materials that Lyno had just provided.

"Rishia?" Itsuki called out to her for me.

"Fehhh?" she replied.

"I still can't use my shield, nor Itsuki his bow. Rishia, can you use the seven star weapon teleportation function to move us back in accordance with a wave summons?" I asked her. We had crossed over to Kizuna's world using the power of an anchor accessory, provided by the ship vassal weapon back when Ethnobalt was its holder. I had originally been hoping to use the wave-triggered teleportation function of the shield or bow to get back. I hadn't counted on our original weapons being rendered useless. The next-fastest way seemed to be Rishia and her projectile seven star weapon.

"Ah, of course. Give me a moment," Rishia responded. Her eyes glazed over for a moment as she checked the remaining time before the next wave. "It looks like that will be possible. Fehhh? The time seems to keep shifting back and forth though, so it's a bit hard to know when it will happen."

"The flow of time is different in each world," I reminded her. "I saw the same thing when I came here the first time." Time here had been a display of the length of time I had left in this world, but the numbers kept changing. After I finally returned from Kizuna's world, the length of time that passed in each world had clearly been different too.

"I'm pretty sure I'll be able to participate in a wave in our world within the next few days," she finally confirmed.

"That's our chance to head home," I replied.

"Okay! Sounds like a plan!" L'Arc boomed, for some unknown reason, punching the air with his fist. He seemed pretty excited about the prospect, even though he was a denizen of this world.

"What're you so worked up about?" I asked him.

"Huh? What do you think, kiddo! We're friends, right? Buddies, no?" came his vague reply.

"Sure, we're friends, but that still doesn't explain it," I responded.

"Don't you get it?" he shot back. "I'm not going to stop you all from leaving, of course, but what if this is exactly what our enemies want? To split us up?" He was likely thinking that S'yne's sister saw us as a threat and wanted to remove us from the board and then attack Kizuna and her allies in our absence. I was pretty sure we could leave things with them—they could handle it—but it also didn't sit right with me, as an ally. The enemy could produce one of the still-missing seven star weapons for all we knew. And yet, I still didn't see that as an argument to all go off to my world together. I understood why he might want to keep us all together, but it would definitely leave this world exposed.

"I hate to point it out, kiddo, but you guys have got most of our weapons. I'd like to beef myself up a bit in your world too, just in case," L'Arc explained.

"True . . . if you guys increase your levels in our world now, it might be useful in a future crisis," I pondered out loud. At the moment, a technique to seal the holy weapons was preventing the shield and bow from being used here in Kizuna's world. The mirror and instrument vassal weapons had therefore come to our aid instead.

"He does have a point," Raphtalia agreed.

"Oh my!" said Sadeena.

"Oh dear!" added Shildina. She casually made it her own, but Raphtalia's katana was actually a vassal weapon from this world, and now Sadeena had also obtained her harpoon vassal weapon by taking it during the battle yesterday. Sadeena had used her expert harpoon skills to free the weapon from its bonds to the resurrected who had been wielding it. This had led to her being appointed as the harpoon hero. Even crazier than that, though, Shildina had gone one rank above vassal weapons. She had been summoned to this world, after all. Having saved the corrupted ofuda holy weapon, she had become one of the four heroes of this world, now an equal to Kizuna. Combine those three weapons with my mirror and Itsuki's instrument and it totaled five weapons that we'd be taking home with us.

"Hah! That only lays plain how worthless and unqualified the pond scum of this world are. Pathetic humans!" the Demon Dragon spat boldly, choosing this moment to mock Kizuna and her allies. She really was one offensive reptile.

"What was that?!" Kizuna and the Demon Dragon started to stare each other down, but I just ignored them.

"Raphtalia and Sadeena being vassal weapon holders is one thing, but the main issue here is Shildina," I mused.

"Oh dear!" Shildina exclaimed. "I'm the problem?"

"Have you forgotten the conversation we had prior to our departure? A holy weapon hero has a much harder time leaving the world they are assigned to," I reminded her.

"Oh my! Does this mean little Shildina is stuck here until she completes her duty as a hero? Good luck with that!" Sadeena laughed.

"Oh dear . . ." Shildina's eyebrows furrowed together at these comments from Sadeena and me. Then she started shaking around the ofuda box in her hands as though she was trying to throw it away. The box did not cooperate, sticking to her hand like glue. It was a pretty cute sight to watch though—almost like Filo having a cute little child's tantrum. She looked a lot like Filo did when someone grabbed her cowlick. "It won't go away! It won't go! I don't want this!"

"If that worked, I doubt any of us would be here," I said wistfully. When I was starting out, I'd wished to be rid of the shield countless times, unable to see a way to survive with a "weapon" that couldn't even attack. Of course, after Takt had taken the shield, I'd been able to fight for a while. The staff had proven pretty useful too . . . and that had been followed by a mirror! I did wonder why the staff had been treated as a weapon exception, but the mirror was handled as though my shield had just been transformed into it.

"Oh dear! I don't want this! I'm going back!" Shildina continued.

"Sorry, but Shildina seems pretty panicked. What can we do?" Raphtalia asked with a concerned expression on her face.

"Talk to the holy weapon," I advised her.

"I'm going home!" Shildina proceeded to shout as loudly as she could at the ofuda weapon—which proceeded to give off a flash of light.

"Oh dear! An exception, just like that?" Shildina exclaimed.

"That was pretty easy," I responded. The weapon must have sensed the situation with the shield and bow and given permission accordingly. The ofuda owed Shildina a lot, which also made it more likely to agree to this. "If you'll fight as the hero here when needed, you'll be free the rest of the time."

"What about you, sweet Naofumi?" Shildina asked.

"Let's see," I said. In my case, I was the one relying on the mirror, and it was highly likely that once I got the shield back the mirror would move on. I'd actually be happy with that— pass on the mirror to a capable new holder and let Kizuna and her friends show them the ropes or whatever. Perhaps it was due to the effects of the shield, but the skills I could use seemed different from normal for the mirror anyway.

"Oh dear!" Shildina had swung around the ofuda for a while, still trying to shake them off, but then she gave up and was now shuffling them. She had always loved card games.

"Don't worry, little Shildina. I've got my harpoon too," Sadeena said.

"Why would that stop me from worrying?" Shildina asked back.

"Oh my," Sadeena responded. I still wasn't quite sure about the relationship between the killer whale sisters.

"What about me? Can I go to Naofumi's world too?" Kizuna asked her own weapon, but the hunting tool made no response at all.

"Looks like you're not getting permission," I told her.

"What's the difference between Shildina and me?!" Kizuna exclaimed.

"Maybe all four holy heroes can't leave their world at the same time," I reasoned. Things were getting back on track here, but if Kizuna was killed by a wave during Shildina's absence, then this world would surely be wiped out. That's how important Kizuna was. "Shildina just happened to arrive here as a candidate, and the ofuda have a debt to her, so that's why it gave her permission. You're one of the pillars of this world, Kizuna, so it can't let you leave so easily," I explained.

"Bah! Unknown fishing spots across the worlds are calling to me, but I can't go to them?" Kizuna moaned. I should have known that's where her mind was at. Seriously, if we were fighting a wave on the beach, she'd probably throw a fishing line into the water. Never underestimate the mind of a fishing addict.

"And L'Arc . . . you're a vassal weapon holder, so no permission needed," I said.

"That's right!" he replied. I still hadn't received sufficient explanation for this level of excitement. "We owe you so much, kiddo, and we're allies. That means we should meet with the king of the nation you belong to at least once."

"You think?" I said. I was acting as a direct agent of our ruler, so I didn't think it was really necessary. If that was all he wanted though, he should have gone over to see Melty and Trash the last time a wave occurred with our world. L'Arc had recently been taking the lead in all sorts of meetings between the nations of this world. In that respect, the selfish actions of these resurrected had actually helped in bringing the other nations together. The enemy of my enemy . . . something like that.

"No problem! Glass is a much more efficient leader than I am anyway, so I can afford to step away for a while!" he exclaimed.

"Don't you feel a little bit bad, admitting that?" I asked him. I looked over at Glass to see her giving an incredibly deep sigh.

"When Kizuna was missing, I often acted in her stead. The

people we're dealing with have sufficient trust in me," Glass admitted. I could imagine she stood in for L'Arc a lot too. When I thought about it now, the first time I met L'Arc had been back in our world—meaning it wouldn't be the first time their king had been away. I guessed a hero was qualified to act as a stand-in, anyway, and Glass had probably handled all sorts of civic duties for L'Arc in her time.

"I guess it would make sense for you to say hello," I said. "Kizuna and the others will be here, and once a wave occurs with this world, you'll be able to come back."

"Sure thing! It'll all come down to which world something happens in, then!" L'Arc enthused. I still wasn't sure why he was so hyped up, but I didn't have the energy to keep pointing it out. His intent to introduce himself to Melty and Trash, with whom he was indeed in an alliance now, also actually did make sense.

"So Glass and Kizuna will be staying here," I concluded.

"It sounds that way," Glass agreed. "We should keep some strength on this side, and if this lets you all take a trip home, then that's for the best."

"I'm still not sure why L'Arc is so keen to go to Naofumi's world," Kizuna commented. I agreed with that.

"What about you, Ethnobalt?" I asked the library rabbit. He had previously been the holder of the ship vassal weapon and had recently become the book vassal weapon hero. Power-ups for the book depended on the rarity of the weapons themselves. It was a little like the rarity boost featured in the sword and ofuda power-ups, but the rarity value of the weapon itself having an effect was more like the bow power-up. It wasn't anything flashy, but just keeping an awareness of it would really boost the abilities of a weapon. The difference was that when a weapon was copied, a kind of serial number was provided. Better-quality weapons meant better enhancements to abilities. Copying a better-quality duplicate would overwrite the previous effect too. As we were dealing with books here, rare elements such as being a first edition might come into play. In the case of weapons from monsters or materials, the quality of the materials themselves would have some effect. It almost felt like a combination of the sword and bow power-up methods but also carried the annoyance of not being able to enhance the weapon directly. It was the kind of thing that was easy to forget about but that you also couldn't underestimate the effects of.

"I'll stay here and protect this world with Kizuna," Ethnobalt replied. I had expected as much. He had learned to use life force and really opened up his latent abilities, making him much stronger than before. I wondered for a moment why all the magical types around me were slowly turning into muscleheads—Rishia was another good example.

In light of this, anyway, I took a moment to consider the two sides. If I took just holy and vassal weapons into account,

Kizuna, Glass, and Ethnobalt would be remaining here. The departing party would include me, Itsuki, Raphtalia, Sadeena, Shildina, Rishia, and L'Arc. Those numbers did give me pause.

"L'Arc, I'm fine with you coming along to show your face, but get back here as quickly as you can," I told him.

"No need to be like that, kiddo! Show me some love!" he replied.

"Quit it," I shot back.

"They've got the Demon Dragon here too; they'll be fine. Right? She's not going to turn down a request from you, kiddo," L'Arc said archly.

"That's true," the Demon Dragon agreed. "I will do whatever the Shield Hero needs of me. I fail to understand why the Scythe Hero is the one pointing this out, however." The Demon Dragon certainly was stronger than a hero on a bad day, that was for sure. Things had gone a lot better yesterday thanks to her presence. "One thing though. If you are returning to your own world, Shield Hero, the connection between us will be severed. That will almost make it impossible for me to provide the same kind of status boost that I did yesterday."

"I'm sure Kizuna can help fill the hole left by Naofumi," L'Arc said brightly. "They're both holy weapon heroes. How difficult can it be?"

"Hah! Scythe Hero, and king. How simple you make things sound," the Demon Dragon replied, a big vein popping out on her head.

"Hold on!" Kizuna exclaimed, also starting to complain. "What's the Demon Dragon going to do to me? L'Arc, what are you expecting her to do to me?" L'Arc really was in a crazy mood ever since crossing over to my world had come up. I wondered what reason he could have to want to cross so badly.

"Answer her, L'Arc!" Glass commanded. "Just what do you expect Kizuna to do?"

"I was just thinking that maybe the dragon could do the same kind of thing as with kiddo here, that's all," L'Arc replied.

"You mean account-hacking," I said.

"Account-hacking?! No way! Keep your scaly paws off my fishing rod!" Kizuna quickly exclaimed. The fact that she called it her "fishing rod" and not the hunting tool said pretty much everything you needed to know.

"Huh!" The Demon Dragon looked over at Kizuna and gave a snort of laughter.

"Hey. That laugh really makes me kind of angry," Kizuna replied.

"If that's the best rage you can manage, Kizuna, that's not going to work. How about giving sloth a try, then? Think you can become the ultimate dragon emperor by feeding on Kizuna's sloth?" I asked. When Kizuna had been under the sloth curse, she had shown no will to do anything at all, a pure blob of laziness. That had likely been an expression of her basic nature to blow things off and go have fun instead. If she

could dig down into the laziness, it might allow her to access power equal to that of my own rage. The curse power of a holy weapon hero becoming a power source for the Demon Dragon seemed to make the most sense.

"My Shield Hero! What terrible orders do you place upon me?!" the Demon Dragon exclaimed.

"I am not lazy!" Kizuna added.

"If you truly believe that, try bringing out a cursed weapon that the Demon Dragon might take a liking to," I told her. She pondered for a moment and then turned her weapon into Hunting Tool 0.

"No . . . not that one. I cannot handle the power of that particular weapon," the Demon Dragon said, uncharacteristically backing down.

"It does work most effectively on corrupt power," I commented.

"That is one aspect of it, but the source of its power is . . . Hmmm, I can't actually remember. In any case, it's a weapon very effective against dragons. I can have no part of it," the Demon Dragon explained.

"Is that even a cursed weapon?" I asked.

"No, not really," Kizuna conceded. "Not that I have much else to choose from—that one forbidden weapon, maybe?" Kizuna did have one weapon she could use to hurt people. The cost for using it was paid in experience—in levels. If possible, she didn't want to use it, which made it a lot like my own wrath.

"That also isn't suited to being used as a power source for me," the Demon Dragon said. "If I were to attempt it during battle, I fear both I, myself, and the Hunting Tool Hero would become so weak we would be unable to keep fighting." I guessed it was a cursed weapon, the only effect of which was to allow Kizuna to fight people. The Demon Dragon crossed her paws, giving Kizuna a bit of a perplexed look, her eyes narrowed. She went on. "That seems to leave us with no other choice. Dragons have the capacity to feed on idleness. I will attempt to draw all the sloth power from the Hunting Tool Hero that I can. You will need to be as lazy as possible!"

"Wow. It's actually really annoying, being told to do it," Kizuna replied.

"You may consider this punishment for the way you normally handle yourself," Glass chided her. The whole incident that brought us here might have been prevented if Kizuna had taken action more swiftly, after all. She really was lazy at heart. Or at least, she only did the things she wanted to.

"Hey, I've been trying pretty hard recently! I can cook almost as well as Naofumi now!" Kizuna fought back.

"Mainly with fish," I added. Due to her love of fishing, Kizuna had been drawn to fish-based dishes, it was true. She'd been great at gutting fish already and had some skills with cooking as a whole. So with a bit of instruction, she had scrubbed up quite nicely.

"Just keep on having her practice ways to get over her laziness," I suggested. "If it looks like it might swallow her completely, send her out in a boat and have her fish the water of the four heavenly kings—that should sort her out."

"Some good ideas!" the Demon Dragon enthused. "Well done, Shield Hero! You really do know everything, even about the laziness of the Hunting Tool Hero!"

"Am I really that simple?!" Kizuna shouted. I refrained from replying, but that was pretty much the exact method we used to overcome her sloth curse the first time.

"It's in her true nature to be lazy . . . however sad it makes me to admit that," Glass said—and she did sound very sad.

"Fear not, Shield Hero. If she becomes so far gone, her mind cannot be salvaged, I will absorb the Hunting Tool Hero and draw from her energy that way," the dragon explained, completely matter-of-factly. That was the trick she tried to pull on me when we first met. "You'll be able to laze around as much as you like inside me, right up until you die. Well, until I die . . . and seeing as I'm practically immortal, that should be a long time." Living inside the Demon Dragon for almost an eternity . . . hell, a living hell.

"That sounds pretty frightening to me!" Glass exclaimed.

"I will master my sloth, you'll see!" Kizuna shouted, her determination firm—for now. If she let it overtake her, the Demon Dragon would swallow her . . . It sounded like some kind of sick horror movie. The sad thing was Kizuna couldn't attack people directly, so becoming one with the dragon might actually make her more useful in battle.

"Yeah, good luck," I said, pretty listlessly.

"All the best with that," the Demon Dragon added, clearly hoping it wouldn't work out. Was Kizuna's laziness going to become the power to save the world? I felt a headache coming on.

That settled that rather unsettling matter, anyway, forcing me to wonder again about L'Arc and his excitement to cross over.

"Whatever the reason," I said, almost to myself, "I've been wanting to enhance the abilities of these heroes." I gave a nod. "Just as an experiment, then, we'll take L'Arc with us. We have the killer whale sisters, who are experts at helping people level up."

"Bring it on!" L'Arc enthused, a bit too energetically for me. Something about his attitude still bothered me, but I just had to consider this a proactive choice and move on. "Your world is calling to me, kiddo!" It really was bothering me.

"That decides what's happening with your people, Kizuna, but what about our side?" I asked. Raphtalia would be coming back, of course. Shildina clearly wanted to make the trip, and Sadeena would go where Raphtalia went. Filo wasn't even in the room because of the Demon Dragon being here, and she definitely wouldn't want to be left behind.

"We need to obtain more information from our captive, Mald," Itsuki mentioned. "I still need to work him over a little more, so we should take him back with us to make sure he doesn't escape."

"Fehhh . . . Itsuki!" Rishia said, unsettled by his casual mention of torture. Itsuki was the Bow Hero, so he'd be coming back, and that meant Rishia too. S'yne was sure to go wherever I went.

"I think the Hengen Muso teacher is going to stay behind," Raphtalia said. "She is getting along very well with Glass's master."

"Okay, I guessed as much." She was pretty strong, making her a good candidate for experiments with our new enhancements. It would be interesting to see if she could come to match a hero in strength.

Anyway, that meant that almost everyone would be making the trip back with us. This had proven to be quite a long visit, so I wasn't surprised everyone wanted to see home again. The situation here had moved back in our favor, so things should be okay for a while.

"Sounds like it's all decided," I said. Having made the decision to travel back as soon as possible, we set about passing the days until we got our chance.

Chapter One: Prisoner Transport

We mainly spent the days until our departure leveling up. As we gathered together just before setting out, Mald was brought to join us. He was a former underling of Itsuki's, whom I called simply "Armor." He had an ofuda attached to his face in order to prevent him from moving around. Apparently, it hadn't taken much, in the end, to get him to start talking. Lyno had been present for the proceedings to see if he said anything she didn't know or if she could catch him in a lie. Sadeena—a self-proclaimed specialist in torture and spotting lies—had also taken part. In the end, Armor didn't really have much information of note anyway—maybe just that some former members of the Church of the Three Heroes had also teamed up with Bitch.

"He spilled his guts pretty quickly. Are you sure you don't want to just execute him here and be done with it?" I asked.

"No, we need Mald to share more information with us over there before we finish him off," Itsuki replied. Armor still wasn't really seeing the reality of the situation, cycling between saying his friends should be coming for him at any moment, wondering why they hadn't come for him yet, and then calling them traitors and scum. He had a slave ofuda slapped on his forehead, making him look like one of those Chinese hopping ghosts. Yomogi had been given the same treatment once, if I recalled correctly.

Unable to even move, let alone speak, Armor managed a few muffled grunts while desperately looking around to try and find some aid. But he was surrounded by our allies, who all knew just to ignore him. He would still try and fight back if given the opportunity though. It was exhausting, but I also had to ask myself if I would give up if I was in his position.

"Mald, Mald, Mald. There's still no sign of your heroes, your so-called 'allies of justice,' coming to save you." Itsuki picked his moment to kick Armor as the lump struggled on the floor. I wondered how this treatment of a prisoner fitted in with Itsuki's own image of such "heroes." I had thought he'd expanded his horizons a bit and was giving things a bit more thought, but this just exposed how deeply the darkness had taken root in him.

"Fehhh!" Rishia exclaimed. For once I wanted to make pretty much the same noise.

"Mr. Naofumi." Raphtalia was quick to respond too, both girls letting me know I should be helping out. It didn't really seem like my fault that Itsuki was beating up one of his former comrades.

"Are you awakening to the path of a dark hero? That sounds like fun," I said.

"Even if he was some kind of hero, this guy has gone too far. That's what I think, anyway," Itsuki said.

"Fair enough," I replied. Itsuki could still be diamond-hard when he had to be—but maybe not all the time.

"I also take exception with him putting all of that old responsibility onto you, Naofumi," Itsuki added. This was something we had discussed when capturing Armor—back when they were working together. He and the other goons had swiped a reward intended for Itsuki. Armor was a traitor who had perverted the course of Itsuki's justice, so I could see why Itsuki wouldn't want to hold back against him now. "I have continued to struggle with the definition of 'justice,' but there is one thing I am certain about; there is no justice in you, Mald." At Itsuki's declaration, Armor struggled to shake off his bonds and speak out, but the pain was stopping him from doing anything. "Look at you! You can't even escape from those bonds. In the same position, Naofumi would have chewed through his own arms to tell me I was wrong. That's the difference between you two."

"Don't bring me into this," I said, although I took it as a compliment.

"This is your punishment for giving everything up so easily when tortured and then saying you want to come back and join us again. Your 'justice' and ours are completely different. I cannot accept you," Itsuki said.

"Me neither," Sadeena admitted. "I'm amazed at some of the stuff he came out with."

"It makes me sick," Lyno agreed, following up on Sadeena's comment. "He leeches onto the strong and powerful. I guess that might make him an ally of some kind of justice." It sounded like Armor had been saying some pretty crazy stuff then—a certain kind of "justice" indeed. The justice of the resurrected. For them, justice simply equaled strength. Joining up with the strongest people who came along could be considered an ally of that kind of justice.

"I don't care if you call me merciless," Itsuki said. "Mercy is more suited to you, Naofumi."

"Like I said, don't bring me into this. I don't have any mercy either," I stated. Atla was the only one who had given me mercy, and that was all I had of it. Even Itsuki was starting to sound a lot like Ren now.

Itsuki kicked Armor while turning to look at me.

"Do you really believe that? Do you believe that the one who accepted us other fallen heroes isn't capable of mercy?" Itsuki asked.

"I talked you down because having you die would cause all sorts of problems, that's all," I said.

"I suppose that's another way of looking at it," Itsuki admitted. "We can leave it at that for now."

"Sounds like you think we'll be coming back to this," I said.

"Not at all. I mean nothing by it. Everyone sees things, thinks about things, differently. That's all," Itsuki said. He was really saying stuff that pissed me off today. I even found myself wondering if he was somehow using his "accuracy" supernatural power on his mouth. I didn't feel like walking further into the swamp of picking a fight with him, so I decided to just let him say his piece. "That's the way I saw it, is all," he finished.

"Sure thing, whatever." I brushed him off.

"I'm sorry, but . . . it's time," Rishia let us know, looking very worried about interrupting us.

"Okay then," I said.

"Well . . . that all got a bit weird just before you set out, but you've done so much to help Naofumi," Kizuna said with a frown as she looked at Itsuki and Armor. We were dealing with a criminal coming over from our world, after all.

"Okay, Kizuna! Take care of things here. We'll see you soon!" L'Arc gave a breezy farewell with Therese in tow. I was still wondering why he was coming, to be honest—and why Therese was naturally tagging along. It was so natural, in fact, that Kizuna and her allies didn't even seem to question it. L'Arc was basically her guardian, now that I thought about it.

"Ah, Shield Hero. This is such a shame, truly," the Demon Dragon said, looking at me with puppy dog eyes. But I ignored her. Three of the four heavenly kings were looking at the scene with highly suspect expressions on their faces. I could sense how they were struggling with this complicated situation, knowing that having me around made the Demon Dragon so much

THE RISING OF THE SHIELD HERO 20   37

stronger. The dragon being stronger meant the four heavenly kings got stronger too.

"Filo! Our new heavenly king of the wind! Obey the orders of our Demon Dragon and protect this hero from another world for us all," said one of the other heavenly kings.

"I didn't ask to be made into a king of anything! Boo!" Filo rasped, obviously not happy to be ordered around. She had a point. She had been made into a king without her consent. In our last battle, that unexpected promotion had led to her being targeted aggressively by the enemy, so she was still a bit prickly about it. That said, she did love being able to fly around freely in this world, taking to the skies and singing whenever she had a spare moment.

"And you, katana vassal weapon holder. I have resolved your issues relating to the use of magic. If you study hard, you'll be able to use magic at the same level as a hero. You can also use my own magical protection, so study them together," the Demon Dragon said, looking at Raphtalia. I'd almost forgotten that Raphtalia couldn't handle Way of the Dragon Vein very well.

"Okay . . . thank you. I'll do what I can to learn it all," she replied.

"Raph!" added Raph-chan.

"Ah, one last thing. Give this to your dragon emperor." The Demon Dragon proceeded to spit something out, something that looked very much like a dragon emperor fragment, and tossed it over to me. It looked pretty horrible to have to carry around. "If your dragon emperor has any intelligence, he should be able to draw out the power of wrath in the same way as I can."

"I don't really want to have to rely on that . . . but it sounds like a good insurance policy," I admitted. Being able to deploy the power of wrath and mercy at the same time would surely make me stronger. If I could access that power without any cost, it had to be worth a try.

"Not to mention . . ." This time, the words rang ominously inside my head. "I have a copy of my personality inside your shield. When you cast magic, I will be able to lend a hand wherever you are." I was seriously, seriously starting to regret having let this genie out of the bottle. She'd help out when I was casting magic, sure . . . but I wasn't sure I liked this arrangement. "This is one of my best features," she said.

"Silence!" I silently raged back.

"I'm going to get into your good graces!" the dragon said, speaking aloud again. "Once the fighting ends, come and see me again!"

"Sure, whatever," I said, brushing her off.

"Boo! I won't let him!" Filo cut in, seemingly at the limit of her patience after this long discourse with the Demon Dragon.

"Isn't that for the Shield Hero to decide?" the Demon Dragon countered.

"I won't allow it! Boo!" Filo retorted petulantly. Her dislike of the dragon seemed very close to her dislike of Motoyasu. We didn't have long left, anyway, so I decided to say what needed to be said to Kizuna.

"Hey, Kizuna," I called to her.

"What?" she replied. I had a serious look on my face, and Kizuna waited for me to continue with a puzzled look of her own. I simply had to say this.

"Next time you get captured, I'm changing your nickname to 'princess.'"

"Where did that come from?!" she exclaimed.

"Every time something happens you manage to get yourself captured," I told her. "I can't stand for it a third time."

"I'm not doing it on purpose!" Kizuna retorted.

"That's just how things have turned out. You can't blame Kizuna for it," Glass said, seemingly coming to her rescue—but there was a look in her eyes! I could tell Glass was also troubled by Kizuna's "damsel in distress" nature.

"I see," the Demon Dragon cut in, never missing a chance to mock Kizuna. "If she is a princess, then that makes things easier to process. I will update my awareness of her from Hunting Tool Hero to helpless princess."

"Enough! I'm not going to let that happen!" Kizuna shouted back. I hoped that would be enough to stop her from getting captured again while we were gone. I really hoped so.

"They are always such a lively group," Ethnobalt said, waving goodbye to us with a smile on his face. He was accompanied by some of the other library rabbits and the old lady.

"Saint! You can leave this with me! I'll make sure to teach them all Hengen Muso style!" the old lady shouted.

"Okay, good luck with that," I encouraged her half-heartedly.

"It's been a long road, but I finally get to return home," Raphtalia said. She was right; we came over here simply to pick her up after the whole Takt debacle, and things had ballooned from there. I was happy to chalk it all up to being Bitch's fault and leave it at that.

"We're moving out, you rabble," I told them. "Make sure you check your party registry carefully so you don't get left behind." It would be a bad joke if that happened to any of them.

"It all looks fine," Itsuki reported, followed by Raphtalia and Rishia.

"We'll be going then," I said.

"And we'll see you again?" Kizuna asked. I took a moment to think about everything that we were likely to face in the future.

"I think so," I finally responded. "The situation has changed a lot since last time, and I'd like to settle things here as quickly as possible. You brush up on your skills and be ready for our return."

"You bet," Kizuna replied. "I need to be able to handle everything, just like you."

"Yep, and I'm sure you can. Also, try and find that one thing that only you can do," I advised her. That didn't sound much like the normal me, apart perhaps from the arrogance with which I imparted it, and it made Kizuna look happy.

"Okay! Good luck to you too, Naofumi!" she replied.

"I make my own luck," I replied. First "the one thing that only you can do," and now this. I was on a cornball roll today.

"Departing now," Rishia announced. "They should be in the middle of a wave over there, so please be ready for anything." Even as she spoke, we waved at Kizuna and the others, and then we teleported away, back to our world.

**You have returned to the world you are
responsible for.
Changing from the mirror to the shield.**

This text appeared in my field of vision, and my mirror weapon changed back to the shield. The trip over had been through a tunnel of light, but we had returned in the blink of an eye. Pondering this difference, I looked across at the familiar split caused by a wave. This looked like . . . the barren wastes in the vicinity of Zeltoble, perhaps.

Then I heard a loud shout, followed by, "Father! You have returned, I say!" Motoyasu was the first to exclaim our return. I'd been hoping to ease back into things a little more slowly. "Why are you back? Has the fighting in the other world concluded?"

"It's a little more complicated than that. There are still issues to resolve, but we thought a visit home was warranted," I explained.

"You'll have to tell me more," Motoyasu said.

"Maybe . . . but it can wait until this wave is finished," I said. "Come on!" Everyone who had just teleported in with me gave a shout in reply, and without pause we headed directly into combat with the wave.

"Ah! Sweet Filo! We finally meet again!" Motoyasu shouted, his priorities as clear as ever.

"Boo! Get away from me!" she responded, equally as predictable. I decided to ignore them both. First things first, take care of the wave.

"Even a wave can't withstand this number of people," I commented as the fighting ended. We had all attacked the crack and closed it with ease. Now we were checking up on any damage it had done and regrouping to discuss everything that had happened on both sides during our absence.

"Hero Iwatani, your return is most welcome. How fared your endeavors?" Trash appeared with Melty in tow.

"Pretty well, actually. The reason we came back is because we got wind of something ominous on this side," I explained.

"I see. Ominous how, exactly?" Trash asked.

"Before you get into that, I need to introduce myself," said L'Arc, cutting into the conversation between Trash and me. "I am L'Arc Berg, the scythe hero over in the other world. This is Therese. Kiddo and his friends have helped us out a lot, so we came to say hello."

"Indeed. My wife told me of the battles with the heroes from other worlds. My name is Trash Melromarc XXXII. I fight the waves in this world as the Staff Hero," Trash replied. I knew his surname was Melromarc but didn't realize his line had been continuing for such a long time. As Melromarc was led by the queen, the husband was the one who took the Melromarc name when he married into the family. Maybe that meant Trash was the thirty-second man to do so—hah, just more pointless trivia. I was itching to comment about him so proudly introducing himself as "Trash" though.

"So you're in charge around here. Kiddo has explained about your name," L'Arc said, a little bluntly.

"Good," Trash responded, with far more pride than the situation really warranted. I was starting to wonder if sticking with the name I had given him was just another ploy from the Wisest King of Wisdom. L'Arc and Trash shook hands, anyway. "I nodded in recognition of my name, and I have been helping here in Hero Iwatani's absence as a hero, but I am not actually the one in charge." Trash proceeded to place his arm around

Melty's back and introduce her to L'Arc. "This is the queen of our nation of Melromarc, Her Majesty Melty Q Melromarc."

"Hero from another world, welcome to our own. We have much to discuss on both sides, but for now please accept this brief greeting," Melty said.

"Sure, sure thing . . ." L'Arc said, a bit surprised. That was probably understandable, considering Melty's age, even though I had explained things to him beforehand.

"She hasn't said much yet, but I can already tell she's got her act together," L'Arc muttered to me while leaning over, still looking at Melty.

"Kings and queens have been known to take the throne at a pretty young age here," I told him. There was Melty, for one thing, then Ruft, who was former royalty, and the nation where the phoenix had been sealed had a kid for a king too. All of them had their own circumstances for why they had ascended to the throne, of course. It was rarer to find someone like L'Arc over here, to be honest.

"Mel-chan, I'm back! Help me!" Filo rushed into the scene.

"Filo!" Melty exclaimed as the filolial leapt onto her and started using her as a shield against Motoyasu. I was surprised at the speed she went from "I'm back" to "help me." Melty had it rough too.

"Motoyasu, cool it," I told him. "We're in the middle of something here. Stop getting in the way."

"But, Father!" he retorted. "I've finally been reunited with sweet Filo! Ah, Filo! Je t'aime!"

"Boo!" Filo replied—she clearly didn't speak French either. Motoyasu was so broken. I shook my head.

"Queen Melty. Can you appease the Spear Hero, please? I will discuss things with the Scythe Hero while you do that," Trash suggested.

"Of course, Father," Melty agreed. "Filo, with me please."

"Okay!" Filo immediately turned into her filolial form. Melty climbed onto her back . . . and then the pair of them flew away!

"Waaah! I can still fly!" Filo exclaimed.

"This is amazing! Filo!" Melty said back. For some reason Filo could still fly here in this world! Maybe it was some side effect of the Demon Dragon having made Filo into the heavenly king of the wind. It was impressive, nevertheless. A freaking flying filolial.

"My god, Filo has flown off into the sunset!" Motoyasu blabbered. "I must catch her! I'm coming!" Filo soared away with Melty on her back, and Motoyasu scurried off on foot after them. Behind him, his own three primal-colored filolials gave chase. I almost felt nostalgic, seeing them all again.

"Hey, kiddo. That guy with the spear is the same rowdy fellow who joined me in sneaking a peek in the baths on the Cal Mira islands, right?" L'Arc checked with me, poking me in the ribs as he watched the pursuit unfold.

"That's right," I told him.

"So what happened? Something shake a screw loose?" L'Arc asked.

"That's a pretty astute observation. It was all Bitch. Bitch broke him too," I replied.

"Same thing as Itsuki, huh? I remember you saying he caused a fuss when you last exchanged information with this side. Now I see what you meant," L'Arc mused. He seemed to have accepted the situation a little easily, but it was the truth, so there wasn't much we could do about that.

It was all Bitch's fault.

"Our conversation has wandered off track. Now that we have introduced ourselves, Hero Iwatani, Scythe Hero, can you tell me exactly what brings you back?" Trash asked. I glanced at L'Arc, and he signaled for me to take this one. I proceeded to explain how we had managed to defeat most of the resurrected causing the problems in Kizuna's world, but after the ominous proclamation from S'yne's sister, we had decided to come and check things out. I also explained what had happened to Bitch and how L'Arc had come to meet those in charge of the forces he was now allied with.

Trash's face stiffened as he took all of this in. It must have been hard on him, hearing that his daughter—Bitch—was planning more trouble here in this world. He had to be worried that even the Wisest King of Wisdom might find himself unconsciously holding back when it came to handling his own flesh and blood.

"That makes sense. I can see why such a thing would bring you back," Trash concluded.

"Glad you agree. What about things here? Anything unsettling to report?" I asked.

"Everything has been most peaceable, most peaceable indeed," Trash responded. "One can only hope that we are not within the calm before the storm."

"You said it," I agreed. If S'yne's sister had been lying, that would be for the best all around. Trash excelled at correctly assessing a situation based on limited information. I had kept it brief, but he probably had a good handle on things.

"Something else. This is Lyno, one of the spies sent out by the previous queen," I said, making the formal introduction. For her part, Lyno was looking at Trash with hints of suspicion in her eyes. She had probably only heard rumors about him, and not the good kind either. Trash had been pretty hard to stomach prior to his recent reform. She had to have detected the change in the air around him though.

"I am Lyno. I was acting as a spy, both on the orders of our dear deceased queen and out of my own personal rage," Lyno explained.

"Indeed. You have my thanks for saving Hero Iwatani and his party from the clutches of my foolish daughter. Allow me to offer my own personal praise for the excellence of your actions. I wish to reward you, if there is anything you desire," Trash stated.

"If you will forgive my impudence, the only thing that I desire—all who belong to the same unit of spies desire—is to see our target punished. That is the intent of all in the unit created by our now-deceased queen." Lyno knew that Trash was Bitch's father, and that he still held vast authority, and yet she did not flinch in the face of him.

"Very well. Your reward is the punishment of Bitch . . . I have heard you, loud and clear. I may find myself faltering when that moment comes. I give you more authority than I in this matter. Please continue your good work," Trash commanded.

"Yes, Your Majesty!" Lyno responded. From the look on Trash's face, I saw he understood exactly what was going on.

In almost that same moment, the whip seven star weapon that Lyno had been temporarily holding onto turned into a ball of light, circled around us a few times, and then vanished.

"Don't go getting captured by the enemy again," I called after it. It appeared again and flickered as though to say it would be okay, then vanished a second time. It looked like it had chosen to hide itself, then, in the same way the mirror and book had done.

"That completes a simple exchange of information, at least," Trash concluded. "This is not the kind of place we should talk for any length of time. Shall we get moving?"

"Good idea," I agreed. We prepared to depart the scene and return to Melromarc Castle . . . when I looked around and noticed that someone important was missing.

"I don't see Ren. Did a wave happen somewhere else and he's off fighting that?" I inquired of Eclair, who was part of Trash's honor guard. "Some kind of double operation?"

"No, not exactly . . ." Eclair said, seemingly struggling to explain further. I looked over at Trash, and he gave me a wry chuckle, also taking a moment to decide how to explain.

"Ren has been under a lot of pressure, from the Spear Hero, Gaelion, and others, and in the end it all proved a bit too much for him . . . and he collapsed. He's resting up in the village," Trash finally explained.

"What a moron," I breathed, shaking my head. He had a strong sense of responsibility, that was for sure, but it was meaningless if it made him collapse! There was no need to even give Motoyasu the time of day. I had been worried about Ren, but I hadn't expected him to collapse in such a short period of time.

"You leave large shoes to fill, Mr. Naofumi. I'm not surprised the pressure got to him," Raphtalia said sympathetically. I wondered if it really was such a hard job. But I guess he couldn't just dump it all on Trash, who was being kept busy enough by Melty. Motoyasu wasn't any help—in fact, he was part of the problem. It made sense that everything was going to roll downhill to the only other holy hero left behind, poor old Ren. He could have at least relied on Fohl a little, surely, even if he was a bit difficult at times. I looked over at Fohl in that moment, but he glanced away uncomfortably. He was just as awkward as ever.

"I did what I could to help!" Fohl stated, reading my mind. So the pressure of responsibility on Ren and support from Fohl were two different issues.

"Very well." I gave a sigh. "Let's just head back to the castle." We hurried away from the scene of the battle.

Chapter Two: Training for an Obstinate Man

We returned to the castle and proceeded to exchange information in more detail, filling in Trash and our other allies about everything that happened in Kizuna's world. Trash, Lyno, L'Arc, Therese, and I were speaking. Raphtalia and the others were there too, but they were only listening. I had sent everyone else back to the village to rest. Sadeena and Shildina had gone right away. As we had already exchanged an outline of information, it didn't take that long to explain the rest of it.

Trash made a thoughtful noise as he absorbed the information Lyno provided, the details of the enemy's internal structure. As for Armor, who Itsuki brought here, he had spilled his guts all over again and had then been taken away. They had used a dragon hourglass to reset his level first, giving him no chance of escape. Once they had extracted everything they could, they were going to execute him. The guys from Zeltoble had been talking about using a bull of Phalaris to do the job, but that was their business.

Meanwhile, L'Arc had explained the battle in his world to Trash in more detail.

"The activities of these ones called 'resurrected' that I have already heard Hero Iwatani speak of . . . the true nature of our enemy, the one who assumes the name of God . . . I still don't have a full understanding of the situation, but it seems most troubling indeed," Trash said.

"Indeed. You got any ideas in that big brain of yours?" I asked him.

"We already thought of them as the vanguards of the waves, so now we simply know who they actually are . . . but hearing a little more about their internal structure may open up some new avenues," Trash pondered.

"I was thinking the same thing," I replied. We got all the information from Lyno too.

"The issue being . . . it is still going to be difficult for us to pivot to the attack. Defense isn't everything . . . but looking at the weapon power-up method information we have now obtained, we are going to need to increase our strength considerably. If we can't do that, it won't matter what kind of plan we come up with—we won't be able to execute it," Trash analyzed.

"Sounds like we're on the same page there too," I agreed with him.

"I'm glad. So whether something happens here or not, you and your allies should work on enhancing yourselves, Hero Iwatani. We too will seek to enhance the techniques of those who could benefit from further training," Trash said. That was more important than forming a more specific plan of action, then. Sound reasoning. I had nothing to offer otherwise. Trash having reached pretty much the same conclusion had told me my thinking had been correct.

"We should send the accessories that Lyno and I obtained for analysis as quickly as possible," I suggested.

"I have already placed requests with research groups in each country for the purpose, including our own. That said . . ." Trash was signaling me with his eyes, asking me to pass this on to someone with a deeper understanding of such technology.

"He isn't involved yet?" I asked.

"I think any talk of accessories would probably appeal to him, but I decided we were more likely to capture his attention if it came from you," Trash explained.

Zeltoble, a nation of merchants and mercenaries. A nation where enough money was said to be able to resolve pretty much anything. I had connections to the one in charge there. The one Trash was suggesting I meet with. The one he wanted help from was like my master in the making of accessories, whom I personally called the "accessory dealer." Simply making accessories using the methods he taught me was enough to increase their quality. It was some kind of secret method that differed from normal accessory-making, and the results had been well received by those around me.

I sometimes wondered if the accessory dealer had really taught me something so difficult or special. All it felt like to me was that he'd taught me a way to imbue magic. In any case, that had put me on the path to making all sorts of accessories and provided me with a working knowledge of how they operated. I had the abilities of my shield too.

Getting the accessory dealer to analyze the pieces we originally carried back from Kizuna's world had allowed him to make an accessory for use in this world that permitted teleportation to the site of a wave when one occurred. He had also looked at the accessories housing a Scroll of Return and the one with the translation function, but he was yet to make as much progress with those.

Then there was the accessory re-creating the drop function for monsters that had been absorbed by the holy and seven star vassal weapons. Analysis of that had proceeded quite promisingly. But ultimately he needed more samples, so I had made sure to bring back plenty this time. We also had the materials provided by Lyno this time. Now we could only pray that the analysis would proceed and methods to mass-produce or counter the accessories would be found. In any case, it was true that we should probably arrange a meeting. He was a dealer—a businessman—first and foremost. There was nothing to say that he wouldn't make a meal out of even someone he knew and liked for the sake of some cash, if they exposed such an opportunity. Trust might be the most important thing in business, but there were also times when—if the other party was becoming nothing but a burden—you simply had to cut them loose. There was meaning in creating a situation in which he couldn't betray us, and I had to be careful to maintain it.

"Hey, kiddo. Thinking of going already?" L'Arc said, almost leaning forward eagerly as he asked and interrupted my thoughts. The accessory dealer had nothing to do with him, surely. That said . . .

"We've pretty much completed the report to Trash, so the choices are to return to the village or go set things up with the dealer," I admitted.

"And which are you picking, kiddo?" L'Arc asked.

"Good question," I pondered. "I don't see much 'rest' in my future even if I go back to the village." Things were likely to be a bit crazy there—just like always. They might not throw a full-blown party for us, but there was a lot of energy in the village and they would be happy to see our return. Of course, this had all been a bit sudden, so there would probably be some people missing. Sending Sadeena and some of the others back ahead of us had partly been to let everyone know what was going on. I should probably give them a little more time to prepare. "I guess I'll clear up these annoyances first."

"Okay!" L'Arc enthused. I tilted my head, still not sure what his angle was. Everyone else present seemed to feel the same way about his reaction, and there was a strange atmosphere in the air.

"Very well, Hero Iwatani. I will return to making

investigations for our future plans, further training, and my public duties," Trash concluded.

"Okay," I replied. The meeting with Trash ended there and everyone started going their separate ways.

"I will take my leave too," said Lyno. She was heading to report to her unit about her dealings with Bitch. It might not have been decisive, but there were plenty of people who would be happy to hear about Bitch being killed.

"Okay. I need to meet up with your people and have a chat sometime. I think we'll have a lot in common," I said with a grin.

"I will make the introductions soon. They will surely be bolstered to hear of your exploits, Shield Hero. Until then." Lyno gave a bow and left.

"I'll invite Ren and Itsuki along too," I said to myself. They were sure to enjoy chatting with some like-minded folks. I was looking forward to it already.

"I would rather you didn't spend too long with those people," Raphtalia said. I understood where she was coming from. A bit of a chat couldn't hurt though. Getting the victims of Bitch together would firm up our desire to see her punished and share the feeling of being allies all working toward the same goal.

We used a portal over to Zeltoble and with materials in hand went looking for the accessory dealer. His main store was located here and had a branch located in the town next to my village. The retail of merchandise originating with me should be making him quite a tidy profit. He had seemed pretty happy with the arrangement prior to our departure, but I didn't know what the situation was now.

"This is a bustling town!" L'Arc exclaimed, eyes darting about all over the place as he commented to me. This country felt like it would suit him; L'Arc the playboy, the easygoing jock. When I first met him I'd thought he was either a merc or an adventurer, and this country was the mecca for folk of that ilk, so it wasn't surprising that he seemed to fit in.

"Bustling indeed. Zeltoble is the nation of merchants and mercenaries," I told him. A place that suited Sadeena's personality too. It was also a great place to hide, with few people prying into the affairs of others. I had entered Keel and some of the others into the coliseum here and caused quite the ruckus as a result. So those parts of the country were more cautious around me now. Motoyasu had benefited from that experience when we held those filolial races during the festival Melty held in the neighboring town to try and cheer me up.

"I've got business to discuss, so you and Therese can go find a tavern and have some fun," I told L'Arc. He had come to introduce himself to Trash, and that had already been taken care of. I would have been happy for him to go home completely now. He had only tagged along to let his crown slip a little—a little further—and have some fun. I knew that much.

"No, no, I'm going with you, kiddo," he answered. I hadn't expected that, and it made me wonder again what he was up to. He was definitely sticking close to me.

"Whatever. Let's just get this over with," I replied. We headed toward the department store run by the accessory dealer. If he wasn't here, we could ask one of the staff where to find him. However, that proved unnecessary.

"Oh my. If it isn't the mighty Shield Hero," a familiar voice called out. Just like when I first met him, there he was, sitting behind the counter.

"I wondered this before," I asked him snidely. "If you're the boss here, why are you working retail?"

"You don't understand?" he responded innocently.

"No, I get it," I told him. "If you don't place yourself on the front lines, dealing with customers face to face, when you have a little time to do so, then it will blunt your edge. You could even let big business chances slip past you. You need to be there, boots on the ground, to catch these things."

"Very nicely put, oh mighty Shield Hero. I can see your edge isn't blunt," he said, eyes twinkling in that way I really didn't like. I wasn't sure where this "mighty Shield Hero" junk was coming from, but I wished he would quit that too. He had some kind of evil presence inside him, like the opposite of life force—some strange power, unique to merchants, that even the old lady and others sensitive to life force couldn't detect.

"And? What brings you here?" the accessory dealer asked.

"I've come to see you, of course," I replied.

"I see. About those accessories you asked me to analyze? Unfortunately, I can't do anything more without more materials. Any chance you can provide a little more capital? A little more support?" he asked.

"What do you mean 'a little more'?" I asked, raising an eyebrow. "Paying you anything would be a complete waste. If someone from my side is paying you, that stops now."

"Oh my . . . I've said too much." He chuckled. Seriously, this guy. I wondered if he had been receiving payments since the previous queen was in power. If that was the case, then I really needed to start seeing some results.

Trash was great in a scrap, but there was a chance he couldn't keep up with the business side of things. If he spent the time to come and deal with this himself, he would probably get a handle on it quite quickly, but there was no need for the king to be doing that.

Maybe knowing that was why he was leaving all of this to me.

"You never fail to impress, mighty Shield Hero. It's been a while since we last met but you are on your game like always," the accessory dealer said.

"Hah. Enough buttering me up. Take a look at these." I showed him the materials that Lyno had recovered and some samples of the accessories we had obtained. Just taking a cursory glance over the materials was enough to change something in the accessory dealer's eyes.

"Oh my. I don't understand the language these are written in . . . but I can already tell I'm very interested in what they say," the accessory dealer said.

"These materials all come from another world. They detail technology belonging to our enemies. I'm planning on having our own researchers take a look at them, but what do you say? Going to ask for more money now?" I teased him.

"Please, that was just my little joke. Of course, I very much want to be involved in whatever this is. Oh, indeed," he said with a chuckle.

"We will need some research capital from you, of course," I said, seeking some funds from him. It sounded like he had already received payments from us, while really he should be the one paying for the privilege. After all, this could end up making a lot of money for him.

"What if I were to say I'd rather not pay anything?" he asked.

"You're a businessman. You know the answer," I told him. I didn't need his cooperation, not specifically. I'd just go and find another wealthy merchant. Once we had obtained the technology, however, this guy would surely get involved again. No matter how large Melromarc had become, and how much Trash and Melty were willing to pay in research costs, money was not infinite. We also might not want the resulting technology to just spread uncontrolled across the world. That was where having a merchant on the hook could really help out—so long as he was on our hook, and not us on his.

"Very well then!" the accessory dealer exclaimed with a laugh. "You may present whatever figure to me you desire. The rights to produce the resulting accessories will be mine, however."

"You don't get to decide that. We have made some progress though. Go see Trash in Melromarc next. You can sort out the details of the contract with him." I gave the accessory dealer the necessary documents, prepared in advance, for him to see Trash. This should make Trash's life easier.

I had heard that, perhaps from technology that had leaked out into the world after the defeat of Takt, an airfield had been created close to Zeltoble, and the accessory dealer had obtained the deeds to that place too. He was also involved with slavery, to some degree—quite a dangerous fellow, when all was said and done.

"Sorry for interrupting while you are getting so involved, Mr. Naofumi, but maybe you should restrain yourself a little . . ." Raphtalia said with concern in her eyes. I took a look around and saw the people in the vicinity were looking on with some worry. It could just be the presence of the famous Shield Hero among them . . . or maybe they were worried about whatever new mischief the accessory dealer and I were cooking up.

"One more thing . . ." the accessory dealer said, pointing behind L'Arc at Therese. He had noticed the Four Holy Beasts Guardian Seal: Starfire and the Demon Dragon's Four Heavenly King's Bell accessories that she was wearing. Being artifacts from another realm, I almost expected the text for them to be corrupted, but everything seemed to be functioning.

"Mighty Shield Hero, this one I take no exception with," he said, pointing at Starfire, "but I think you let yourself slide a little with this one," he continued, pointing at the bell with an uncomfortable expression on his face.

"It's a prototype I made just to check out the quality of the materials. Cut me some slack, okay?" I told him.

"That's hardly any excuse," he chided me. I shook my head and beckoned Therese over, then silently handed the bell to the accessory dealer. He started to inspect it with a magnifying glass at once.

"Yes, this work here is very rough . . . I'm amazed you are willing to let it out in public like this," he muttered.

"I bet you think just anyone could make it, right?" I said, knowing what was coming next.

"You said it, not me," he replied. With a few swift

movements he broke the piece apart, transporting the bell into its components in the blink of an eye. Then he applied a file to some of the parts before fitting them back together with far greater precision. "You are certainly using some pretty tricky materials, but you should have at least achieved this much."

Demon Dragon's Four Heavenly King's Bell (Demon Dragon's Four Heavenly Kings blessing, four elemental magic power-up (large), power of darkness and soul, bond of loyalty)
Quality: highest quality

The additional "bond of loyalty" had been added. I wondered what kind of effect it might have.

"If you imbue too much, it will affect not only the quality but also the balance of the entire piece. The wearer will need a powerful desire to defeat the darkness to make this work," the accessory dealer said.

"I could alter things around, but over there, higher quality means better weapons," I explained.

"I see. It's a fun little piece, I'll give you that." The accessory dealer touched each of the places that had moments ago been a separate part. "It seems close to that mystery material with the corrupted text, but the magic contained in this is being forcibly changed into something else," he pondered.

"I'm impressed by your eye, as always," I told him. "This was indeed created with materials from a powerful monster originating in another world. It would likely be difficult to draw out its true power here in this one." I'd now provided him with a reasonable volume of information. A merchant of his standing wasn't going to expect much more for free.

"Okay. How about we call it a day there, Shield Hero? If you can put together a report for me on the unknown materials you encountered in this other world, I will be happy to pay additional money," he offered.

"I'm happy to give it a try, but I'll be interested to see what you can make based on just that limited information," I told him. The dealer just gave a chuckle. We were about to wrap things up when L'Arc suddenly got involved in the conversation.

"You're the one who taught kiddo how to make accessories, correct?" he asked. Maybe this was the reason he seemed so keen to tag along. "I'm L'Arc Berg. Everyone calls me L'Arc, so feel free to do the same."

"Okay, ah, sure thing." The accessory dealer looked away from the incoming L'Arc and over at me. He wasn't sure what to make of this sudden interruption either. We were all looking at L'Arc with suspicion in our eyes, but he just carried on like normal. At least, that was probably his intention, but there were hints of what looked like panic on his face as he sought a handshake from the accessory dealer.

"You are an ally of the mighty Shield Hero, I take it? What do you want from me—from my store?" the accessory dealer asked.

"This place you've got here is so sparkly! Don't you agree, Therese? Amazing!" He sounded really cheesy—like some kind of pickup artist.

"I know. All of those stones are sparkling so brilliantly. Proof that he is skilled at his job," Therese agreed as she looked around. "I can also tell . . . these pieces are just for display. They aren't even your best work, are they?"

"Smart lady," the accessory dealer said, instantly more taken with Therese than L'Arc.

"I appreciate you trying to put your best foot forward. I personally prefer the work of the Master Craftsman here," she said, pointing at me. I pondered for a moment on the differences between our work. I sought practical capabilities while the accessory dealer sought sales. That could lead to some differences. I myself had once sold all sorts of uniquely shaped accessories to nobles in order to make money, of course. That all came down to personal taste, in the end, so everyone would probably feel differently. For my work, I was influenced by anime and games and so liked to put some fun little gimmicks in there—the kind of stuff you might find in a cheap souvenir store. Accessories featuring butterflies in their designs or accessories designed based on Filo's wings had all sold pretty well.

But I'd have to really commit to it to hone my senses for that kind of thing. It wasn't exactly my main profession.

Aside from all of these factors, the pieces on the accessory dealer's shelves were greatly influenced by designs that were popular out in the world. He tried to retail popular designs.

"Are you looking for something for your discerning female companion, then?" the accessory dealer asked with his best salesman smile in place. It appeared plain on his face that he wasn't happy dealing with the likes of L'Arc—but when I thought about it, I realized he had that look on his face most of the time. He'd even worn it when I first met him.

"Nope, that's not it," L'Arc replied. The accessory dealer had clearly been expecting a positive response and had been reaching beneath the counter to bring out the good stuff. Now he paused and tilted his head. I did too.

"L'Arc, just what are you here for?" I asked him. He had barged into the discussion between the accessory dealer and me, but then he started talking to Therese. When asked if he wanted to buy something, he said that he didn't. Just what did he want, then?

"I might ask the same thing. If you are a companion of the Shield Hero, you may speak plainly. I have limited time," the accessory dealer said. He was one of the top merchants in Zeltoble, so I'd been told, and one who hated wasting time with pointless conversations. "Time is money" was his philosophy, and he apparently stuck to it pretty strictly with almost anyone other than me.

"I was hoping to chat a little more before we reached this point, but here goes." L'Arc took a deep breath and placed both hands together to beg the accessory dealer. "Can you please teach me your secrets of accessory making?" I made a surprised noise. I'd already done that, far above and beyond the call of duty, while we were in the other world. Yet here he was, asking the accessory dealer! Did he have some kind of issue with my skills?

The dealer looked L'Arc up and down, then looked away, making it pretty clear he wasn't interested.

"I'm sorry. I have nothing to teach you. You're not suited to the work of a craftsman," he reported. Just that glance had been enough to tell L'Arc sucked with his hands. In all fairness, anyone could make the same assessment with a similar glance. In his own world, he was the king of an entire nation, leading negotiations with other kings. But that suited him, like some feudal-period warlord. Having a guy who looked like he might proclaim unification of the world suddenly talk about becoming king of accessory making was totally out of left field. If it was already his hobby, maybe it would add some flavor to his character in an unexpected way, but that wasn't what this was either.

"Please! I'm begging you!" L'Arc said, standing firm in the

face of rejection. He bowed his head low, uncaring of the fuss he was causing out here in public.

"I think walking up with a pile of cash and picking something out for your discerning female friend there is more your speed," the accessory dealer said again, his eyes cold, as he finished bringing out his pieces from beneath the counter and showing them to Therese. He kept on calling her "discerning," didn't he?

"Wow . . . these are amazing. They maximize appeal with the minimum possible polishing. You certainly have the skills to call yourself the master of the Master Craftsman . . . but you didn't actually make these either, did you?" Therese said.

"I knew you were discerning," the accessory dealer said. He seemed taken with her eye, but also perhaps a little annoyed by how good it was. This kind of customer had to be a pain for a salesman, I could see that. Perhaps finally realizing that he couldn't get anything past Therese, the accessory dealer reached into his clothing and produced what I presumed was a secret piece, some kind of ultimate work.

"I see," Therese said, finally satisfied. "You are indeed more skilled than the Master Craftsman. However . . ." She returned the necklace to the accessory dealer. "As I already said, this isn't quite to my taste. I'm sure many others will feel differently. You should get a pretty penny for it." The accessory dealer seemed to understand what Therese was trying to say and nodded.

Therese continued, "There is another way to increase the appeal of the stones and appeal to the person who will wear it. That is a fact too."

"I understand that," the accessory dealer replied. "But what do you mean by it? This is suited to me, is it not?"

"Oh, most definitely," Therese replied. "I'm not saying it is a waste. There are some people who can only allure with such heightened emotions." She had clearly seen through to the very merchant soul of the accessory dealer—that making these accessories was, for him, just a way to make money. Therese had understood the true reason he made accessories. But pointing that out to him wasn't going to make him change his ways, of that I could be certain.

"If you want a piece that will really please her," the accessory dealer said to L'Arc, suggesting that it was time to give up, "you should ask the mighty Shield Hero to make something special for her. Do you understand?"

"I can't do that!" L'Arc wasn't backing down, bowing deep to the dealer again. "I need to achieve the same level of skill as kiddo, if not better!" So a playboy-type was begging to become his student and wouldn't back down no matter what he was told. He appeared too casual, so flighty that even if the accessory dealer agreed, L'Arc was likely to run off in less than three days, sick of the whole thing. That had to be what the dealer was feeling. "This is the whole reason I came over here!"

"What? L'Arc, this is why you came?" Raphtalia had been listening silently up until that point, but his proclamation was so dumb it even made her speak up. Not that I cared to finally discover it, but this was the reason he had been acting so strangely. I almost found myself wishing he had been planning something else—anything else, other than this. It seemed impossible. It was awful now that I was faced with it. His whole reason for crossing between worlds was to become the student of the accessory dealer!

I thought back on it now. Before we left, I had dropped in on L'Arc in his private chambers, and there had been a lot of ore lying around. I'd also heard talk of him visiting Romina's workshop a lot, and he had been keen to listen to any tips I might have for him.

Even with all of this, his technique hadn't improved at all.

"I don't want to just hear about you from kiddo and the others. I'm here to learn from you, directly at your feet!" With this further declaration, L'Arc took out a rough-looking Orichal Starfire Bracelet. It was poor quality, a bad copy of the one I had made—and yet it had to be the very best that L'Arc could make at the moment.

"Please, teach me how to make accessories! Teach me the same things you taught kiddo. Just make it easier to understand! I'm not good with my hands, I know, so I need some serious help!" L'Arc pleaded. The rest of us were starting to feel quite sorry for the guy. I wondered what it was that was driving him so hard.

There was a fatal flaw in his logic, however. Seeing as my teachings weren't helping him, he believed that he just needed to be taught by the one who taught me. He was hoping the techniques that one needed to learn and hone for oneself could simply be picked up from someone else. Talk about a schoolboy error. I'd known otaku friends with the same problem—thinking that getting into a vocational school was all they needed to work in the industry and learned nothing as a result. Wherever you went to school, you wouldn't get anywhere without the will to learn. In some cases, the inflated ego and air of faux professionalism provided by attending such a school only made things worse out in the real world.

"I'm sorry, but I have nothing to teach you," the accessory dealer maintained, still holding his ground. Emotions didn't come into the equation for a merchant—but this was a stark contrast from when he beat his teachings into me, without me even asking.

"If you want to learn so badly, ask the mighty Shield Hero again . . . or you can pay me an introductory fee and I'll introduce you to one of my students. They can meet your needs, give you the full experience," the accessory dealer suggested smoothly, the conversation always managing to come back around to money. His use of "experience" also suggested he still considered L'Arc nothing more than a tourist.

"No! It has to be you!" L'Arc replied. Although I very much wanted him to, he wasn't giving up. The issue was we were dealing with a merchant, not a craftsman. His only intention was to use his accessory skills to make money, nothing else. His salesman's smile finally slipping, the accessory dealer dropped the affable front. He took out out a smoking pipe like it was the most annoying thing in the world to be forced to do and starting to smoke it.

"Look . . . I didn't want to have to do this, not in front of the mighty Shield Hero," he said. He looked like the whole thing was a massive pain but also like he was resigned to the fact that he was going to have to spell things out. "To be perfectly honest . . . L'Arc, was it? I don't want to teach you. Why, you ask? Because I sense nothing of the merchant's soul from you. That is completely different, I might add, from having a talent for simply selling things." It was true. Going this far was the only way to get through to L'Arc. He was the king of an entire nation and pretty good at talking people around to his way of thinking. If he did start selling a product, he could quickly gather talented people to him who would surely choose him as company president. He had the charisma for that. Simply having L'Arc in the lead would gather people to him, people who would follow his orders and make their sales a success. In that sense, then, he probably did have a talent for selling things—but that wasn't the "merchant soul" that the dealer was looking for.

The accessory dealer liked hardcore merchants, dyed-in-the-wool hagglers who would count and crimp over every last coin. The type that wanted more money, no matter how much they got, and would do whatever it took—legal or illegal—to make it. The kind of merchant soul that didn't care about capture and was unafraid of crime; that was the altar at which the accessory dealer worshipped. Even if it led him to his eventual demise, he surely wouldn't regret it. When I considered it all together like that, he really was a piece of work. He had this look in his eye when he finally revealed himself, glinting suspiciously in the darkness. From this perspective, I much preferred... Okay, "preferred" was not the right word, but I could still put up much more easily with Motoyasu II, the crusty old pervert who had trained the weapon shop guy, even if he only made weapons so he could fuel his drinking and womanizing. That also made him so much easier to handle, though—you just had to tempt him with some women.

"You need to just give up on learning for yourself," the dealer continued, "and have someone else with some talent make the accessories for you. I'm not running some kind of touchy-feely workshop experience here," he finished, really putting the boot in. This was for the best though. We needed L'Arc fighting for the future of the worlds, not mucking about making trinkets here. That could be his hobby, something to relax with, that was all.

"No! I'm not giving up! I'll never give up!" L'Arc said, looking up with a strange aura flicking around him. I was starting to get suspicious. Had L'Arc gone and got himself cursed? I wouldn't be happy about that. Maybe thinking about Therese too much, he had gone and got himself cursed with jealousy, meaning we would have to fight him! No, I wouldn't like that at all. "You know more about this stuff than kiddo, right? You can tell me anything that I don't understand, right? I can't take subtlety. I need it straight!" It looked like L'Arc might jump onto the accessory dealer any moment and try to take a bite out of him. The dealer was shrinking back a little, starting to get overwhelmed.

I could even see where L'Arc was coming from. You couldn't learn to make accessories just by copying. Even working from an example that I had made wasn't enough. I even liked how hard he was trying to overcome his shortcomings and make something that Therese would like. But on the flipside of that . . . I couldn't really understand why he was so fixated on accessories.

"L'Arc, can you just give up on this please?" Therese pleaded. "I haven't started to dislike you, and I'm not thinking about moving on from you either. It's all okay."

"I don't need your empty praise!" L'Arc said. "I want to be

a man you can truly be proud of, Therese! I can't compromise on that!" I could understand her feelings wavering at a playboy like him now coming on so strong. From his perspective, he didn't want her just hanging around because the guy she might prefer already had attachments. Although I wasn't exactly giving her any impression of fidelity, I wasn't sure how I would feel if Raphtalia intimated that there was someone she preferred, but she was sticking with me out of habit.

"I want to learn these skills!" he declared. But the truth—that he didn't want to lose his woman—was plain for all to see.

"L'Arc suddenly has a look in his eyes a lot like you, Mr. Naofumi!" Raphtalia said with bewilderment on her face. I did a double take, wondering if that was really what I looked like all the time.

"Okay then . . . very well. I guess I can accept you as my student," the dealer finally said. I wasn't the only one who gave an exclamation of surprise. Cowed by L'Arc's persistence, the dealer had finally caved and agreed to the situation.

"That's great!" L'Arc struck a victory pose, face beaming, his shout as loud as I had ever heard him go—which was saying something. He was probably hearing some rousing music playing in his head right now. Then I realized he was actually crying. I wondered if he could really be that happy. He certainly went all in.

That said, I had to give him credit for crossing to another

world just to become the student of the accessory dealer—
even if I would have preferred he spend the time leveling up in
preparation for the coming battles.

"Hey," I said to the accessory dealer.

As people around all applauded the conclusion to our little
performance, I prodded the accessory dealer, who had his hand
theatrically raised to his forehead. "Why did you agree to this?"

"I regret it already, I assure you," he replied. "But I was
simply unable to turn him down. There was a light in his eyes,
a burning light that said he could achieve it, he would achieve
it, no matter what." L'Arc's eyes, that had made even the mi-
serly accessory dealer change his tune . . . They had apparently
looked a lot like mine. Maybe that was what had broken down
his stubborn heart, then.

"Something feels wrong about all this," Raphtalia
commented.

"You can say that again," I agreed heartily.

"If you're going to do this, I want you to see it through
to the end," Therese said, also seemingly at a loss with how to
respond to L'Arc. "There's no helping you sometimes, now is
there? I really wish you would learn to compromise a little."

"Looks like we're doing this," I said with a sigh. "You can
work out the fee for his lessons during your contract negotiations," I told the dealer.

"I am partly to blame here, so I will keep it as cheap as

I can," the dealer replied. With that, the opening of negotiations between the dealer and me came to a close. The lesson I learned from it all was never to bring someone like L'Arc along to such a meeting ever again.

Chapter Three: The Sword Hero's Sense of Responsibility

It took longer than expected, but we finally rolled back into the village. L'Arc and his allies had remained behind. Just as I had expected, everyone from the village had gathered to welcome us home. However, they managed to stop themselves from throwing a full-blown festival.

"Bubba, welcome back! I can't wait for dinner tonight!" shouted Keel, the one voice I could pick out. Others shouted "welcome home!" or "I can't wait for dinner!" or "feed me!" Everyone was hungry; that was the impression I got. The preparations had already been made, and no sooner was I home than I was forced to start cooking. I guessed this was to be my lot in life, no matter my destination.

"Hey, Imiya," I said. "Your accessory was a big help over there."

"Ah, well . . . thank you," she replied.

"We'll be receiving a visit fairly soon from someone who was really impressed by your work, so I hope you'll have a chat with her," I continued.

"Of course," Imiya said. I carried on, chatting with everyone in the village in a similar fashion.

"Brother, Sister . . . you have returned to the village," Fohl said, coming in as I continued to prepare the meal. We had seen each other briefly when fighting the wave, but I had prioritized talking to Trash, so we hadn't really caught up yet.

"That's right. I'm not sure exactly when we will go back over, but for the time being we are going to be keeping an eye on things here," I told him.

"Understood," he said.

"How have things been with you?" I asked him.

"Bubba Fohl has been hanging around the village like a bad smell . . . He doesn't like talking to Staff Hero Trash, not one bit!" Keel said gleefully.

"Keel!" Fohl was quick to chastise her, looking most uncomfortable. Trash was Fohl's uncle, meaning he had familial feelings toward Fohl that were along the same lines as those that he had for Melty. I could understand Fohl not quite knowing how to handle them.

"Atla did tell you to look after the village," I reminded him, giving him an out. "If there hasn't been any trouble, that's fine."

"Okay! Everyone in the village has been training! Everyone is trying hard!" Fohl reported. I took a moment to check over the levels of those who were assembled and saw that they had indeed seen an increase across the board. Next we needed to implement the whip power-up method and work to create an invincible force that could take down any wave.

"Naofumi . . . welcome back." Ren appeared in the refectory, looking pretty worse for wear. He greeted me unsteadily. I'd been thinking of giving him an earful, but his condition actually looked pretty bad. I couldn't get angry with him over this. His sense of responsibility was even stronger than I had expected.

"I'm sorry . . . I know you left me in charge," he said, sounding truly exhausted.

"I didn't mean for you to take responsibility for absolutely everything," I told him. The medical analysis had determined he was suffering from a gastric ulcer and intense mental exhaustion. He also faced a lack of sleep due to stress, with some people reporting he had been training instead of sleeping. Perhaps the pressure of fighting to protect the world had just proven too much for him. It all seemed a bit silly to me. He took everything too seriously, which only accelerated the troubles he faced. I knew that I had been helping to reduce that burden on him, but I didn't realize it would get this bad this quickly without me around. It could be a result of Motoyasu and the others running so wild . . . or just Ren having such a strong sense of responsibility for everything.

"Kwaaaaaa!" One of those moments that had been causing such a hassle for Ren came—quite literally—flying in. It was Gaelion.

"Hold on, Gaelion!" I shouted. All he did was squawk, so

I was forced to take action and defend myself—just in case. "Shooting Star Shield!" With a thunk, the incoming dragon crashed into my barrier.

"Kwaa! Kwaa!" he squawked, clearly complaining about the wall keeping him away.

"The taunts of the Demon Dragon really got him riled up, or so I heard," I commented.

"Kwaa!" Gaelion responded.

"That's true! He went on quite the rampage and caused a lot of trouble for the Sword Hero. I'm so embarrassed . . ." Wyndia explained.

"The Demon Dragon is also to blame, taunting him like that," I said. I didn't know exactly what she had said to him, of course, but I was concerned enough about what the additional fragment she had given me might contain that I wasn't sure if I should hand it over or not. "Even so, you're the king of the dragons, aren't you? Shouldn't you be acting a little more regal?" I pointed out. I wished the old Gaelion would suppress him a bit, but the personality of the young one was too dominant.

"Kwaa . . ." Gaelion squawked.

"It seems Gaelion wants to know if you had relations with the Dragon Emperor in the other world," Wyndia asked.

"He really thinks that's something I would do?" I asked, with some venom. I wondered if I was really considered so unprincipled. The way the Demon Dragon came on strong reminded me of Atla, which I didn't hate. But taking it any further than that would be going too far.

"Really, as if you would do such a thing," Raphtalia agreed.

"Raph!" added Raph-chan. I wondered how he could even think such a thing was possible. Maybe he thought she had turned into a beautiful girl to tempt me. Gaelion's face brightened at my response, seemingly forgetting that he was going to have to be punished for his misdeeds while I was away.

"After all the trouble you've been causing for Wyndia and Ren, I'm not going to be talking to you much for a while. I don't know what kind of taunting message it contains for you, but I have a gift here for you from the Demon Dragon, so just take that and let's see what happens!" I told him, tossing him the fragment I received from the Demon Dragon.

"Kwaa . . ." Gaelion said pitifully at my words, moving over to have Wyndia console him.

"So now you finally calm down. I told you, there's no way the Shield Hero was going to fall for that madam dragon," Wyndia said, unable to resist an "I told you so."

"I can't say I like her on a personal level, but she's definitely more capable than you in battle," I told him. He squawked in surprise. "If you don't like it, you'd better start training harder."

"Kwaaaaaa!" The dragon grabbed onto Wyndia, crying. I had no sympathy for a selfish reptile who couldn't even keep things together while I was away. Hopefully, the regret he was feeling now would propel him forward.

Old Gaelion was choosing to keep quiet, the situation being what it was.

"There, there. Let's go back to the monster stable before you upset the Shield Hero any further," Wyndia said, carrying Gaelion away. As they left, Sadeena and Shildina came in, bringing Ruft—with Raph-chan II in his arms—along with them.

"Shield Hero, welcome back," said Ruft. He was in his demi-human form and was also starting to look a little taller than everyone else. If I compared them all directly, I could see a definite change in him. Just like Raphtalia, he seemed to be developing faster than the others around him. Seeing him with Sadeena and Shildina like this also helped to reinforce a similarity to that of Raphtalia. I guessed that it meant even after everything that happened, he was indeed the king of Q'ten Lo. Seeing Melty and Trash in action up close had probably been having an effect on him too. Raphtalia seemed to be having similar thoughts about the demi-human Ruft, because she had a complicated expression on her face. She had lost her parents and probably saw some of her departed father in Ruft's face.

"Raph!" said Raph-chan.

"Dafu!" said Raph-chan II. I basked in their cute greetings for a moment, and then I turned to Ruft.

"Hey, Ruft. How are things?" I asked him. With a poof, Ruft turned into his therianthrope form, a happy expression on his face. I felt conflicted about the fact that when he was a therianthrope he looked his actual age, but I wasn't going to let it bother me. After all, he also looked like a giant Raph-chan.

"Queen Melty and the others know more about the political situation. Rat has been conducting research into my own transformation," he explained.

"I see. How is that looking? Do you think we can perform the same thing on Raphtalia?" I asked. As soon as I said that, Raphtalia grabbed my shoulder, turning a fixed smile in my direction and giving off an aura so strong it was like she might have been cursed herself.

"I know I have been away for a while, but none of that, please," she told me.

"Are you sure?" Ruft pleaded, looking up at her with a slightly frowny pose that even Raph-chan never used.

"Oh my!" said Sadeena.

"Oh dear!" said Shildina. "You've gotten bolder than before, Ruft."

"I'm not going to allow it, no matter what kind of look you give me. It sounds like you and Mr. Naofumi have been cooking up all sorts of trouble while I was away . . . Ruft, don't you take issue with being experimented on?" she asked him pointedly.

"Not at all," he replied. He had asked for the class-up experiment himself—and that had led to the birth of this incredibly sweet Raph-type therianthrope. It looked so cute. . . but it was also starting to feel a bit dangerous. I had also learned that both raccoon therianthropes and the race called war raccoons looked different from what Ruft had become. "When I'm like this, I get along so well with the other Raph species. I can understand what they are saying, and the text for cooperative magic just appears in my head, making it so easy to cast! It also makes the Melromarc language easier to understand too." That almost sounded like some kind of translation function. I would have to ask Rat what was going on there.

"Raphtalia. You know I always tell the village slaves that they get to choose for themselves when they take a classup—that I'm not going to choose for them. Ruft wanted this Raph-chan class-up for himself. You'll just have to accept it."

"You really believe that? I can only see you having pushed him into this, to be honest. Making all these comments about Raph-chan being cuter than filolials, things like that," Raphtalia responded.

"I only speak the truth," I replied. Of course, that was also all based on the reaction Ruft had shown when we first met him. Ultimately, Ruft had taken a liking to Raph-chan and started to play more with the Raph species.

"Dafu!" said Raph-chan II, looking a little upset about the whole thing. Raph-chan consoled her by patting her on the head.

"There's no changing what has already been done, but we are not finished discussing this issue, Mr. Naofumi," Raphtalia said. She could be stubborn too when she wanted to be.

"Brother, Sister, I'm glad nothing has changed with you," Fohl said, nodding to himself in acceptance. I wondered if this situation was really something to be accepted so easily.

"Now things should be easier on me . . ." Ren breathed.

"You need to learn to relax a little, Ren, that's for sure. Fohl, he needs more backup from you," I directed.

"I did what I could! The Sword Hero collapsed anyway!" Fohl protested. He had always done a good job of looking after Atla, giving him the flexibility to handle a certain degree of problems that the village might throw at him. The issue was really Ren's fragile mental attitude and lack of means to blow off that stress.

"I'll be watching over things for a while, anyway. You just concentrate on getting better, Ren," I told him. He managed to mumble his agreement.

"Little Naofumi, are we expecting a meal anytime soon?" Sadeena called.

"It's like every day is a party recently! What fun!" said Shildina, both of them clearly very hungry.

"It's almost ready," I told them.

"Master, I'm back! Save me!" Filo came flying in and immediately rushed into the kitchen and hid herself. I wondered where Melty was—maybe Filo had dropped her off somewhere. With or without her, anyway, I knew what was coming next—Motoyasu.

"Everyone with their hands free, stop Motoyasu and his filolials from getting through! They can eat later!" I commanded. There were shouts of agreement.

"Naofumi! Should you really be giving orders like that?" Ren asked.

"It's fine. Everyone here has such energy, as I'm sure you've noticed. This is how you handle the villagers, Ren. Watch and learn," I told him. I ignored the chaos my orders triggered and went back to cooking.

Dinnertime was always crazy. This was one of the big differences between here and Kizuna's world. There were so many mouths to feed that I could cook and cook and I'd still need to cook some more. I got sick of it in the end. I told anyone else who was still hungry to eat some bioplant veggies. Then I settled down to my own dinner. Everyone stuffed themselves and then went their separate ways for the night.

"Hey, Filo," I called out to her. I had chased out Motoyasu and his filolials after feeding them, and Filo was now eating some bioplant nuts in the refectory. "Can you get in touch with Fitoria?"

"Huh?" she replied, stuffing her mouth. I couldn't believe how much she could eat. Then her cowlick started twitching. "Yes. I hear her, and she can hear you. She wants to know what you want," Filo reported.

"You know at least something about what we are fighting

against, right?" I asked, speaking to Fitoria directly. "About Takt and the others called the vanguards of the waves." Via Filo, I proceeded to explain the truth about the vanguards of the waves and those who appeared to be behind them. "But you already knew all of this, didn't you?" She had been around for a long time, so it seemed unlikely to me that she didn't have some inkling about this stuff.

"Hmmm. She says it was all so long ago. Her memories are unclear. But she knew about enemies being sent here by the waves," Filo relayed.

"You can't do any better than that?" I asked.

"It's all blurry, she says, and the waves try so many different things. She doesn't know," Filo reported. She was still just a filolial at the end of the day. They were a pretty easygoing race.

"No matter. We learned a lot over in that other world—the second other world, for me—but I take it you already know about Ethnobalt through Filo, correct?" I asked her. I waited for Filo's cowlick communication to be completed and then continued. "He's a monster that occupies the same position that filolials do here, basically. It seems that there was once a legendary library rabbit, much like you, but they were killed at some point in the past." The one who assumed the name of God had shown a tendency to wipe out anyone who could act as a threat to the waves. In that case, it wouldn't be surprising if they decided to come for Fitoria. I went on to explain to Fitoria what had happened in Ethnobalt's home, the Ancient Labyrinth Library. "It seems that the ones we have been fighting are active in this world too. They might be targeting you, so please be careful," I warned her. We had no idea what might happen, after all. S'yne's sister's forces might even try to capture Fitoria alive and do all sorts of things to her.

"She says that she understands. She's also saying . . . that there are some things she wants to check with you, so she wonders if you would come and see her in the near future," Filo told me.

"Things? Like what kind of things? She isn't looking to cause trouble for us with more strange requests is she?" I replied. I had yet to forget the antics with Motoyasu—I would never forget them, to be honest.

"She says it sounds similar to the Ethnobalt issue. It's getting dark today, so she wonders if you can make time tomorrow," Filo relayed.

"Hmmm. Okay then," I replied. As I gave the nod, Filo's cowlick stopped moving.

"A visit with Fitoria. It has been a while, hasn't it?" Raphtalia commented.

"You know what? It really has. We haven't seen her since the whole Spirit Tortoise business," I replied. We had been in the middle of the monster war at the time, meaning we didn't really have time for a chat. Since then, the only real contact had been the request that had led to whacky races with Motoyasu, and thanks to that, I hadn't really had the time of day for her since.

I just had to hope things would go better this time.

Chapter Four: The Filolial Ruins

The next day, we arrived at the filolial sanctuary, guided by Fitoria. It seemed different from the place we had come to before.

"I have to say though . . ." I said, looking around.

"What?" Fitoria asked.

"Haven't you ever heard of tidying up?!"

Fitoria had come to the village and then teleported everyone who wanted to come. I hadn't said anything yet, but Fitoria's carriage was super suspicious. The thing could teleport around, after all! In Kizuna's world there were eight vassal weapons, but in our world there were only seven. Fitoria had lived for a long time too. These facts had me considering a certain possibility . . .

"Fitoria. There's all sorts of things I want to ask you about your carriage, but could it be a vassal weapon?" I asked. "The eighth seven star weapon, as it were?" She stayed quiet as I asked and didn't provide any answers. There had to be some reason for that too—like something that was better kept secret, or maybe it was at the request of a past hero.

Investigating the filolial sanctuary came first. When Fitoria and her filolials turned up at our village earlier, they had brought for us various pieces of gear that the heroes in the past had owned—other than the holy or seven star weapons. But there had been some real junk mixed in among them. So we had decided that the heroes and others from the village should come to Fitoria's sanctuary and sort through the stuff to find those items we could actually use. Trash had not joined us; he was busy working things out with other nations. L'Arc was, of course, training in accessory making in Zeltoble, and Therese was with him there. Gaelion and Wyndia were absent too.

It looked like we had arrived in some kind of ruins. There was a forest around us and what looked like the remains of an abandoned village. There was also some sort of shrine in the ruins nearby. This reminded me of something Melty had said once about the filolial legends of a place called the Lost Woods. As the name suggested, anyone who went inside got lost. I was beginning to think we were in the Lost Woods right now. This was a different place from the whole Church of the Three Heroes incident. I would have to bring Melty to see this next time.

Motoyasu immediately gave a shout. "This sanctuary shall become my new paradise!" he exclaimed.

"Why did you bring the Spear Hero?!" Fitoria squawked.

"I thought you might like to see him," I said innocently. I had registered a portal, returned to the village, asked Motoyasu if he wanted to join us, and then came back. In the moment Fitoria saw Motoyasu, she backed away from him at incredible speed. Motoyasu was not deterred, still leaping toward Fitoria, who promptly kicked him away.

"You won't stop me!" Motoyasu had taken almost no damage, immediately springing back to his feet and starting to chase Fitoria around. This was her punishment. I had been pissed off too many times to count by Fitoria's attitude in the past.

We left Motoyasu to his own devices and started to investigate the inside of the ruins. The reason I had made that cutting jibe about tidying up was because the narrow interior of the ruins was packed with what looked like little more than trash. All the sparkly things were likely because we were dealing with birds. I remembered Filo collecting her "treasures" in the past.

"Wow! It's so sparkly! I love sparkly!" Filo shouted. She was pretty much the same right now. This was Fitoria's nest. The sparkly things scattered around ran the gamut from rare-looking treasures to cheap-looking crystal.

"Let's tidy up," I said. What a collection she had amassed though! These were large ruins—or a temple, maybe—but the collection was rough and ready. The setting might have given the impression of dungeon treasures, but that wasn't what we were looking at here. It was more like a random collection of trash. There were loads of bird feathers mixed in as well, and it was all pretty dirty.

"Shall we just burn all the feathers away?" I suggested.

"What if there's something here that we don't want to burn up?" Raphtalia warned me. She was right, of course. Better not to start burning stuff. All of Fitoria's long years of collecting had turned her nest into a veritable trash pile, anyway. It made me sad to think rare items might be slumbering amid this muck. We were planning to recover anything promising and get it analyzed, which meant we had to sort through all this crap by putting it into the heroes' weapons, of course.

"Split up and start the cleaning operation!" I ordered, and so the spring cleaning of Fitoria's stink pile started. I found myself wondering which was preferable, rabbits that lived in a mysterious dungeon with a load of strange rules or birds that didn't have any dangerous dungeon-like elements to deal with but also couldn't keep their nest tidy.

"What's this? It's all sparkly and beautiful! Some kind of crystal?" Filo said.

"That's trash! A literal ball of trash!" I told her.

"This is rare ore, I say! Naofumi, what shall we do?" Motoyasu asked, pulling his weight for once.

"Keep a hold of it. I'll requisition it later," I told him.

"Why is there a sword here? It doesn't look rusty either. Ren, what do you make of this?" Rishia asked. She was here too, helping to clean up with Itsuki.

"Huh?" Ren looked over. "That's a sword I don't have yet. Let me have a look . . . Ascalon, is it? What's this? Effective against dragons?" The name of that sword sounded familiar to me, for some reason, but for now we needed to keep working. I was just glad we didn't bring Gaelion along.

"Why is there a spear wrapped up in cloth and suspended here?" Rishia continued. "Motoyasu, please take it and have a look. You can pick up feathers and sniff them later."

"Very well! Bah! I can't reach it!" Motoyasu quickly exclaimed.

"Dafu!" said Raph-chan II. She was up on the spear-like item suspended in the air. It looked like something a hero must have made—like a yokai-fighting spear bound in red cloth from that one famous manga.

"Why don't you just copy it?" Rishia suggested.

"Good idea! Beast Spear? Oh, this one works automatically. A convenient-looking weapon," Motoyasu reported. We had some pretty yokai-like creatures among our allies. I had to hope it wasn't going to be effective against the Raph species in particular. We didn't need Motoyasu having that power.

"Dafu," said Raph-chan II—who was the past Heavenly Emperor. After making sure Motoyasu had copied the spear, she tapped the tip of the spear, making the cloth fly off it, then took it into her hand. It had even shrunk down to her size! I was starting to feel like we were finding all sorts of crazy items. We could think about it all later.

Shildina gave a groan, using me as—appropriately enough—a shield as she watched Raph-chan II powering up. She didn't get along well with that one.

"There's no need to be scared, Shildina. You're stronger than her now, surely," Ruft told her.

"But still . . ." Shildina said nervously, tightening her ofuda defenses even as Ruft tried to bolster her courage. She just needed to keep powering herself up. So long as she did that, she should be able to handle anything that came her way.

We continued to clean the interior of the shrine, picking our way through the mixture of various rare items and trash.

"There are some dragon bones here. I guess we should take those," I said. It looked like a couple of skeletons' worth. Just how much history was scattered across the floor in here? We were lucky to find things still intact, too, because the entire collection had been exposed to the elements for who knew how long.

In one room of the ruins there were all sorts of weapons lying around, including one used by the high priest of the Church of the Three Heroes. That had to be a replica, but I still wondered what the hell it was doing here. Maybe it could be used for something—but it would need to be refilled with magic and looked difficult to handle. We should probably carry this stuff to the castle or village and have the old guy and the others analyze it.

A shield also turned up for me, which I copied. It was called the Ancient Shield. It wasn't all that effective either. An unlock effect that increased magic defense, that was about all it had to offer. It was the same for Ren and the others—all the Ancient series. These were weapons that could cause a status effect called "magic blocker." That sounded kind of useful, but it was only for use against humans.

"Big lady filolial!" Motoyasu shouted.

"Boo!" Fitoria rejected him using the same type of line as Filo. I hadn't heard the reasons why, but Fitoria seemed to dislike Motoyasu as much as Filo did.

S'yne was pointing at Motoyasu, and I realized she was asking if maybe she should stop him. As I waved at her not to worry, I looked between S'yne and Fitoria. They were wearing different clothing, and there was the issue of feathers, but . . . they actually looked kind of similar. S'yne was taller, but they had a similar atmosphere about them. Fitoria, originating as a monster, and S'yne, a resident of a destroyed world . . . there was a real connection between them. Maybe they just happened to look alike. I wondered if it could be that simple.

"Ah! Filo!" Motoyasu quickly changed target.

"Boo! Stay away!" she replied. As Motoyasu closed in, she leapt up into the air and flew away.

"Oh wow, she's flying!" said one of Fitoria's minion filolials who could talk.

"That looks like fun," said another.

"How did she learn to fly?" a third asked, all of them watching her with jealous eyes.

"What? Someone is making her fly with magic?" a fourth one said.

"Let's get them to do that for us!" said a fifth one. I wasn't sure where they had heard it, but all filolial eyes turned to Shildina.

"Help me!" Shildina hugged Raph-chan II to her, going on the defensive with Ruft.

"Dafu," said Raphtalia II, looking a little perplexed at Shildina's change of heart. Then she used magic to make Shildina and the others vanish, turning the awareness of the filolials away from them.

"We aren't making much progress here! If you're only here to mess about, you can leave!" I shouted.

"Hahaha! Father! I'll do everything I can to turn this filolial sanctuary into a paradise!" Motoyasu exclaimed.

"Stop flapping those lips and start tidying up!" I replied. How easily these airheads got distracted! I could hardly deal with them. Kizuna's bunch were even more lively, perhaps, but they also had a clearer sense of purpose.

"Seriously, there is so much trash in here. What's going on back there?" I asked. We pushed deeper into the ruins, eventually coming to what looked like a large altar. There wasn't any trash on the ground here. The floor was paved with stone, and it looked to be decorated like a clockface.

"The air feels kind of heavy in here," Raphtalia said.

"Agreed," I replied.

"My, my, this house of filolials is full of such special things!" Motoyasu exclaimed.

"Motoyasu, stay back," I told him. Ignoring me, he stood in the center of the clock and stuck his spear into the ground. It made a clicking sound, followed by an ominous rumbling.

"Motoyasu!" I shouted.

"Oh my! Whatever do you think is happening?" he asked.

"Don't ask me! Shooting Star Wall!" I shouted. Picking the wall version just to be sure, I created a barrier to protect everyone other than Motoyasu and his own band of filolials.

"Fitoria, you got any idea about this?" I asked.

"No idea," she replied, tilting her head to the side. She wasn't any help at all!

"Oh? Oh? Oooh!" Motoyasu breathed. There was light starting to shine out from the hole he had placed the spear into. Then the light was absorbed into the spear, leaving flickering images in its wake.

"Fehhh!" Rishia exclaimed. "What just happened?!"

"No idea," I said. Nothing else seemed to change. "Motoyasu, anything different?"

"There is something . . . a weapon called Dragon Clock Hand has appeared," he reported, transforming his weapon. It was a long, thin spear. Simple, almost, which might have sounded refined—but it looked more like the minute hand from some old clock.

"Does inserting your weapon into that hole trigger something?" I pondered aloud. I felt around the hole Motoyasu had used and experimentally tried to stuff the shield into it. Nothing happened or even looked like it was going to happen.

"First come first served?" Ren wondered, also giving it a try.

"Motoyasu!" I shouted.

"I have no idea, I say!" he replied. One would not normally just stick their weapon into any hole that presented itself . . . I would like to believe. But I couldn't be sure, it being Motoyasu. I gave a sigh.

"Just more unexplained shit. Come on, let's keep moving," I said. It didn't look like we had any monsters to contend with, anyway. This was filolial territory, so with their boss Fitoria along, it wouldn't matter even if we did bump into some monsters.

Traps were a different matter. All the classics sprang off around us, from rolling boulders to spikes on the ceiling, but they meant nothing in the face of a party of heroes. My Shooting Star Wall blocked them all, and I even gave a chuckle when the boulder stopped dead. Eat your heart out, Indy.

I also expected some light puzzle-solving, but there was nothing so complicated. We had a read on the shape of the space thanks to Sadeena and Shildina's sonar ability. That was a useful one to have around in places like this, places filled with secret doorways and passages. At the heart of the ruins, we came to a stone room that appeared to be floating in the air via magic. Floating stone . . . It was known as "glawick," I recalled.

We climbed the steps carved from it and reached the room at the top, then looked around.

There was a seriously heavy atmosphere in the room. It felt like this was the origin of the magic.

"Mr. Naofumi, we've seen a place like this before," Raphtalia said.

"Indeed we have," I recalled. It was exactly like the stone chamber assigned to the curator in the Ancient Labyrinth Library, Ethnobalt's home.

"After hearing your description of that place, I thought I had better bring you here," Fitoria explained.

"So there's one on this world too," I said. Here, in the depths of the ruins—of Fitoria's home—a small vial was floating in the air. Behind it there was the same mural on the wall as we had seen in Ethnobalt's place, depicting some kind of winged cat-like creature. There were images of the holy weapons . . . and the vassal weapons too, when I looked more closely. Some of the images were glowing. To start with, I thought it was the exact same image as before, but it was actually different in multiple places. The cat part was different too. There were two whale-looking creatures hanging around in the background. Seeing where I was looking, Rishia started to investigate the wall herself.

"It looks very similar to the one we saw with Ethnobalt, but there appears to be text written on this one," she reported.

"There is?" I asked. Rishia pointed to a section of the wall. At a glance, it had appeared to just be another kind of pattern, but now I saw it was covered with text. It was almost like a piece of art, forming an image from a distance but turning into text when you got close. I appreciated the effort—almost—but kind of wished they had just written it out in more legible lettering.

"I'll leave the analysis to you," I told her. Time for our true main character and the greatest intellect present to step up to the plate.

"I'm sure I'll make all sorts of interpretation and translation mistakes," she replied, unsure of herself.

"You've got incredible analytical skills, I'll vouch for that. You can do this," I told her.

"He's right, Rishia. I believe in you too," Raphtalia offered.

"Fehhhhh!" came her predictable response, but she seemed ready to give it a try.

I turned my attention to the vial of red liquid that we had also seen with Ethnobalt. I picked it up. No problems. There was also a lot more left in the vial here than there had been over there. I wondered if that meant something. It might be related to how long Fitoria seemed to have lived. Over there they had been forced to use it more frequently. Maybe that was the reason.

"That is the medicine that guardians from other worlds should drink, correct?" Fitoria asked, pointing at the vial.

"What is it? What is its purpose?" I asked her.

"It's a poison, but I don't really understand it. I drank it before," Fitoria said.

"Okay. What about people? Can they drink it too?" I asked.

"I think I remember hearing that they'd better not," she replied. So it sounded like it was only for monsters but had the effect of extending their life span—like some kind of elixir of eternal life. "What I do remember is one drop means eternal pain, two drops means eternal loneliness, and three drops . . . means something truly terrible." That was the exact same thing that Ethnobalt had said.

"The thing is, using the weapon produced by this to attack a wave crack greatly increased the time before the next wave. There's more of it here than there was in Kizuna's world—enough for all of our heroes, most likely," I explained. A mysterious liquid left by a hero in the past. We were going to have to make good use of it . . . but I was still wondering what this wall meant, with all the same images as the one in a totally different world. That was not an issue that could be resolved by simply thinking about it, however.

I dripped a drop of potion onto my shield.

Conditions for Shield 0 unlocked!

Shield 0 (Awakened) 0/0
<abilities locked> equip bonus: skill: "Shield 0"
special effect: Judge of Reason, World Protector

It turned out to be a shield even lower on the ladder than the Small Shield, with everything at 0. Kizuna had obtained the same thing for her weapon, but I wondered again just what this was. I changed to it to see what would happen. It looked the same as the Small Shield.

"Shield 0," I said, using the one skill it had. Light flashed out and the shield started to shine. It looked pretty cool. I'd have to experiment more with it later. The potion hadn't produced any strange side effects, and so it seemed safe to use. The shield itself was far too weak to use, but it might offer some excellent effects. Games often had weapons and armor of the same type.

"All of the heroes should have this, in order to overcome the trials ahead," Fitoria said.

"You heard the crazy bird lady. Let's have everyone put some of this into their weapons," I said. Each hero present proceeded to place one drop into their own weapon, releasing the same 0 series for each of them, with the same effects for each.

"Do you want to try some?" I asked Filo.

"You're asking me again? Boo!" she said. I had indeed

asked her the same thing when Ethnobalt underwent the drinking ceremony. She hadn't wanted to drink it then either, but in the end, I thought—one day—she was probably going to have to. She was Fitoria's successor, after all.

"You are the next queen, Filo, so one day you will have to drink it," Fitoria said, confirming my own thoughts.

"Boo!" she replied again. I wondered about this past hero who had made Fitoria drink it, even though he probably knew it was poison. I couldn't see Fitoria accepting it easily—but here I was, trying to get Filo to drink it.

I looked at the wall, with its cat creature, and wondered when that little mystery was ever going to be solved. With our track record, maybe never. Always seen close to materials covering the waves, it didn't really feel like the one behind the waves . . . but maybe it was. I wondered if this was the one who assumed the name of God.

If so, there should be images in the ancient texts that Rishia had been reading.

"Fitoria," I asked. She looked over at me. "Have you met this thing here?" I said, pointing at the creature on the wall.

"I think . . . I probably have," she replied.

"You normally sound more confident about things than that," I commented.

"I can remember what it looked like moving around. I don't think it is a bad creature . . ." she said, trailing off.

"Is it the one who assumes the name of God?" I asked. If so, we needed to be ready to dispatch immediately, if we ever encountered it.

"No, that doesn't sound right. But I remember it talking with the heroes," she replied. That sounded like the one who made this wall was trying to impart something about this creature—but also that the cat wasn't an enemy. No answers there. ". . . moru," Fitoria said softly, almost inaudibly, placing her hand on the wall.

"Whatever is going on here, the one behind the waves has been trying to kill those just like you, Fitoria, all across history, so you need to be careful," I told her.

"I understand that. Now maybe you see why I rarely show myself," she replied. That was true. Ethnobalt worked in the library, but there was no telling where Fitoria might show up next. Her nest was in the Lost Woods—even the resurrected would have trouble finding her. She might be like the Demon Dragon, living so long that she had come to look down on humans and distanced herself from them.

"I've met those trying to kill me many times. They have to be ones under the influence of whoever is behind the waves. They had led the people and betrayed my trust over and over," she continued. It sounded like she'd experienced her fair share of trouble, eventually leading her to only deal with humans through her underlings.

"Ah, here . . . I can read this part," Rishia said, still looking at the text on the wall. "This weapon is highly effective against those who possess eternity . . . for defense against those who would take the name of a god . . ."

"That suggests the 0 series weapon cluster would be effective against the one behind the waves, the one who assumes the name of God," I pondered aloud. In Kizuna's world, attacking a wave crack with the 0 weapon had extended the time until the next wave was going to arrive. That also seemed to suggest these were special weapons that would be effective against the one who assumed the name of God. It was mainly an assumption for now, but we were starting to see some proof of it.

"The heroes . . . are intended as stopgaps, until help can arrive . . . and that's all I can read," Rishia finished.

"That's more than enough. It overlaps with what we heard in Kizuna's world," I told her. It seemed that the heroes fighting the waves presupposed the eventual arrival of help from somewhere, otherwise text like this wouldn't keep saying it. I didn't know who or what we were meant to be counting on . . . but the expectation to do so made me feel pretty uneasy. I wondered if we could really rely on whoever it was who was meant to be coming, looking again at the creature on the wall. Maybe that was who we were waiting for.

We completed the cleanup and returned to the village. I still had the vial in my possession, and it was doing a good job of keeping Gaelion away.

"Kwaa!" he squawked.

"What's wrong with you?" I asked. As I moved toward him, he slid back the same distance.

"Stay away!" I heard his voice in my head. "I feel something from you, something sending shivers down my spine!" I handed the vial to Raphtalia and moved closer to Gaelion again. This time he didn't move away. It seemed the poison was also good at warding off dragons. I tried to remember if we had experimented with it on the Demon Dragon. It might work on her too, I thought hopefully.

"Ah, I think I get it," I said. When I applied what Rishia had discovered, the Dragon Emperor was a little different but still something close to being immortal. Even if it died, it could be revived, and it lived for so long it was hardly worth counting the years. The poison was effective against all creatures that "possessed eternity," after all.

"I can use this to help keep the Demon Dragon under control. It's almost like Kizuna is already using it," I commented.

"Kwaaaaaa!" Child Gaelion didn't miss the chance to leap at me, flying onto me as I got closer in an attempt to get some attention. I was amazed again at how he could push down base instincts with emotion. I still didn't understand why he was so attached to me either. I hadn't done anything in particular for him.

"Okay, enough of that. The experiment ends here," I told him. Fitoria had asked that I return the vial to her once we had unlocked the weapons for all the heroes, so I proceeded to do that—including L'Arc—and then returned it to her. There hadn't been much left in Kizuna's world, but we still had quite a lot here.

I turned my attention to the skill called Shield 0 . . . indeed, the entire series. After unlocking the skill, I tried activating it and then having a monster attack me, but—as I had expected—nothing happened. I couldn't even resist the attack. The skill simply shattered in an instant. It was the same with the others—the skill looked super flashy when triggered, but it was unable to cause a single scratch. It wasn't about holding back or anything like that—it really was just a zero-damage skill. It had zero cooldown time and consumed zero SP.

With that, anyway, the cleaning of Fitoria's nest and our excavation of ancient gear that had been slumbering for who knew how long came to an end. We had acquired some pretty fine new gear, and so I was quite pleased with the final result.

Chapter Five: Village Abnormality

It was the day after we returned from the filolial sanctuary. We had gone to report our progress to the old guy and others at his workshop and then returned to our own house.

"Ah, Naofumi. Welcome back." We were greeted there by Melty, sounding for all the world like this was her place too and reclining on the sofa in the middle of the house where Raphtalia, Filo, and I lived. She was dangling her legs, looking totally relaxed.

"Melty, just who do you think you are?" I asked her.

"The queen of the largest nation in the world," she replied. That was true. She was indeed the queen of what had become the largest nation in the world. But it also wasn't what I had meant.

"That might be your title . . ." Raphtalia started.

"Indeed, it is. So go do some queen stuff," I told her.

"I have today off," she said.

"Do queens get the day off?" Raphtalia asked. "What's going on? Are you okay, Melty?"

"I've been through a lot as queen recently, so my father told me to come see you guys and spread my wings a little. Blow off some steam. This is about the only place I can do that," she

admitted. While I was away, Melty had been dealing with meetings and reports from all across the world. She was trying to
hold together so many threads of disparate information I could
actually understand where she was coming from. That didn't
excuse her acting like this in my house, of course.

"He also wants me to report back on how things look
here, what with the large collection of heroes you have now
amassed," Melty admitted.

"That sounds more like Trash," I replied. So Melty got a
break from her punishing duties while being pushed almost
forcibly onto me. It also displayed to the other nations how
close the Melromarc royals were with the Shield Hero. All under the pretense of her duties as queen. Quite the cunning plan.
Trash had proven himself one to watch out for since he came
back to himself. Still, this could trigger advances on me from
the Siltvelt side as well—marriage advances—so I wished they
would back off a bit. Maybe he was handling that side of things
via Fohl.

"Okay, I understand why you are here now, but where's
Filo?" I asked. Melty was here but Filo was nowhere to be seen.
It wasn't like she spent long here, even if this was her home, but
it seemed far too quiet for her to be in another room.

"Bubba Fohl! Eat this food I made!" came a voice from
outside.

"Why are you bothering me? Ask Brother to do that!" said
a second voice.

"There's so much pressure in getting Bubba to eat it! I want to practice on you first!"

"Why are you bothering me though? Go ask Sadeena!"

"Sadeena and Shildina aren't here! They are probably off drinking on the island until Bubba calls for them!"

I was pretty sure I could put faces to the voices that I heard through the window. The village sure was a lively place. I tried not to concern myself with whatever it was they were discussing. Filo wasn't out there, anyway. So she really wasn't with Melty. That was rare.

"Filo was spotted by the Spear Hero and had to go on the run. I tried to stop him, but you know how he is. We said we would meet up again here, so that's what I'm waiting for," Melty explained.

"Okay, so that's why she isn't here," I said. Motoyasu simply never gave up. Stalkers were scary. I could sympathize, having the Demon Dragon and Atla stalking me to some degree. I didn't mind that they liked me; that wasn't the issue. In Motoyasu's case though . . . he was just sick.

"So I'm just waiting for Filo to get back and enjoying my free time. I've had so many meetings and other official business recently. I'm worn out . . . and I don't get any real freedom, with all the fear of assassination," Melty complained.

"Queen of the biggest nation in the world. That all comes with the territory," I said. We had the Raph species here in the village, so assassins couldn't get in. Just like Raphtalia, the Raph species could all use illusion-type magic. Any outsider trying to conceal themselves would be outed in an instant. That would make it very hard for assassins from other nations to get in here and kill Melty. Melty had also been going to train with Filo. That meant she could probably handle herself against anyone who wasn't a hero anyway. The only thing that could cause any trouble was an attack by S'yne's sister's forces.

"My father has created a firm foundation, but we are still in a dangerous time," Melty said. Most everyone with connections to Takt had been executed, but some of them might have escaped or still be in hiding, which meant security was being kept tight. There were other groups who would profit from Melty's demise too. But surely a fate worse than death awaited anyone attempting to harm the beloved daughter of the Wisest King of Wisdom. His other daughter was now a wanted criminal across the world, of course, but he likely didn't consider her his daughter any longer.

"You have your own burdens, don't you, Melty?" Raphtalia sympathized.

"You're one to talk, Raphtalia. I think you should pay a visit to Q'ten Lo before they forget what you look like," Melty said.

"You have a point," Raphtalia said unsteadily, "but I'd rather leave that to Ruft, if I can."

"Unfortunately for you, on paper Ruft is dead—executed,"

I reminded her. "It's going to be a few more years before we can pretend he's a distant relative."

"That kid is something else, let me tell you," Melty said. "He can speak the common Melromarc language already and knows far more of it than I taught him too. He's definitely related to you, Raphtalia." Melty went on to tell us how Ruft had been while we were away. He had been observing as Melty's aide, but perhaps due to being former royalty himself, he had displayed an innate sense of anticipating what Melty and Trash wanted. He had been there to provide Trash and Melty with the correct documents just when they needed them. He had a fresh blackboard waiting before they even thought of asking. He could also respond to the approach of assassins and was able to spot attempts at reconnaissance from other nations.

"I'm happy that you think so much of him, but that's also complicated for me, emotionally," Raphtalia admitted.

"He's very warm and loving, and he loves that therianthrope form of his. He's always turning into it and playing with his fur any chance he gets," Melty said. She seemed to be sympathizing with Raphtalia too. I wasn't into that. This was Ruft growing up! The very reason he had come so far so quickly was because he was related to Raphtalia.

"He's starting to ask more and more questions that I can't answer and I have to tell him to ask my father. My father has started to take notice of him as a result. He even said he was going to talk to you, Naofumi, about whatever plans you might have for him," Melty told me. I thought for a moment.

"I really want him to choose for himself," I said. He had been the ruler of a nation, true, but everyone under him had been self-serving scumbags. That wasn't the case anymore. If Ruft learned how to be a proper king, it would probably be better than the current situation of Raphtalia acting as queen in pretty much name only. "I guess Raphtalia and Ruft should chat together and sort that out between themselves," I concluded.

"You mean, the future of Q'ten Lo?" Melty confirmed.

"That's right," I said. Raphtalia gave a sigh. From my perspective, I was thinking of taking her back to Japan with me once the waves were finished. So if possible, I wanted Ruft to handle Q'ten Lo. This was all working toward setting that up.

"Okay, Melty. You heard anything else from Trash? About S'yne's sister or Bitch and her goons making their way back into this world?" I asked her.

"At the moment, everything seems quiet. While you were away, the only real problem we faced was some small-scale resistance from forces displeased with me becoming queen," Melty reported. Incidents too small to bother reporting to us. "There was a small scuffle in Faubrey yesterday, and Father did have his eye on that . . . I'm not sure if he'll report it to you or not." With everything going on in the world, it was impossible to tell which of our enemies might be involved. Often when reading a story or watching some movie, you would sit there in amazement, wondering why the dumb main characters couldn't see what was right in front of their faces. I'd done that myself, back when such entertainment was available to me. Now, though, living in a more dynamic situation myself, I could see things differently; I could see how difficult it was to spot the smallest, but ultimately significant, change in your everyday life. Say there was a small pebble in front of your door that wasn't there the day before. Would you even spot it, let alone think it was strange? If so, you would probably make a fantastic detective.

Swing a stick and you'd probably hit trouble, especially in this world. But if I took the current size of Melromarc into account, it wasn't going to be one or two hundred instances; it was going to be one or ten thousand. There was no way to know which of those was the one we needed to focus on.

"If Trash is interested in it, then there's likely something there," I said. He had a habit of picking up on important things, like some incredible fictional tactician himself.

"Still, Father wants you and your team to build your strength as much as possible," Melty said.

"I'm sure he does," I commented. For all we knew the enemy was active in Kizuna's world right now. We might have been tricked into coming back here. Kizuna and her gang might be fighting in full force now.

In either case, we were going to hang out and keep an eye

on things for about two weeks. We needed to use that time to raise our levels and improve ourselves as much as possible.

"Hey, Melty. You're going to be staying here tonight, right?" I said.

"I guess so," she replied.

"How about we go hunting later?" I suggested.

"I guess just lounging around is a bit much. What about Filo?" she asked.

"We'll invite her along if she can get away from Motoyasu," I said.

"That's mean," said Melty.

"Raph!" As we were trying to plan our schedule for the day, Raph-chan started to look around, her fur standing up, suddenly on high alert. "Raph?!" I tilted my head, wondering what was going on, but everyone assembled took it as a warning to get ready for action.

"Iwatani, get out of there at once!" It was S'yne's sister's voice, suddenly coming out of nowhere. "What?" I exclaimed in surprise, but in the same moment, a heavy feeling completely overtook my body.

"Mr. Naofumi? Whatever is the matter?" Raphtalia asked. It seemed like none of the others had heard the warning. Then S'yne, who had been waiting at the doorway, basically kicked in the door and burst inside. There were crackling shafts of lightning running along the ground outside, making it obvious that something big was happening—like some kind of super-dense magical magnetic field. It was like a more powerful version of the magic that Gaelion, the Demon Dragon, or Filo used to create a sanctuary, swelling to fill the entire vicinity. Panicked voices rang out from the villagers, who were wondering what was going on and shouting to get back inside. I, meanwhile, rushed outside, turning my shield into something ready for combat and preparing myself for anything. I didn't have a clue what was going on yet, but I was ready to defend Raphtalia and Melty as required.

"Melty, be ready to get out of here!" I told her.

"I am!" she replied, rushing out of the house alongside me. The next moment, lightning crashed down in the middle of the village. It was a blinding light covering everything in the vicinity. That was followed by an intense floating feeling. Sparks crackled off my shield as though it was protecting us from something.

"What's going on?" I shouted. S'yne's sewing kit and Raphtalia's katana weapons were giving off a similar response as my shield. I blinked a few times and then we all looked around.

It didn't look like anything much had happened. The same village scenery spread out around us.

"What was that?" Fohl asked. "It was so bright!"

"I saw it," I replied. He was covering Keel and Imiya with his body to protect them, while the others in the village were looking around, blinking and shaking their heads. I checked again to see if anything had changed—everything seemed the same.

Inside the village, at least.

"Bubba, hey, was there a mountain like that outside the village before?" Keel asked. I looked where she was pointing, and that immediately told me something was seriously wrong.

"What's going on here?" I asked. The familiar scenery outside the village had now totally changed. There was a mountain I'd never seen before and a whole forest that spread out from the village. I immediately checked my Portal Shield to find that every location other than the village had vanished from it. In that moment, I had no idea what had happened or what new trials lay ahead.

Chapter Six: Encounter with Extinct Monsters

"Brother . . . do you recognize that mountain at all?" Fohl asked me, tilting his head in puzzlement while pointing to the "new" mountain outside the village. Unfortunately for all of us, I couldn't say I'd ever seen it before.

"Nope, no idea. Does it look like a mountain we would recognize?" I asked.

"I'm not sure," Fohl replied. "I do feel like I've seen it before somewhere, but only vaguely." That was no help. Whatever the situation was, we needed to gather information.

"I need some of you suited to recon . . . Filo, Gaelion . . ." I started to give orders, the monster seal registration still in place, but then realized communications were cut off. The status of Gaelion and the others was the same as it had been while I was in Kizuna's world. "How about Sadeena and Shildina . . ." I muttered but then realized that now that they were heroes, I couldn't track their slave seals anymore. With something big like this happening, I would expect them to hurry back immediately. But the fact that they weren't here meant we couldn't count on them showing up. "Before we explore outside the village . . ." I thought for a moment. "Everyone, gather up! Take a proper roll call of whoever is here!"

So we were out of contact with Filo and Gaelion. Raph-chan was here, but I thought about sending her out to scout a bit later. If we didn't get a handle on who was actually here, there was a risk of failing to respond effectively.

"Don't worry, just fall into line!" Ruft said, helping to keep everyone calm.

"That's right!" Keel said, helping out. Raphtalia and Fohl were helping to gather everyone together and take down their names.

"What's going on?" said one filolial.

"I'm scared," said another.

"Raph . . ." added one of the Raph species, all of them looking around with concern on their faces. It looked like we didn't have that many filolials with us. Maybe only half the Raph species too.

"Naofumi," said Melty, sliding up to me, looking worried. She really looked her young age at times like this. "Filo is okay, isn't she?"

"It looks like we're the only ones caught up in this. I bet Filo is worrying about us just as much right now," I told her.

"Yes, you're right," she replied. Finally coming back to herself, Melty slapped her own cheeks a couple of times and her expression returned to normal. "If I look too worried here, I won't be able to call myself a queen, will I?" I expected no less from Trash's daughter. She had been trained well in how to be royal. She dashed off toward Ruft to help identify everyone we had with us.

"Whatever . . . is going on here?" Ren appeared, still looking worse for wear.

"Hero Iwatani, what is the meaning of this? I was just checking on Ren, and then . . ." Eclair said. She was with Ren. She must have come as protection for Melty and then gone to check on the convalescing Ren.

"No idea. We were just counting up the villagers before starting to investigate further," I said. I was using my registered slave seals to check on which slaves were here and which were missing. Ren was here, anyway. That could turn out to be good or bad luck.

"Ren, have you seen Motoyasu or Itsuki?" I asked.

"Sorry, no. I haven't," he replied.

"Okay then," I said. There was no way that self-centered Motoyasu wouldn't come bursting out amid a crisis like this. Itsuki and Rishia had still been at the filolial sanctuary, attempting to read the information we found there.

I really needed to work out why I couldn't portal to any of my registered locations. I could still come into the village, so I wasn't simply being blocked. I couldn't believe every location had been stopped somehow.

"Archduke!" Rat ran up with Wyndia. Rat was an odd one, choosing not to call me "Shield Hero" or by my name, but by my rank. "What's going on?"

"No idea," I replied. I had left her in charge of analyzing the technology we obtained from Kizuna's world. She had moaned about it not really being her specialty. Complaints or not, she still did a good job of it. Most of her recent research seemed to have been focused on the Raph species and the filolials, but I didn't really know the details of what she was mucking about with. She was also responsible for the care of the village monsters, so she was far from useless, but some of the stuff she was doing with the Raph species seemed a bit icky.

"Wyndia, where's Gaelion?" I asked her. Wyndia had been entrusted with Gaelion as a kind of surrogate parent. She shook her head, indicating she didn't know.

"After you got angry at him, Gaelion had semi-run away from home. Don't you know where he is, Shield Hero?" she asked. "Semi"-run away, huh? I wasn't sure how to respond to that.

"I guess that means he's not in the village," I concluded. That wasn't just limited to Gaelion; it included Filo too then. Many of the slaves and monsters registered to me were in the same boat.

"Oh no! What's happened to Gaelion?!" Wyndia started to panic.

"Stay calm. Neither Filo nor Gaelion are the types to be defeated so easily, you know that. It seems far more natural that we're the ones who have been caught up in something, not them," I said.

"That makes more sense. Try to calm yourself," Rat said, soothing Wyndia. Rat knew more about monster biology, making Wyndia like her student.

"When was Gaelion going to be back?" I asked.

"Mealtime. That's normally how it works," Wyndia replied.

"And that's him 'semi'-running away?" Raphtalia asked.

"Gaelion is such a softie. I'm sure he would have come back. No matter how rough things get with the Shield Hero, he would come back complaining, but he would come back," she said. So it was all a little act to get some attention, which was pointless if I wasn't even hearing about it. He was just taking a stroll. That was all you could really call it.

I rarely understood anything that these dragons did, to be honest. They were so peculiar it was almost impossible to understand what they were thinking: old Gaelion, so paternal while calling himself the weakest dragon, the Demon Dragon, magical queen of evil who came onto me like Atla on steroids, and the child Gaelion, who in some ways was even harder to fathom than the Demon Dragon and old Gaelion.

"We just have to believe Gaelion and the others can handle themselves and work out what's going on with us," I decided. "Raph-chan!" I called out.

"Raph?" Raph-chan replied, tilting her head at being called upon.

"Anything you can share with us?" I asked. Raph-chan had

saved us many times before in all sorts of ways. She was probably going to understand our situation the fastest, so that's why I asked her.

"Raph . . ." Raph-chan responded.

"Dafu," added Raph-chan II, both of them shaking their heads to indicate they didn't have any ideas. They had been doing something in front of the sakura lumina growing in the village, but they didn't seem to know where we were either. I was just thinking the Raph-chans weren't going to be any help when Raph-chan pointed behind Melty.

"Indeed. It iz my time to shine, zo to zpeak," said a Shadow, appearing out of nowhere. He even had a Raph species dressed like a ninja on his shoulder! Cosplay, I liked it!

"It's you!" I said. It felt like a while since I'd last seen him, but I immediately recognized his voice. It was the same Shadow who had done so much during the Church of the Three Heroes incident as the body-double for the queen. I hadn't seen him at all since then and wondered what the hell he had been doing.

"I waz protecting Queen Melty, concealing myzelf just in case," he explained.

"Hey, Raph-chan. Didn't you think you should mention this potential assassin?" I asked her.

"Ah, don't blame your monsterz, Shield Hero. Of course, they zensed me. I explained the zituation to them and they have been letting my prezence zlide," he explained.

"Raph!" said the Raph species in the ninja getup. I was starting to feel that village security might not be as tight as I would have liked. I would have liked Raph-chan and the Raph species to react to Shadows as well, if possible. At least let us know they were there.

"Shield Hero, are you okay?" Ruft asked me, noticing I was a bit pissed off.

"Did you know about this too, Raphtalia? Ruft?" I asked them.

"Well . . . Eclair told me that he has been placed as protection for Melty," she hesitantly replied.

"You mean the spy guy? Sure. I thought you all knew about him too. He's right there," said Ruft. These two had concealment abilities, after all. It had to be nice to be able to see this guy wherever he was. I certainly couldn't. "If the Spear Hero was using this to follow Filo around, I would point him out. But it's someone we know, so I didn't think I needed to," Ruft explained. Obviously, Motoyasu would have to be stopped. He could confound even Filo's natural instincts in his attempts to snap unwanted images of her, so capturing him would be a given . . . but I couldn't help but wonder if they really should be letting a Shadow slide so easily.

"I have been in contact with individualz from Q'ten Lo, in a mutual exchange of information, and have honed my craft as a rezult. I am a Shadow . . . and also a shinobi, making use of the artz of Q'ten Lo. Your village, Shield Hero, is the one place where people gather who can still zee through my enhanced artz," the Shadow explained.

"Yet the hero himself can't see you at all. What a farce! I'm not sure you are worthy of the title of 'shinobi' either," I told him. I might have to put Raph-chan on his head at all times, to track him for me.

We needed to deal with this emergency, anyway.

"Okay! Is that everyone from the village gathered together? Make sure we don't have anyone hiding away!" I shouted.

"Bubba, I don't think anyone would be dumb enough to hide themselves at a time like this," Keel said. Sure, that was a good point. Everyone was gathered in the village square. I proceeded to look over the assembly.

There was Raphtalia, Melty, Raph-chan, and S'yne. They had been with me since this all kicked off. Fohl, Keel, and Imiya were there, central village figures. There were a lot of other village folk too. Many of them looked like lumo, a pretty technical-type species. Then there was Ren and Eclair. He had been convalescing in his own home—which might turn out to be a stroke of luck—and Eclair had been visiting him there. After that, we had the monster-lovers—Rat, Wyndia, and Ruft. After having them count up the Raph species and the filolials, I found out the number of monsters had apparently been pretty reduced. There was also the past Heavenly Emperor, Raph-chan

II. She had all sorts of other silly names, such as Dafu-chan. And finally, the Shadow who had been guarding Melty.

On the flip side, the people we couldn't contact were Filo, Gaelion, L'Arc and his party, Itsuki, Rishia, Motoyasu and his retinue, and of course Trash. Sadeena and Shildina weren't here either. From the slave seal responses and what Keel had told me, those who had been away from the village for trade also weren't responding.

"The common connection between all of us here is that we just happened to be in the village when this—whatever it was— happened," I pondered aloud. Just what "this" was though, I was still left guessing.

"Has some kind of technology moved the entire village?" Raphtalia wondered. The scenery outside our familiar boundaries was quite different—but there were still points that didn't line up.

"It's not impossible . . . but I can't understand why only the village can be selected when I try to portal," I replied. This was a different phenomenon from when we had been on the Cal Mira islands.

"Maybe some kind of barrier has been put up?" Raphtalia hazarded another guess.

"Okay. That sounds like a thread worth pulling on," I agreed. Perhaps a barrier had been put up to stop us from teleporting out, and then we had been teleported away somewhere.

That seemed like one possibility, considering we didn't recognize this place. I had first wondered if we had been sent to some unfamiliar new world completely, but when I looked at our levels and other data, it didn't seem like that was the case.

"How long until the next wave?" I wondered aloud and looked at the number. For some reason it was unstable. "Raphtalia, can you use Scroll of Return?"

"No, I can't," she replied. Raphtalia had tried using teleport skills herself, a number of times, but was having no luck either. "To be exact about the issue, we are outside the specified range of a dragon hourglass teleport," she reported. Outside the range—I wonder how something like that happened.

"S'yne, what about you?" I asked, but she was already shaking her head. She was suffering from the same issue. "Looks like we have to leave the village and see what's out there," I concluded.

"Okay! Let's do this!" Fohl seemed keen to get started. The Shadow would probably prove to be better at collecting information, but Fohl was light on his feet. That would count for something. We needed to gather as much information as we could—and quickly.

"Hold on, Naofumi. We have no idea what is happening here. Should we all be rushing out there?" Melty said. She had a point.

"Better than doing nothing. Our fastest, most flexible

members should take the lead and search out the vicinity," I said. It definitely hurt that we didn't have any powerful fliers among our team—Filo and Gaelion, basically. "We don't know what might show up, so the heroes should go along too. Split up into teams and start getting the lay of the land," I told them.

"Leave it to me," the Shadow said.

"Yes, I'll be counting on you in particular," I told him. With that, we split up and got started. Raphtalia, Melty, Raph-chan, and S'yne headed north with me. Fohl put together a team of the more competent fighters from the village, led by Keel, and headed east, while Ren took Eclair and Wyndia and headed west. The Shadow planned to take the Raph species and strike out to the south. Ruft, Rat, and the remaining villagers would remain behind to protect the village. The range of the search was to be the ground covered in thirty minutes. If nothing was found, we would return to the village after that time, collate our information, then expand the range and strike out again. Seeing as we didn't even have a basic map, it didn't hurt to start out prudent. If anything did happen, the affected party would shoot some magic up into the air to let the others know. We decided to use the filolials remaining in the village to get around. From among them, I was to ride the one known as Chick, Filo's immediate subordinate and the one leading the village filolials.

Immediately prior to our departure, I was looking at the ground with Rat.

"It seems this is the boundary line," Rat stated, pointing to the ground just outside the village. A single, clean line extended all around the village from there. We had investigated, and it encircled the entire thing. "If some kind of power or technology has transported us, it looks like it moved everything inside this circle."

"That would make sense," I agreed. It was a big chunk of real estate to move, however. The entire village, pretty much, apart from the filolial stable. One of the monster stables had remained, so it was hard to guess the reasoning behind the selected area—and impossible to guess how it had been achieved too. I couldn't help thinking that S'yne's sister had tricked us after all.

"Well then, Archduke. I'll let you proceed with the survey," Rat said.

"Okay. You take care of the village," I told her. Then we crossed the line and started out on our investigation of whatever lay beyond.

"Everyone, go your separate ways!" I said. Following my instructions, each group moved away in its designated direction. The sky was clear and blue, with no clouds in sight. We had been a village on the coast, so there was normally the smell of salt on the air, but I couldn't smell a hint of that now.

"Huh?" We hadn't walked far from the village when we encountered a monster. I considered having Chick just smash it away, but I wanted to conduct this search carefully, so I climbed down and went into combat.

Red Snake Balloon

A long and thin, pencil-shaped balloon was wriggling in the air and coming toward us. It looked like something you might use for balloon art.

"A snake balloon? Those monsters don't live in Melromarc," Melty said with a frown, pointing at the balloon that was clearly intent on attacking us. I had already grabbed it with my bare hands, of course, holding it still in the air. The part that looked like the head was biting eagerly into my hand, but it didn't hurt at all—it didn't even tickle.

"So where do they live?" I asked. This could be useful information.

"Siltvelt and demi-human countries. However . . ." She trailed off, still frowning.

"Yes?" I prompted.

"Being a shape suited to use as pool inner tubes, and after a boom in balloon art, I heard their numbers are close to being wiped out. They have various uses you can't really do with other balloons, something like that . . ." she explained.

"Okay," I replied. As we wasted our time on balloon trivia, a load of more snake balloons showed up and flew toward us.

There was a lot of them to say they were meant to be close to being wiped out. I used a skill called Hate Reaction, one I hadn't popped off recently, and drew the attention of all the monsters to me. It also served to draw even more of them out of hiding. I was already protecting Melty and the others with Shooting Star Wall, and quickly found myself surrounded by a gaggle of snake balloons. They were even trying to get in through gaps in my armor.

"I'm sorry, Mr. Naofumi. I'm sure you are okay, but shall we defeat them now?" Raphtalia asked.

"Okay. I'll throw out a Shooting Star Shield, so match your timing with me and finish them off," I ordered.

"Okay!" she replied smartly.

"Shooting Star Shield!" I shouted. Countless snake balloons were suddenly sent flying away by the barrier I created. At the same moment, Raphtalia swung her katana, Melty unleashed some magic, and S'yne swung her scissors. Raph-chan was riding Chick and had the filolial kick the snakes away. The snake balloons were defeated in an instant. Talk about weaklings. I guessed being rare didn't make them strong.

"I bet there are still some live ones, so let's capture them," I said.

"Naofumi? Can I ask you why?" Raphtalia asked.

"To sell. If these things really are rare, I bet collectors will pay through the nose for them," I said.

"You're still thinking about making cash at a time like this? You're an archduke now!" Raphtalia exclaimed.

"Why does that matter?" I asked.

"I think I can understand why the accessory dealer wants you as his successor," Raphtalia said, a little dejectedly.

"Raph," said Raph-chan, but I wasn't giving in. These were rare monsters. There was no reason not to make use of them. There was a load of them here too, so it would surely be okay to take some back with us.

"We can do that later, anyway," I said. For now, I put one into my shield and unlocked the corresponding shield. To say how rare these things were meant to be, it only had the specs of a balloon variant. It wasn't even worth discussing in detail.

Taking some of these balloon corpses back with us would give the kids in the village something to play with, at least. We pressed on, carving our way through the balloon party.

"Melty, these snake balloons are definitely monsters found in the vicinity of Siltvelt, correct?" I confirmed with her. She nodded. It was pretty convenient, being able to work out where we were by the monsters around us. Fohl had said he recognized the place so it had to be somewhere he knew.

"Let's assume this is Siltvelt for now and expand our search area. Raph-chan, Chick. Do you have anything to add?" I asked the motley pair.

"Raph?" questioned Raph-chan, her nose twitching. Chick

also made a puzzled noise. Neither of them seemed to know anything. Melty was looking around, making similar noises.

"What's up?" I asked her.

"This place is just so strange. I kind of recognize it and kind of don't," she replied.

"Fohl said the same thing," I told her. If this was close to Siltvelt, then it made sense that he might recognize it. "What about you, Raphtalia?" I asked. She was always great at remembering people's names and other details, so I hoped I could count on her memory here.

"Oh . . . I'm sorry," Raphtalia said. She didn't know this particular place then. Fohl and Melty had been pretty well-traveled before meeting up with us. That was probably why they recognized it and we didn't.

We continued onward, over ground that was gradually getting drier. We were just walking in a straight line.

"Hey. I think I see a road there," I said. I stepped out onto the well-worn route and looked left and right. There could be a town or village in either direction, but if possible, I wanted to go to the closest one. I registered a portal here, just in case. "If we continue along this path, we might find something. Come on! We'll start by going right." That was what we did, for the rest of the thirty-minute search, but we didn't reach a town or village before the time ran out. It was starting to feel like Siltvelt to me, though, just from the atmosphere. It might be the mountains that looked so worn down by the elements, like ancient hermits were living in them. They looked kind of Chinese in style. That said, they probably weren't the best reference material. I saw Siltvelt as being a pretty mixed-up place, topographically speaking. There were jungles and then suddenly barren plains, thin, narrow mountains, and then suddenly fat ones covered with trees. Even Melromarc felt more unified. The Japanese-style hot spring towns there could be explained away by heroes spreading their home culture.

"We should drop back and see how everyone is doing," I said. It looked like thirty minutes hadn't been long enough. I only had to register a portal here and we could be back in the blink of an eye. So none of our efforts would be wasted. Even the smallest piece of new information could prove vital.

With that, we returned to the village.

"Archduke! This is incredible!" The moment we arrived Rat was there, waiting for us, lifting up the corpse of a monster.
"Are you talking about the almost-extinct snake balloons?" I asked her.

"No! The others have found a monster that actually is extinct!" she replied. Someone always had to one-up me. "This is the discovery of the century! It could rewrite everything we know about monsters!"

"Great, sure . . . but how much is such a discovery really

worth in a place with waves occurring in an attempt to literally fuse worlds together?" I said.

"You could at least try to sound excited, Archduke," Rat said sullenly.

"I understand how you feel, but none of the creatures here can be found where I come from—in Japan. So it's pretty hard for me to get any more excited over another weird blob of goo or whatever," I replied. I had been quite into all the creatures when I first got here, but every time a new monster attacked us now, I only thought about kicking its ass—and turning it into cash, if possible. What Rat was feeling now might be the same as a Japanese person finding a live dinosaur. Okay, a dinosaur might be a little much—how about a dodo? They were extinct too, if I recalled correctly. Of course, in the worlds Ren, Itsuki, and Motoyasu had come from, there might be dodos everywhere. That was what this felt like for me . . . but I was getting lost in pointless thoughts again.

"I'm interested in studying new breeds of monsters, of course, but isn't it even more amazing to rediscover a monster that everyone thought was wiped out?" Rat asked, still all hyper.

"Yes, you might have a point," I conceded. Capturing a monster thought to have been wiped out probably was more impressive than discovering a new continent or some unknown creature.

"Brother, you have returned," said Fohl, noticing us and coming over.

"Bubba, did you find anything?" Keel asked, following behind him.

"We found a road and were running along it. What about you?" I asked back.

"We returned just after discovering a river," Fohl replied.

"Okay. There might be a village or town along that river too," I said. Fohl agreed. "And then you showed the monster you defeated to Rat?" Fohl nodded. So there were extinct monsters out there too. Keel was already happily swinging around the corpse of one of the snake balloons we had brought back with us. I had to warn her not to play with balloon corpses too much. It wasn't fair to turn monster's lives into toys—they needed to be processed a little first. Then it was fine.

"What about Ren?" I asked. It wasn't like him to be late. If he wasn't back here at the appointed time, that suggested something had happened. Even as I had that thought, a flare went up in the direction Ren's party had headed. That certainly suggested they had gotten themselves into some trouble. I clicked my tongue in annoyance and climbed back up onto Chick.

"Naofumi!" Melty shouted.

"We'd better not risk your life, Your Majesty," I said, a little sardonically. "Stay here. If anything happens, Fohl, you protect Melty."

"Okay. Be careful yourself, Brother," Fohl replied with a nod, putting his fist in front of him.

"Hey, don't I get a say?" Melty whined.

"We need to work out what is happening, but even more importantly, we need to ensure the village is well defended. Ruft, you help protect it with the Raph species," I said.

"Sure thing!" Ruft replied.

"Raphtalia, S'yne, Raph-chan! Let's ride!" I said. With Raphtalia and S'yne behind me and Raph-chan riding up on Chick's head, we started out. It shouldn't take too long to reach the point the flare went up. I started to carefully enchant Liberation Aura X.

"You called?" The Demon Dragon's voice popped up at once in my head, coming from the shield. She was hot on her protection—or magical assistance, whatever you wanted to call it.

"Liberation Aura—huh?!" My voice stifled as I tried to cast the spell. I tilted my head.

"Mr. Naofumi?" Raphtalia asked.

"This is strange . . . I can't enhance the magic any further?" I said. All I had managed to complete was a regular Liberation Aura. I wondered what was going on. I'd felt something similar when I cast Shooting Star Shield during our balloon battle. I had been rendered unable to use magic, and unable to use my shield recently, and while I'd done my best to adapt to each situation, it was confusing to have a mix of things I could and couldn't do. I was just trying to come back from that.

"We need to get to Ren as quickly as possible!" I said. The normal Liberation Aura would have to do, and I applied it to Chick to boost her speed. She put her head down with a squawk and rushed forward, carrying us swiftly toward whatever trouble Ren and his party had bumped into.

Chapter Seven: Double the Shield Heroes

"Wait! Just listen, please!" Ren was shouting as we arrived at the spot the flare had gone up.

"Listen to what? A holy weapon hero, here to assault us?" said his opponent, an unknown enemy.

"I can't believe how hard he is to fight! He seems so similar, but he moves so differently!" Ren exclaimed. I noticed a village nearby, which I'd also never seen before. Eclair and Wyndia had been bound up in threads that almost looked like spiders' webs. It seemed possible to cut through them, but there was a vast volume of them spread across the area. Ren was fixated on protecting them both, meaning he was barely holding his own in defending the attacks from his enemies.

"Who are they?" I wondered. There was a woman with an air about her a lot like S'yne—she even carried some large scissors. And what I presumed to be a man in full-body armor and holding a shield was also there. They had to be pretty tough if they were giving Ren a hard time.

Even as I took in the scene, Chick sensed what I needed and rushed toward all the threads.

"Stardust Blade!" Raphtalia shouted. "Mr. Naofumi! I've lost all my skill enhancements too!" she promptly reported. So the katana was on the fritz too. Her Stardust Blade still managed to cut through all the strings.

"We've still got to fight! S'yne!" I shouted.

"Okay," she replied, briefly but with confidence. Then she leapt down from Chick to defend Eclair and Wyndia. She released her own threads, binding them to the ones her opponent was freshly creating and opening a path for Chick.

"Naofumi!" Ren said.

"Are you all okay?" I asked.

"Yes, thanks for coming!" he replied. Luckily, no one seemed to be hurt. I turned to these new attackers. I still had no idea who they were, but if they wanted a fight, then I'd pick up the tab.

"More of them?" said the scissors woman.

"Dammit, can't we catch a break?" said the shield guy, both of them facing us down as we prepared to join the fray. Behind them, a bunch of demi-humans were all facing off with us, holding a bunch of weapons. The situation looked pretty bad. It wasn't like all demi-humans were my allies, after all. If we were in Shieldfreeden right now, then there would be plenty of demi-humans filled with rage toward me.

"What's that strange monster?" the armored guy with the shield muttered, looking at Chick. "It doesn't matter! We still have to fight them!" I was puzzled that he was hanging out with demi-humans but didn't know what a filolial was, but for now I needed to confirm the situation with Ren.

"What's going on?" I asked him.

"We found this village and so we stopped by. We were explaining who we are and asking some questions when the villagers ran off. Then these guys attacked us," Ren explained.

"I don't think we caused any problems. I started by explaining that we don't know where we are but that we're with the Sword Hero," Eclair responded. That all sounded fine. The job of being a hero had all sorts of side benefits, but trying to conduct yourself covertly was not one of them. Ren and Itsuki wouldn't go around hiding their past anymore. But to come seeking help in an emergency and instead get attacked—something was going on here.

"Whatever is all this?" scissors woman asked. "We need to capture them and find out."

"Good idea. Everyone, pile on!" the shield guy shouted. His command was met with shouts of agreement from the band of allies behind him, and then they rushed us. These guys were spoiling for a scrap, that much was clear. Fighting our way out seemed to be the only option right now.

"Raphtalia, Ren, you unleash your skills the moment I pin him down! S'yne, you interfere with the thread-user. She's a lot like you! Everyone else, stop this other rabble!" I ordered.

"Understood!" Raphtalia leaned down, ready to unleash a skill as soon as it was required.

"Naofumi!" Ren shouted. "Watch out! This guy—!" Ren

started to shout. The shield guy seemed to want to fight me. I also raised my shield and intoned some skills.

"Air Strike Shield! Second Shield!" It took me a moment to realize that the other guy had shouted the exact same skill names as me, almost exactly as I said them. Familiar-looking shields appeared at my front and back and tried to hem me in. In that same moment, my own two shields tried to pin down the shield guy, but he grabbed my shoulder to restrict my movements.

"Now!" he shouted. Two more shields came in from the sides to try and prevent my escape, but I blocked those with two of my own float shields. The grating sound of shields clashing filled the air. In the next instant, the demi-humans fighting with the shield guy came to attack me with swords and spears.

"Hah!" I shouted as I created a wall of life force, blocking their movements.

"Haah! Instant Blade! Mist!" Raphtalia shouted, quickly circling around and unleashing her skill at the shield guy's neck, but it was cut short with a sound like it had crashed into a wall.

"Mr. Naofumi, he fights just like you—" Raphtalia started.

"Raphtalia, Raph-chan, fall back! Ren!" I shouted, cutting her off. The two of them quickly did what I asked.

"Naofumi!" Ren said, a bitter expression on his face, knowing what I was going to ask.

"Don't worry about me! Hit us both. Go ahead!" I told him.

"If you say so!" Ren still didn't sound convinced. "Hundred Sword X!"

"Shooting Star Shield!" There it was again—both shield guy and I launched the same skills at the same time. They caught Ren's incoming attack but were unable to stop it, hitting us both. Ren had intentionally directed the attack more toward our opponent, preventing it from hitting me too hard, but it definitely hit.

Ren was getting stronger too. I couldn't handle this attack without enhanced skills. I'd used some life force, which had definitely helped, but my stamina wasn't going to handle repeated hits like that.

"Mr. Naofumi!" Raphtalia shouted.

"Naofumi! Why did you let that happen?!" Ren exclaimed, his face asking why I had taken the attack on a weak version of my skill.

"There are reasons, but no time to explain right now. Focus on the fighting," I told him.

"You attacked your own ally?!" the shield guy shouted. He seemed to be in pretty good shape, even though he must have taken more damage than me. That only made me angrier! "Do you think so little of those you fight alongside?" he accursed, turning his rage and attention onto Ren.

"That's not what this is . . ." Ren stammered with a confused look on his face at this turn of events.

"You've got the wrong idea, so let me explain." I stepped in to defend Ren. "Ren only unleashed his skill like that because he thought I could withstand it. If you have a stronger defense than an ally's attack, you can defend against it, right? And if you can't, you just have to do . . . this."

"It's one of my best features!" the Demon Dragon said, although everyone around me didn't hear that part and so was probably quite puzzled. Her assistance was super useful, anyway. I had to give her that much. I might even pet her a bit next time we met.

"Liberation Heal!" I incanted. Light appeared around me and the pain was immediately whisked away. Excessive pain could sometimes interfere with casting, but with the assistance of the Demon Dragon, I reckoned I would be able to handle anything other than the most serious, limb-removal-type situations. "Now do you get it?" I asked.

"You're still crazy, getting him to attack you," the shield guy said. Sure, I'd give him that. "Crazy" was not the worst thing I'd ever been called. If this was like most games, in which you couldn't damage those on your side, then we wouldn't be having this problem. Unfortunately, this was not one of those games. I didn't want to get hit by friendly fire, of course, but needs must be met and all that.

"Ren, press your attack! He's pretty well pinned down now!" I shouted.

"That's not going to happen!" shouted the scissors woman, who S'yne had been doing a pretty good job of controlling until that point. That was before butterfly wings of light popped out of scissors woman's back, filling the air with countless more threads.

"Sword Wire! Spider's Poison Web!" she shouted.

"What—" S'yne said in confusion, and then her cheek was cut and blood splashed out. She had barely managed to block the attack but was unable to neutralize it completely.

"We've got some magic ready!" Wyndia shouted, accompanied by a bird squawk from Chick. "Cooperative magic, Tornado!" The two of them combined their skills to launch off some magic. A vacuum of wind descended from the sky toward us.

"Don't expect to stop me with magic like that!" scissors woman shouted. The magic and threads started to clash off each other.

"Brave Blade! Crossing Mists!" Raphtalia brought her sword down on the threads but it only created a shower of sparks. They were tougher than they looked.

With a shout, Ren took up swords in both hands and locked himself in combat with the scissors woman. She grunted, holding her own. The shield guy was bad enough, but she was a problem too.

"Phoenix Gale Blade X!" Ren shouted, unleashing a fiery

bird with what looked like deadly timing, but the scissors woman grabbed his shoulder and flipped over in the air to avoid it. Her lithe movements were already impressing me. She would probably give Sadeena a run for her money.

"Shield Bash!" shouted my assailant in the full-body armor as he unleashed a skill toward me with a heavy thunk. This was a skill with a short stunning effect. Against stronger opponents it only caused mild dizziness—really nothing to write home about. The impact, though, felt stronger than when I had used it in the past. There was also some life force mixed in, I noticed. So he could use life force too—but not very well. I guided the life force through my own body and then returned it to him.

"You've got some skills!" he grunted, then gave a shout. Slamming his rear leg into the ground, he let the life force I tried to return to him seep away into the ground. The impact shook the earth beneath our feet. It looked like he was better with life force than I initially thought. I was going to have my hands full with just this guy.

"As Eclair taught me! Multistrike Demolition!" As I was dealing with my own issues, Ren unleashed one of Eclair's techniques—I noticed he was keen to credit her with it—toward the scissors woman. Being a technique, rather than a skill, meant it didn't have any cooldown time to worry about. However, it was also easily avoided. "Straight into . . . Liberation Magic Enchant!" Ren seemed to have guessed it would be avoided and proceeded to unleash some magic right away. As he raised his sword to the sky, the cooperative magic that Wyndia and Chick had unleashed—which at this point was about to fade away—gathered around his blade.

"Tornado Edge!" he shouted. "Naofumi! You'd better get out of the way this time!"

"Okay! Air Strike Shield! Second Shield! Dritte Shield, Chain Shield!" I deployed a series of shields all around me while attempting to bind up the shield guy using Chain Shield. But the moment I released him, he dropped back a distance and threw out three shields of his own.

"Air Strike Shield! Second Shield! Dritte Shield!" Then he bound them into a barrier that was different from my Shooting Star Shield. "Tri Barrier!" This completely stopped my chain shield.

"Vorpal Comet Sword X!" Ren didn't miss a beat, launching a skill mixed with magic at both scissors woman and the shield guy as soon as he dropped away from me. Countless powerful stars turned into vacuum blades, becoming a whirling tornado heading directly for our foes and tearing up the ground in the vicinity as it did so. Dust and smoke were thrown up into the air.

"Naofumi, are you okay?" Ren asked.

"I'm fine," I replied. I was also suspicious of whether this would be enough to end the fighting, and I kept my guard up. There was a high likelihood they would avoid the attack completely.

"Shield Boomerang!" The shield guy's shield whistled out of the smoke, spinning like a flying saucer. I deflected it with my own shield. But maybe due to life force imbued in the shield again, I really felt the impact.

"That was pretty powerful," came the shield guy's voice.

"Don't give up now," said scissors woman. I groaned inside when I saw both of them still alive as the dust cleared. They were super tough, that was for sure—or super good at avoiding things.

"I'll hit them with the next one!" the shield guy shouted.

"There iz no need for that," said a new voice. Everyone looked in the direction it had come from to see the Shadow with his knife at the throat of one of the demi-humans. There was noises of surprise from both sides. "You might want to reconzider making any zudden movez," the Shadow warned. "Thiz izn't a zituation you can rezolve by force." I wondered how he had even slipped in there.

"Gah! Cowards!" the shield guy shouted. Taking hostages felt a lot like something Takt would do—indeed, something he had done to us—which I didn't really like the feeling of. Not that I was going to start trying to play the good guy now.

"You're the onez who attacked uz. I will be happy to free thiz hoztage if we can reach an underztanding," the Shadow replied.

"What do you want? Let him go!" the shield guy shouted without continuing the attack. The demi-human being held was also a man. If we were dealing with one of the vanguards of the waves, he would probably just call this a necessary sacrifice and continue the attack anyway. The guy with the shield didn't move at all, however. Same thing for scissors woman. Raphtalia and the others seemed to notice this too and ceased attacking while remaining on alert.

It looked like we might actually be able to talk to these guys.

"First," the Shadow asked those immobilized by his hostage strategy, "can you tell uz why you attacked uz like thiz? Are you also one of the vanguardz of the wavez?"

"Certainly not!" the shield guy answered without hesitation.

"Then what iz the meaning of thiz battle?" the Shadow asked.

"What do you think? The sword holy weapon hero has launched an attack on our world, even bringing someone with a copy of the shield holy weapon, and is trying to kill us!" the shield guy said.

"There we have it," the Shadow said, turning to me. "What do you make of all that?" Something about being attacked by the Sword Hero stuck out first. I didn't know why they were fighting, but these guys seemed to have mistaken us for someone else.

"I hate to break it to you, but this shield isn't a copy of

anything. It's the real shield holy weapon. We also haven't launched an attack on anything. We've been caught up in some kind of incident and brought here," I explained. If only my shield was some kind of copy, then maybe I could get rid of it!

"And you expect us to believe that?" came the reply.

"I guess it could be a lot to swallow. You get to decide for yourselves if what we're saying is the truth or not. How does that sound? While you're doing that, start talking. Who are you?" I asked the guy in full-body armor who used the same skills as my shield. We at least needed to find out what we were dealing with here. From the way he reacted to the hostage being taken, he seemed to care for his allies. That was something. He had also said that my shield holy weapon was a "copy."

At my question, the shield guy and scissors woman looked at each other, and then scissors woman took a step forward and introduced herself.

"My name is R'yne. I am the hero from another world chosen by the sewing kit vassal weapon. I am cooperating with the others here for . . . various reasons," she said.

"Sewing kit?" S'yne said. I looked over to see her eyes wide in surprise. It was starting to look like there could be multiple versions of the same vassal weapon. We had waves causing worlds to literally crash together, so anything seemed possible.

"A strange coincidence. This is also the holder of the—a sewing kit vassal weapon. Unfortunately, the world she comes from was destroyed," I explained. As I did so, S'yne held up her scissors to be seen, changing them into a form that was absolutely identical to the ones held by scissors woman—R'yne. Even their names were almost identical. I didn't need to see it written down to know R'yne also had that dumb "fantasy" apostrophe. That said, she also had wings on her back, and the weapon itself seemed to be in good shape, so there were some differences too.

"A strange coincidence indeed," R'yne said.

"I agree," I replied. Then she pointed at me, expecting an introduction in return. I didn't have much choice. After all, I wasn't one of these vanguards of the waves, asking people to tell me who they were but then thinking they didn't need to do the same.

"My name is Naofumi Iwatani. I was summoned here from Japan, and I'm one of the four holy heroes—the Shield Hero," I said. As I spoke, the shield guy in his full armor finally removed his helmet and let us see his face. He looked like a young, agreeable youth, at a glance. Not overly handsome, but with warm and appealing features. He also looked to be around the same age as me.

"My name is Mamoru Shirono. I was also summoned here from Japan, and I'm also the Shield Hero. I'm fighting in this world to overcome the waves. I don't know what world you wandered in from, but you'd better get back there right away," he suggested. Hearing these words, the Shadow released his hostage and moved swiftly over to join us. They seemed relieved to have that threat lifted from their head.

"The Shield Hero, huh?" I said. From the skills he had used, it seemed to fit. I didn't know where we were, what place—or what world—this was, but it wouldn't surprise me to find the same holy weapons here. There weren't that many types of possible weapons anyway, so it wasn't unnatural for them to start overlapping. In fact, it was more miraculous that between our world and Kizuna's, which had a total of twenty-three types of weapons, all of them were different from each other.

What this seemed to mean, anyway, was that this new Shield Hero was in conflict with a different Sword Hero—someone other than Ren—who also came from a different world to this one.

Just to be on the safe side, I checked whether I could use the sakura stone of destiny shield on him. Weapons made from that special stone were very effective against heroes—and I was pleased to see that, yes, I could use it. If negotiations collapsed, then that's what I would turn to.

"Sounds like we're both heroes," he said.

"Yep, Shield Hero," I replied, trying it out.

"That's right, Shield Hero," he said back, doing the same. It looked like the forces to which S'yne's sister belonged had moved us to some other alternate world. Our levels hadn't reset

because it was very similar to our own, perhaps. It was probably something like that. There were other things that also didn't quite fit together, but it sounded like we'd been drawn into the conflict between two opposing worlds.

In that moment, the core parts of both my shield and the shield of the other Shield Hero both flashed. It was like they were telling us to trust each other, almost.

And that was the meeting of the two Shield Heroes.

"Hold on. Did you say four holy heroes?" asked Mamoru Shirono.

"The four holy heroes, one for each of the four holy weapons," I told him.

"There are four holy weapons in your world?" Mamoru said incredulously. In every world I had visited so far, there were four holy weapons and then their vassal weapons. This world seemed to be different. I wondered again what kind of place we had ended up in—but for now, all we could do was keep talking.

"Our investigations on the subject have led us to believe that, at some point in the past, two sets of waves caused a total of four worlds to be merged together, thus allowing for there to be four holy weapon heroes. Just to avoid confusion here, let me clarify that the first and second bouts of waves—that is, the merging of worlds—have been completed, and we are now experiencing the third bout," I explained.

"I see," Mamoru pondered. "Things sound pretty different from our world. Here we are known as the 'two holy heroes' or the 'holy weapon heroes.' From what you just said, it sounds like we are in the second batch of waves, then?" Okay then. It really sounded right to say we were in a totally different world. This was all S'yne's sister's doing! She'd sent us right into this trap!

The otherworldly Shield Hero looked over at Ren.

"Ah, this guy with the sword is Ren Amaki, the Sword Hero. We're both heroes together," I explained. Ren relaxed his stance too, showing that he didn't want to fight any longer. Those we were talking to seemed to pick up on this, and while they didn't move any closer, they seemed willing to keep talking.

"I see. I'm sorry for attacking you without talking first," Mamoru said. Sometimes these situations required sudden action, so I did understand—but accepting an apology too easily could put us on unsteady footing in future dealings.

"We didn't have any intent to fight you, so you could have stopped and asked. Ren clearly wanted to talk with you, right?" I pointed out. The other hero seemed to be feeling sufficiently guilty about it, averting his gaze apologetically while saying nothing.

"Mamoru . . ." Raphtalia muttered, looking across at him.

"What's up?" I asked her.

"No, it's nothing . . ." she replied.

"Sorry, who is she?" Mamoru asked, pointing at Raphtalia.

"This is Raphtalia, my right hand in combat. Her weapon is the katana vassal weapon, which we obtained in a different world to this one—and different from our own world too, actually," I said. I was starting to juggle a lot of worlds.

"You've got quite a collection of weapons," Mamoru commented.

"You too, from the look of it," I replied, looking across at R'yne.

"I guess so. Sorry, I was just surprised how much she looks like someone else I know," Mamoru said, still looking at Raphtalia. I wondered if that was just a line.

"I see. Even more strange coincidences," I commented.

"This person comes from far across the eastern sea, a place called Q'ten Lo. Do you think they originally were summoned from your world, perhaps?" Mamoru inquired. Raphtalia and I both did a double take. Q'ten Lo! That was clearly what he said.

"Maybe someone like your parents, Raphtalia, cast out of their home nation, were summoned here," I theorized. Their bloodline had survived by being caught up in a summoning. That sounded possible. We knew from Shildina that summoned heroes didn't only have to come from modern Japan—or some version of Japan, anyway.

"Do you know of Q'ten Lo?" Mamoru asked, puzzled at our exchange.

"It's the name of a country on our world," I replied.

"We have one here too," he responded. I shook my head. Something wasn't fitting together here. It felt like we were making some kind of fundamental error.

"Ah!" Raphtalia suddenly exclaimed. She turned away from Mamoru and had a look of surprise on her face.

"Mamoru . . . no, it can't possibly be . . ." Eclair had also seemed to be chewing something over since hearing that name. If Raphtalia and Eclair had both realized something, it was likely pretty good information.

"What is it? Do you know something?" I asked.

"No . . . it doesn't seem possible," Raphtalia said.

"You know everything that happened with Rishia, right? Nothing is impossible. We need to find out what's going on here. Ideas about what's 'possible' only get in the way. Let me decide for myself if something sounds right," I told her.

"Okay, very well." Raphtalia looked at Eclair for a moment and then gathered her breath and continued. "There are lots of fairy tales mixed into the legends of the four holy heroes. Some of them, dealing with the waves that caused the previous cataclysm, talk about an object of worship and the founder of Siltvelt itself—one of the most famous of the Shield Heroes. Well, his name was . . . Mamoru."

Chapter Eight: Hero Worship

"What?!" I immediately exclaimed in surprise, looking at the other Shield Hero. Just as Raphtalia had said, that seemed impossible to me . . . but power-up methods that we could only partially use, levels not resetting even after being transported, monsters that were meant to be extinct, and Fohl and Melty kind of recognizing the scenery—all of these mysteries suddenly seemed to make a lot more sense.

"What's going on?" Mamoru asked.

"You are Mamoru Shirono, correct? From modern Japan?" I confirmed with him.

"Yes, I mean, I would call it modern, obviously . . ." he replied.

"Maybe you can understand this, then. It seems highly likely that we're from far in your future, caught in a trap and sent back into the past," I explained.

"In other words . . ." he pondered.

"Right. From my perspective, you're one of the Shield Heroes who came before me, tackling the waves long ago in my past," I said. At this revelation, Mamoru looked at us with disbelief on his face.

"From the future?" He tilted his head. "Still, seeing as we

already know that being summoned to different worlds is a thing, jumping across time . . ."

"Isn't such a stretch, is it?" I said. I was pleased he caught on so quickly, but everyone else seemed to have not caught up yet. They were all looking at each other, tilting their heads and wondering what we were talking about. I had to wonder how we reached this point. The occurrence of waves that fused worlds together was also sending people back in time. This kind of timey-whimey tomfoolery could be very volatile.

"Anyway, can we prove it conclusively?" Mamoru asked.

"Good question. Maybe if we could predict some future events for you, like in a movie or something . . . but in our time all sorts of historical documents have been destroyed or disappeared. You're little more than a fairy-tale character, so we've no way to tell you about anything other than large events," I explained. This would be the time to chat with someone who knew a lot about the legends of the four heroes, but thanks to the one who assumed the name of God, it was hard to tell if these things were facts or just fiction. "What we can tell you, if you are the Shield Hero from our past, is that you'll eventually start a nation of demi-humans called Siltvelt," I revealed to him.

"Siltvelt . . ." he said.

"The only way we can try to get you to trust us is by sharing whatever we know with you," I said.

"Okay then," Mamoru finally agreed. "If you don't want to

fight with us, we don't need to fight you either. Explain whatever you can." He paused again. "One thing though. If you really are from the future, isn't there a chance that coming here will change whatever you go back to?"

"That's the issue. If everything we're doing is already part of our past, including our coming back there, then we can do whatever we want," I said. The other choice was being able to do things like save people who should have died in order to make the future a better place. In either situation, we weren't going to get anywhere without more information.

"Tell me something, predecessor (TBC)," I said.

"Can you not give me strange nicknames?" he remarked.

"Don't worry. Once we confirm the truth, I will remove the (TBC). I just need you to understand that if you try anything violent, try to trick or trap us, or attack us for any reason, we're not going to hold back on you," I warned. I had to keep my guard up, but squabbling wasn't going to resolve anything. We needed to find out the truth of our situation first—and the only way to do that was to talk to these guys and the others in their village. "I'm a Shield Hero too, remember, which means I know where to hit you. Try anything and I'll hit you back ten times as hard."

"You are very cautious," Mamoru replied.

"I'm looking to send more than my bones back to the future, after all. I've encountered lots of problematic people in every world I've visited so far," I told him.

"Sorry about that . . ." Ren said, dipping his head. I actually hadn't meant that one as a shot at him! "I got too carried away to help," he said.

"Ren, this isn't about you. Stay out of this," I told him. When he heard all of this, a strange look came over Mamoru's face.

"I understand what you mean," he eventually admitted, nodding. It sounded like he'd experienced some of the same stuff. "There are people who want to use the heroes for their own advantage or who want to—as you put it—trick or trap us. Even the heroes themselves don't always make all the right decisions."

"Have you realized that the waves are running interference here too?" I asked. Mamoru nodded. They understood it even in this era, and yet that information hadn't made it to the future. The vanguards of the waves had been doing their evil work too well, of course.

"I got caught up in all sorts of stuff when I was first summoned. There are nasty people everywhere," Mamoru said. From my perspective, the whole system was shot the moment they started relying on summoning people from other worlds. But I didn't want anything to bounce back onto me, so I kept that opinion to myself.

In order to further understand the situation, anyway, we decided to show Mamoru and his party back to our village.

"There definitely wasn't a village here before," Mamoru said, nodding as he looked around. The boundary line running all around it was clear proof that we were the interlopers here.

"Naofumi, welcome back," said Melty.

"Brother, everyone! You have returned!" said Fohl, the two of them spotting us and running over. Then they spotted Mamoru and his allies. They looked at me with questioning looks on their faces.

"Those weapons . . . If we're right about everything, makes him the Gauntlets Hero of the future, right?" Mamoru asked.

"If we're right," I confirmed.

"Brother, who are these people?" Fohl asked.

"That's pretty complicated," I said. I proceeded to introduce Melty, Fohl, and everyone else in the village to Mamoru and the others, and then I explained that maybe we had been sent into the past. "Does anyone here know a lot about the Shield Hero legends?" I asked. "That might lead to some more clues."

"There is a lot that's spoken of as fairy tales. However . . ." Melty signaled to me that she wanted a more private discussion. Whispering among ourselves might make a bad impression on our new friends, but we couldn't worry about that.

"There sure are some strange monsters in the future," Mamoru said.

"Raph," said one of the Raph species.

"What was that?" asked a filolial as Mamoru and his allies looked over at them. He did hang out with a lot of demi-humans, so maybe he was an animal lover. This seemed like my chance to get a few words in with Melty, anyway.

"What do you want? Something you can't say in front of them?" I asked.

"I know something of the Shield Heroes summoned by the waves before you, Naofumi. My mother told me a lot. I'm sure she would have loved to see this, if she was still alive," she said. This sounded promising. Her mother had been a history buff. Like queen, like princess. "There are numerous heroic tales remaining with a motif of the hero most worshipped in the creation of Siltvelt—like how he taught the demi-humans how to fight for themselves."

"If that's true, it means we've hooked up with a real celebrity here," I said. Nothing was confirmed yet. I wasn't even sure we'd be able to prove it. However, adding to what Raphtalia said, this guy seemed really well liked!

"There's something else you'd better know, Naofumi. Where there is light, there are also shadows. In Melromarc, which is the enemy of Siltvelt, he was the most hated of the Shield Demons . . . the hero known as the Demon King," Melty continued. That was what the guys who hated me called me— guys like the Church of the Three Heroes. And Armor, the guy Itsuki had captured and brought back, had called me that too.

"The Shield Demon King, huh?" I said. There wasn't much I could do about that now. It came down to the difference in the awareness of justice and evil, that hot topic that Itsuki and Rishia were always worrying about. Which side was right could depend on the values of the time—and the side you picked made the other side your enemy. These were the kinds of issues that always emerged once you got involved with authority.

"There's something else my mother said. If you search through the heroic legends from our world in the countries prior to Melromarc, the Shield Hero just suddenly appears at one point. That suggests he didn't exist until that time," Melty said. It must be the effects of the fusion of the worlds, meaning there had been no Shield Hero when the waves first occurred.

"Does that mean the place that is Melromarc for us is the world the Sword and Spear Heroes came from?" I said.

"That sounds correct to me. There are more legends about those two than there are of the shield and of the bow. Tracing back my father's lineage leads to the Spear Hero too," Melty commented. That reminded me of something the queen said once about Trash's name before they got married, something like "Lansarz" or "Lansarose" or something like that. That probably explained where his preferential treatment of Motoyasu had come from.

"We need to find out if we have really come here from the future or not. Melty, can you share what you know with Mamoru and the others?" I asked her.

"Sure thing," she replied. That finished our private chat. Then I saw Fohl.

"Fohl." I called him over.

"What is it, Brother?" he asked.

"With your bloodline, you might be able to share some info that these guys will be interested in. Can you talk to them about the Shield Hero along with Melty?" I asked him. Fohl was a member of the hakuko, one of the representative races of Siltvelt. They probably had some tribal stories or something passed down through the generations.

"I could manage that . . ." he replied. Mamoru and his allies were still distracted by the village monsters. But then I introduced Melty and Fohl to them.

"Thank you for coming to meet with us, Shield Hero. I am Melty Q Melromarc, the queen of the nation of Melromarc." Melty gave them the full royal performance, including a regal bow. I had seen her like this before, but it was so different from how I normally knew her that it still seemed funny to me.

"Your Majesty. Melromarc is not a name I have heard before," Mamoru replied.

"Most likely a nation that does not yet exist in this time. Likely, it will be coming from a completely different world, thanks to the waves," Melty said.

"Being the queen of a nation that doesn't exist yet means you've been demoted to 'ordinary girl,' Melty!" I quipped from the sidelines. She gave me an elbow of considerable force right in the side, which also wasn't very regal. Also, unfortunately for her, I was the Shield Hero. It didn't hurt me at all. Probably not the best impression to make in front of guests though—Mamoru already looked perplexed by this interaction between us.

"And this is Fohl, the Gauntlets Hero. He is one of the most knowledgeable people in our village on the topic of Siltvelt," I continued, introducing Fohl to Mamoru and his allies.

"Archduke Naofumi Iwatani, who we know as the Shield Hero, has explained the details of the situation to us," Melty said, continuing with her sickly official persona and continuing the discussion. She even put "Archduke" in front of my name! It was nice to feel noble sometimes. I was getting goosebumps. "I can only hope that this works, but we will be able to share with you some stories from our time of the Shield Hero."

"I would like that very much. We also wish to confirm the truth of this situation," Mamoru said. The discussion was led by Melty and Fohl. We started to talk about the Shield Hero with Mamoru and his allies. The basic outline was pretty simple— Mamoru was summoned as Shield Hero to the ancient nation of Siltvelt, the weakest nation in the land. He taught them how to fight, took on the waves in order to save the world, and after many struggles and hardships, he secured the continued existence of the world. The part about teaching demi-humans to fight probably wasn't that difficult to do, considering the hero's blessings he would have been able to offer. Still, he had faced tribulations along the way, but there simply wasn't time to share all of the stories in detail. I was actually somewhat interested, but there was no way of telling if they were true or not—in particular, there were things that hadn't happened here yet.

"Angered at the invasions by other nations, Shield Hero Mamoru combined his strength with his allies to drive off—" Melty continued.

"There are plenty of records of that in this time," Mamoru said.

"So that is true?" Melty confirmed.

"Yes," he replied.

"Okay, moving on. It is said that ancient Siltvelt was comprised of those who learned how to fight from the Shield Hero. The four main races that benefited from this were the hakuko, the aotatsu, the shusaku, and the genmu. The Gauntlets Hero here with us is a member of one of these races, the hakuko," Melty revealed, pointing at Fohl to direct attention to him.

"Hakuko?" Mamoru said, puzzled.

"You don't have that race?" I asked.

"No, I don't think we do," Mamoru replied. I wondered what that might mean. If this was the past, the hakuko race should be here too. Perhaps they were a race that emerged after this but before our time.

"That does sound like the kind of name you would give

something," R'yne said to Mamoru, looking intently at Fohl with a smile on her face.

"That's rude!" Mamoru said.

"I really think it sounds like one of your names, that's all," she teased.

"R'yne!" he exclaimed.

"You have trouble thinking up names, do you?" I asked. So this was the hero who had given the races all those dumb names. "They're a little better than strings of random letters. I bet you give things really simple nicknames too, don't you? Like 'doggie' for a dog-type monster?"

"I couldn't possibly comment . . ." Mamoru said, turning his eyes away.

"Bingo!" said R'yne, pointing at me like I'd won the jackpot. Just as I expected.

"You're not one to talk, Mr. Naofumi. You just add 'II' on everything," Raphtalia chided me. Friendly fire, at a time like this! Friendly fire that was hard to avoid, too, because it was aimed so accurately.

"This isn't about me. None of those names will be going down in history either," I said. I just made up nicknames for people who wouldn't share their names with us—mainly our enemies.

"Oh really? You deny calling Wyndia 'valley girl' and almost calling Ruft simply 'cousin' because of his relationship with me? If we do succeed in bringing peace to our world, can you be sure that your nickname for Wyndia isn't the one that will go down in history?" Raphtalia said pointedly.

"Wow, Raphtalia. You've really upped your game," I said.

"We've known each other for a long time, after all. We've had this discussion before too," she said. We both almost looked off with glazed eyes into the distance. We'd come a pretty long way—too long, to be honest. "We met those people in the Demon Dragon's castle who didn't tell us their names, didn't we? What nicknames did you give them?" Raphtalia wasn't giving up. It sounded like this habit of mine actually really bothered her. She was so good at remembering names herself. That's probably where this was coming from.

"Cool and affected people get labeled Ren II. People with a strong sense of justice, Itsuki II," I said, deciding I had nothing to hide anymore.

"Hey! Are you talking about the stuff that happened in the other world? Stuff that you told me about yesterday? You were calling the enemies by my name?!" Ren said, suddenly getting involved.

"I had to call them something. They weren't forthcoming with their names, and there was one of them who was exactly like you used to be," I replied. Now Ren was much more of a team player and gave due consideration to his allies—he was a totally different person, really.

"I know I was like that, and I regret it, but how long am

I expected to drag it around? Next time someone else like me shows up, you're going to call them Ren III, aren't you?" he accused me.

"Of course," I shot back. "I'm up to III with Motoyasu and Trash already. Trash II got sliced in half, and Trash III is currently locked up after getting all muscular," I said.

"I know who you are talking about. III is a woman!" Raphtalia had her hand pressed to her forehead. Motoyasu III, by the way, was Therese. Then Raphtalia suddenly looked over at me again, having seemingly realized something else. "Hold on. I've had this thought before, actually. Don't you actually know the name of Trash II, Mr. Naofumi?" I wasn't about to answer that question. I needed to deflect before Raphtalia became sure of it.

Quite honestly, who gave a shit about the vanguard of the waves that Tsugumi had once had the hots for? Tsugumi herself was now completely fixated on Kizuna anyway. For a moment, I thought I saw both Kizuna and Tsugumi shaking their heads in the back of my mind, but no, that couldn't be a thing. The two of them were basically scissoring every time I saw them. Then add Glass into the mix and you had a right romantic comedy going along.

"Hmmm," Eclair pondered. "In the case of Hero Iwatani, knowing the model for the nickname could be an effective way to understand the kind of impression these others give off. It might be a good way to remember people," she continued. I hoped she was just making a joke, but that seemed unlikely from her.

"Eclair?!" said Ren in surprise. "This isn't something you should be copying!"

"Where did 'valley girl' come from?" Mamoru asked unexpectedly. Wyndia looked sullenly interested in the answer too.

"You'd like to know?" I asked.

"Just a passing interest," he replied.

"Okay. Even though you say you're from Japan, we already know from among ourselves that you might not be coming from the same Japan as me, so I'm not sure if you'll get this, but here we go." I gestured to the Raph species from the village that had originally been a caterpilland and directed it to move around behind Wyndia. "Now turn into your bug form," I told it. The caterpilland popped back into its previous form. "Before I won everyone in the village over, Wyndia and the others living there were raising these monsters and keeping them hidden from me. Even when I finally found out, she did everything she could to hide the monster by standing in front of it like that, telling me there was no monster at all." Mamoru was clearly picturing the scene, and his eyes narrowed. It looked like he was thinking back, remembering something. "From that reaction, I think we have the same thing in both of our worlds," I said. There had been plenty of examples of geeky guys being selected as heroes already, so it made sense—and in this case, we were talking about an internationally famous anime.

It had been a long time since I saw any anime, I thought wistfully. Just another thing I missed.

"Okay, I see it. Valley of the—" Mamoru started. Yeah, he got it.

"I don't like these explanations that only you heroes understand!" Wyndia cut in petulantly.

"Ask Ren and he'll explain it to you," I said.

"I wouldn't like that either!" she said curtly. Wyndia really disliked Ren.

"Maybe one of the other heroes has already brought this story over? That might help you to understand," I said.

"You know what . . . I think I may have seen something like this," Melty muttered. She was a royal, after all. She might have seen it in a play or something.

"Hey . . . if you keep this up, then Wyndia's name really will go down in history as 'valley girl.' Is that what you are aiming for here?" Raphtalia asked. She made a good point. Spreading the origin of the name might indeed turn her into valley girl forever.

"Please, don't allow that!" Wyndia said emphatically.

"Okay, okay," I replied.

"If you are allied with Mr. Naofumi, please make sure to tell him your name. Multiple times, if necessary. Otherwise, who knows what will happen?" Raphtalia stated. It sounded like she was okay with me giving names to our enemies, then. Most of them probably wouldn't share that information even if we asked—or would just come out with a made-up name. Even that might be better. But then I'd end up calling them "Mr. Fake Name" or something if it ever came out.

"We are getting pretty off track here," I said. "You don't have hakuko, correct?" I asked for confirmation. Mamoru stayed silent. "This might be something we really shouldn't be telling you," I continued. "The hakuko might be a new race that you are yet to discover, like a powerful race that chooses to hide itself away from the habitats of others."

"There are stories like that too," Melty said, stepping in to back me up. Perhaps like Hengen Muso Style, pushed to the brink of extinction by the effects of the vanguards of the waves, but somehow just managing to cling on. This was all still just supposition, of course. They might also be in a country like Q'ten Lo that sealed itself off from the outside world or might literally be sealed off somewhere. Maybe Mamoru would meet them at some point after this and win them over—or maybe they were refugees, using the waves as a means to cross to this world. The waves had warped history so badly it was hard to uncover the truth any longer.

"I'm still not sure I believe any of this . . ." Mamoru said.

"The name sounds so much like one of yours, Mamoru. I believe it," R'yne said brightly.

"We aren't going to get anywhere without a little trust, and you don't seem to want to fight. To be honest, I thought maybe you were going to just mob us," Mamoru admitted. If we were invaders, that might have been a tactic we used. If we used everyone we had here to launch an all-out attack on just Mamoru and the allies he had with him, we might have been able to win.

"I could say the same thing to you," I countered.

"Indeed. I've decided that we'll accept you as our guests and cooperate with you however we can. We need to find a way to get you back," Mamoru said.

"Okay," I said.

"One more thing. Those monsters with wings on their backs, who are they?" Mamoru asked.

"Huh? The filolials?" I replied.

"Is that what they're called?" Mamoru said. He was looking at the filolials, furrowing his brow. He seemed pretty interested in them.

"From your reaction, it looks like you don't have them in this time either, right? They're pretty odd monsters who like to pull carts around. In the future, wild filolials can be found pretty much everywhere," I said. They were versatile beasts, used for everything, like transport to food. Unfortunately, Filo was the only one who could fly.

"Filolials, huh," muttered R'yne, also looking at the birds. I was starting to get suspicious again, but I wasn't sure what could be causing it. The filolials had noticed the attention and a few of them asked what was going on. "Nothing to worry about," R'yne said. "Can I ask you something? You've been transported somehow to this strange new place, potentially the past—aren't you scared?" The filolials thought for a moment.

"No, we're fine. Iwatani and the others will sort this out. If they can't do it, I'm sure Kitamura will come to save us," one of them said.

"Yeah, that's right," another agreed. They were as airheaded as ever, pretty much giving up on thinking about anything altogether. Mass-produced Filos at their finest. Unfortunately for them, Motoyasu was not going to come to the past—or at least, I very much didn't want him to.

The scary thing was he might find a way to do it.

"I think that covers everything. We are going to go along with your conjecture for now," Mamoru said after listening to everything we had to say.

"I do have a lot I want to ask you, but really, we just want to get back to our time as quickly as possible," I said. In the past, before I was framed, and if I could fight—if I had nothing holding me back, basically—then I probably would have quite enjoyed ending up in the past like this. Now I wanted to make getting home my first priority. We'd been hit by an attack that moved us through time. Back where we came from, I was betting that S'yne's sister—and Bitch and her goons too, probably—were going to town in our absence. I had to do something about that situation. I needed to get back as quickly as possible and wipe them all out.

"You've kindly explained the situation to us, Naofumi. I want you to see my base of operations too," Mamoru said.

"I understand where you are coming from . . ." I said, trailing off. I looked at Melty and the others from the village. The most pressing question was still how the hell we were going to get back to our time. Maybe we could negotiate with the shield or request a transfer from Raphtalia's katana? When I checked on those possibilities immediately after arriving here, however, neither had looked very promising. As I pondered these issues, I saw Rat looking pretty pleased with herself. She probably wanted to make a start on investigating these extinct monsters. She could do that later.

I looked away from her and back at Mamoru and his allies.

"Hold it, Archduke," Rat said, following up after I ignored her. "You aren't going to ask for my help?"

"Quite honestly, when actual achievements such as reading ancient texts are considered, the only ones among my allies I consider truly intellectual are Rishia and Trash—both of whom aren't here," I told her flatly. Rat was a researcher, so she said, but working under me, she had been more of a monster doctor/veterinarian, and there wasn't a great deal I relied upon her for. For another thing, she'd been taking her sweet time deciphering the technology we'd collected from other worlds. She had originally been conducting her research in Faubrey, but Takt had shut that down and so she'd drifted into Melromarc. I did know that after we defeated Takt, she had expanded her research facilities.

"You are pretty full of yourself, even though you don't achieve much," Wyndia said, coming in with an unexpected boot from the sidelines. Rat winced and gave her a nasty glare. I knew she had her talents, but Wyndia also wasn't wrong.

"I just don't like research that doesn't look far enough forward—that gives no consideration to its subjects! The proof of that is all the medical checks I've been giving the Raph species, some of the archduke's favorite monsters. I'm working as hard as I can to reduce the complications of an interspecies class-up!" Rat said indignantly.

"Hold on. There have been complications?" I asked.

"Of course. If your entire body was suddenly transformed into a new shape overnight, Archduke, I'm sure you would have trouble moving parts of it or keeping it all working. I'm helping the Raph species adapt to their new circumstances," Rat explained. She was claiming to be working hard beneath the surface, then . . . but it was still hard to evaluate her based on these kinds of results. That said, what she was doing was worthy of praise, so I had to be careful with my reply. She went on. "I've also been keeping an eye on the technical stuff you've been asking other people to handle, Archduke. The texts translated by the projectile weapon hero, the Ivyred girl, have passed through my hands too—and the reports on the pieces you've been bringing back from other worlds." She was starting to sound like a jack-of-all-trades. Maybe I should have been calling her "Rishia II." She specialized in monster-related stuff but seemed to actually know a reasonable amount about other stuff too. "You must be aware, Archduke, that alchemy requires a wide base of varied knowledge. You have your own skills, after all, such as accessory-making and cooking, so you understand," Rat said. She did have a point. The Demon Dragon blood I had used in the cooking, for example, was more a magical material if you were going to categorize it. Rat had specialized knowledge, so she clearly thought this was her time to shine.

"Raph!" came a gaggle of calls. The Raph species monsters clustered around Rat. I guessed this meant it was okay to trust and rely on her. The monsters trusted her second only to me, after all. I would like to see how she reacted to the Demon Dragon, that was for sure.

"If the Raph species are vouching for you, I guess I can roll with it. What have you got, Rat?" I asked.

"I'm not sure I like the way you're asking," Rat said.

"I have some resistance to the Raph species recommending this. Are you sure you want to proceed?" Raphtalia asked. Neither of them seemed that happy, but Rat herself had asked me for this!

"Raphtalia, we'll discuss this later or we're going to get distracted again. In the first place, do you think Rat can't be trusted?" I asked her.

"No, of course not. She performs health checks for everyone, and I think we can trust her," Raphtalia replied.

"That settles it. Rat, we're going to search with you for clues, okay?" I said.

"It's not my specialty, but I'm the biggest brain you've got around here, Archduke. And I'm very interested in this world of the past," Rat said. So that was what she was really after. A researcher like Rat was clearly going to react to having all these extinct monsters around. She wanted to get materials on them, no matter what that took.

"We'll take you along then, Rat, but we need to firm up the defenses of the village too. If we go out in force and fall into a trap, it will be hard to escape," I said.

"You still don't trust us?" Mamoru asked with a frown.

"I didn't say that," I said cautiously—but quite obviously, believing anyone too quickly could only lead to pain.

"As your predecessor as the Shield Hero, let me remind you of something. What is the shield's power-up method? Trust, right?" Mamoru said. I grunted. He certainly knew where to place his punches. The shield power-up method could raise abilities through trust and being trusted. Trust itself could become power. In some respects, the Shield Hero could be called the "hero of trust."

"I understand, but I only survive by being careful," I told him.

"Just how dark are things in the future?" Mamoru said, shaking his head. "It's like being told that everything we're fighting for here is meaningless." I couldn't comment on that. I had no way of rating the difference his actions were making. We didn't even know how many years into the past we were. It certainly wasn't ten or twenty years. We were talking hundreds of years here, at least. Considering the lack of records, it could even be thousands. How many years ago was the founding of Siltvelt anyway? I seemed to recall hearing a number . . . and it had been pretty long ago.

"I don't think we need to worry too much about that," R'yne said, giving what seemed to be a typically cheerful reply.

"I'm not suggesting hostages, but why don't we have some of our allies remove their weapons and stay here in the village? That should give you some insurance," R'yne suggested. Some of Mamoru's allies immediately put down their weapons and put up their hands.

"I can do that," said the guy whom the Shadow had taken hostage. One wrong step and he would have been dead, and here he was, offering himself as a "hostage." That was how much he believed in Mamoru.

"How does that sound?" Mamoru asked.

"Fine then," I eventually said. If they were going to these

lengths, it didn't seem like we had much choice.

"Naofumi, I'll go with you too. I'm a representative of this world. I can just hide back here," Melty said, in a rare proactive moment. She still had to be feeling considerable distress with Filo not being here. I guessed it was her royal colors showing through. "Or do you think you will be unable to protect me?" she asked pointedly, questioning whether I would be able to protect my queen or not, almost like a threat. I wondered if I should take that as an example of how much she had grown— or maybe an example of how Trash's education was pushing her development in unexpected ways.

"Okay then, fine. Ruft, you and Fohl can take over from Melty in managing the village," I commanded.

"Okay!" Ruft said brightly. I honestly would have preferred to leave Melty here with them, but that wasn't the situation we were in. Ruft could look out for the villagers in Melty's stead, I was pretty sure. Everyone under my command was getting pretty mouthy in their old age, I thought, shaking my head. I just hoped they could back that up with action.

"Melty, you'd better stay close to me at all times," I told her.

"Of course. Being close to you is the safest place to be anyway!" she replied cheekily.

"Hey! Melty, no fair!" Keel protested, pointing accusingly at Melty.

"Don't start!" I warned them. "We don't know what's going

to happen here, so I need you guys to just keep protecting the village while you wait for us to return! We won't be gone for long. Don't worry!" I told them.

"I shall alzo accompany you," said the Shadow, giving a salute to Melty. He could definitely prove useful, for both spying and protection, so I had no complaints there.

S'yne didn't speak, but she seemed very interested in the hero with the same weapon as her and clearly wanted to come along. Even if I told her no, she would probably ignore me. So I decided to include her in our numbers. That meant it would be me, Raphtalia, Raph-chan, Melty, Rat, S'yne, and the Shadow leaving the village again. Not the usual lineup of faces, I had to admit. There being no Filo, the Shadow being out in the open, and Rat leaving her lab were all standout features. Eclair had wanted to join us, out of worry for Melty, but eventually she decided to remain behind for Ren.

"Let's go," R'yne, the Sewing Kit Hero, said. Then Mamoru and R'yne both sent us party guidance. There were also limits to consider on the number of people they could teleport.

"Jumping Needle!" said R'yne.

"Portal Shield!" said Mamoru. Everything flickered around us and we moved into what looked like a castle courtyard.

Chapter Nine: Ancient Siltran

I looked around to see plenty of human activity, but the building itself looked older than Melromarc and seemed to be under
repair due to battle damage.

"Where are we?" I asked.

"Siltran. This is the nation that summoned me," Mamoru
said.

"Ancient Siltran, right?" commented Melty, providing some
useful additional information. "I've read about this in ancient
texts. The country that came before ancient Siltvelt." I wasn't
sure how to express it, but the castle seemed smaller . . . more
cozy when compared to Melromarc and Siltvelt. It probably
meant that Siltvelt had become more flashy and bigger as history continued. "So this is what it looked like. From what I
can see here, it looks like Vanira construction . . . but hold on,
something is a little different," Melty continued, tilting her head.
I wondered what she was thinking—and to be honest, I didn't
know what Vanira construction was.

"This castle isn't here in the future?" Mamoru asked.

"Much has been lost to conflict," Melty reported.

"I'm sorry to hear that," he eventually said. This was probably just the vanguards of the waves again, working behind the

scenes to ensure such assets didn't remain for future generations. I was getting sick of hearing such stories myself, but I
also thought that maybe we shouldn't be sharing such tales of
a dark and gloomy future with these people. They were going
to have trouble getting out of bed in the morning if they knew
the nation they currently lived in wasn't going to make it into
the future.

"Still, there's something about all this . . ." Even I wanted to
pick my words carefully, which was a rare occurrence. It was just
that the castle looked so bleak, and—for all the people—the
town did too. There was a lot of rubble and destruction, likely
from the waves. It all felt like something out of the Middle
Ages, old and dated. But it was almost taking it too far. It felt
old in a way that was different to L'Arc's nation over in Kizuna's
world.

I had been to Siltvelt, and I also wasn't seeing the same mix
of Western and Chinese styles that I had experienced there.
The town here was comprised of simple houses that mixed
rough stone and wood.

"Do you have a dragon hourglass?" Melty asked.

"Yes, in that building over there," Mamoru replied, pointing
to a building in front of the castle. Placing the dragon hourglass
in the vicinity of the castle was definitely a theme in this world.
That would at least let me line this location up with the future.

"Naofumi, I think I know what you're thinking, so let me

tell you something. Just like how a river can change its course
over a long period of time, a dragon hourglass can shift po-
sitions too. I don't think its location will be much help as a
reference point," Melty explained. It was the first I was hearing
of this—another arbitrary annoyance.

"Okay then, let's see what else we've got," I said and looked
around. But I didn't see anything that suggested further links
with the future. The scenery in the distance did look a bit like
what I had seen in Siltvelt, but if I had to say that this place
would definitively become Siltvelt in the future . . . that was a
tough call. There was a jungle close to the castle town in Siltvelt,
but here I was only seeing what looked like barren plains. I
mean, this was just from a quick glance around.

"Please start by coming to the castle," Mamoru said. "I
want to keep everything legit."

"Okay," I agreed. Mamoru let us into the castle of the nation of Siltran. Just like the exterior suggested, it was a pretty
cramped place. Melty walked on as though it was the most natural thing in the world, however, and so I just followed her lead.

I wondered if this really was the nation that would later
become Siltvelt again. The demi-humans I could see walking
around didn't look all that strong. When I had been in Siltvelt,
I'd been exposed to a melting pot of savage-looking individuals.
But everyone I was seeing here looked far more kind and gentle.
The therianthropes were also smaller races such as kobolts; I

wasn't seeing any of the big guys. I saw some sheep therian-thrope, and a lizard-man type too, like a muscular crocodile, not something I had encountered in Siltvelt. They looked pretty strong, but there wasn't a large number of them. In any case, the races here seemed closer to those in Q'ten Lo. Taking the shape of the demi-human ears and tails into account, I noticed there were lots of mice and weasel types.

Then I noticed Raphtalia looking over at a demi-human with weasel features.

"Something up?" I asked her.

"No, it's . . . it's nothing," she stammered.

"Raph," said Raph-chan, leaping up onto Raphtalia's shoulder and making more noises. She seemed to be saying that it was rude to stare.

We continued on and were allowed into the Siltran audience chamber.

"Welcome back, Hero Mamoru. Baah!" We were welcomed by a sheep therianthrope. It was wearing a coat and tails, making me want to make an impromptu crack about a mutton butler for some reason. I was also very distracted by the bleating noise, but I decided to let that one go. "Whatever is going on here, Hero? Who are these people with you? Baah!"

"It seems they are heroes from the future, sent to this age for as of yet undiscovered reasons," Mamoru explained.

"What! Baah!" said the sheep.

"This is one of the ministers of Siltran," Mamoru explained to us.

"What about the king?" I asked.

"He recently passed away, I'm afraid, due to the betrayal of our castle magician," Mamoru said. "The king was a good man." I frowned as soon as the word "betrayal" came up. I wondered why there was so much of that in the world. "So my friend here has taken on a lot more of the detailed public duties," Mamoru continued.

"I do whatever I can to aid the Shield Hero Mamoru in his defense of the nation of Siltran, in place of our departed king," the sheep explained.

"You make it sound like Mamoru is basically the king now," I commented.

"Not the king, but a representative, maybe. I'm supported by so many other people though. I'm just more like window dressing," Mamoru said self-depreciatingly.

"Maybe a bit like the position you hold in Melromarc, Naofumi," Melty said.

"You need anything, the minister here should be able to arrange it." Mamoru turned back to the sheep. "How about we start with some maps? Our nation and others?" he suggested.

"Very well. I will arrange for them at once. Baah!" the minister said. Maps would be a big deal. Learning the terrain would be super useful for all sorts of reasons. If they were willing to show them to us, I wasn't going to turn them down, but I wondered at their security. I wondered why they would give such information up so easily.

"Please, take a look, heroes from the future," the mutton minister said, having ordered his underlings to bring in maps for us. I spread a few of them out. I had been paraded around inside Siltvelt, so I had some idea of the lay of the land. The nations had different names, the locations of towns and villages were different, and the actual size of the nation was smaller too. But I did recognize the mountains and general terrain. When I looked at the world map . . . there was something I had no idea about. It did feel similar in some places though. Melty was taking a look too and was looking just as baffled as I was. So this was the world prior to being fused by the waves. At some point in the future, then, the first world and second world would merge to create a third world.

There was an island called Q'ten Lo in the east, so that was a definite commonality, but on these maps, the shape of the island itself was not depicted; it was more just supposition that the island was located there.

"Something I'd like to ask about. This magician who betrayed you, tell me a little more about that," I said.

"A worm who took the head of our king as a prize to our sworn enemy, the massive nation of Piensa," Mamoru explained.

"I guess scum like that can be found in any age!" I raged.

"He asked me and the king to save the world from the waves, begged us, and then turned around with this betrayal. To be quite honest, I would love to find some way to punish him," Mamoru admitted. It almost sounded like he was asking for my help with that. That was a topic I could actually get behind, but I also wasn't in the market for another revenge quest at the moment. "The scariest part is that we don't know when they will attack, just that it is coming," Mamoru continued.

"We have you though, Mamoru, so we'll be okay," R'yne added. It sounded like his enemies thought quite a lot of his abilities then. "They are a big nation, and they try to solve everything with strength. They claim to be free from discrimination, but that's just a claim. They believe that their national view of justice is the justice of the world." That sounded a lot like Shieldfreeden. I'd only heard about it secondhand from Melty and Trash, but they talked about their ideals of freedom while wielding tight authority over their people. That made sense; it was the nation ruled by the aotatsu race, one of whom we had encountered as part of Takt's retinue. She had been seriously warped as well, triggered so badly by defeat it had been difficult to watch.

"They have vast lands and yet always want more, believing that the hero is more suited to their own nation," Mamoru explained.

"And they are now trying to wipe you out, after you wouldn't do what they asked," R'yne said.

"That's right. They've sent assassins to try and kill me countless times," Mamoru admitted. At that comment, Melty gave me a poke in the ribs with her elbow, telling me she needed to talk privately.

"Historically Piensa is described as a tyrannical nation that often attacked others. In the end they were defeated in a war with Siltvelt and wiped out," she told me. Based on that final result, it didn't sound like something we needed to get involved with.

"So what next? Are you going to let us use that spot for our village so long as we help you with your revenge?" I asked.

"I've no intention of asking you to help with our war efforts," Mamoru replied.

"I hope that's the truth," I said, still not sure about the guy.

"Of course it is. However, you are going to need to be careful. If it gets out that we have a second Shield Hero now, that could bring trouble down on you and your friends, Naofumi. Your village is in a bit of a hotspot, to be honest," Mamoru told us.

"Hot spot how?" I asked.

"We were in the region because we highly expect the enemy to attack from there," he said. I took a moment to consider that. It sounded like our village had popped out right between

Siltran and Piensa. If an all-out war did break out, we would probably need to evacuate the entire village. We could fight to protect it or run for the hills. "I just need you to be careful," he reiterated.

"Okay. In light of that warning, can you allow us free passage through this country?" I asked.

"I'll set that up," he said, giving orders to the mutton minister to prepare the paperwork.

"We don't want to rile up Piensa unnecessarily, do we? I'll make sure everyone, Ren and Fohl included, doesn't spread around the fact we are heroes. That should help to keep all this quiet," I said.

"That's a good idea," Mamoru agreed.

"That does leave the question of exactly what we should be doing next though. I'd really like to find a way to get back to our time period, but I guess ideas for time travel aren't going to just pop into my head," I said. I could really use a time-traveling car around now. Over in Kizuna's world, they had the Ancient Labyrinth Library, a really convenient resource at times like this. I almost wouldn't be surprised if we found freaking DeLorean plans in there somewhere.

"Archduke, I would like to take this opportunity to start surveying our surroundings, if you agree," Rat said.

"Maybe check and see what materials you can find here in the castle first," I suggested.

"Okay, good idea," she replied.

"We have someone most talented here who might be able to help with that. I will make the introductions," Mamoru said, looking over at the mutton minister again.

"A fine idea. I'm sure she will be a great help to them," the sheep bleated. "I am afraid, however, that such a meeting will have to wait. She only just departed the castle. Baah."

"Ah. We missed each other," Mamoru said.

"Correct," the sheep confirmed.

"Who are we talking about?" I asked. Someone "most talented," huh. There was a phrase that tickled me the wrong way.

"An excellent researcher, most intelligent. Someone we could not do without," Mamoru replied. "She's also the Whip Hero." That only made me think of Takt, which I really didn't like. We had managed to save the whip seven star weapon from him in the end, and I was still hoping it would choose someone in the future.

"I guess she wouldn't like it if we just go check out her lab," I said somewhat hopefully. Before I got an answer, however—

"Mamoru! Welcome back!" A horde of demi-human kids poured into the throne room, all shouting happily. I did a double take just to confirm it, but yes, they were all kids. They all looked at us and started talking at once.

"Hey! Who are these people?"

"They look like humans!"

"This one looks a bit like Mamoru!"

"You think? He looks scary!"

"I think he looks kinder than Mamoru!" The kids were staring especially hard at me. It made me uncomfortable, to be honest. I lifted my chin a little to highlight my arrogance. I didn't need more kids getting attached and annoying me all the time.

"Did he just say Naofumi looks kind?" Melty quipped, clearly unable to resist.

"Not overflowing with ambition?" Rat added.

"I am zurprised too." Even the Shadow got in on it, all three of them looking at me with puzzled looks on their faces. I had to agree with them though—it was hard to understand why any of these kids would say I looked "kind."

"He's got Mr. Naofumi pegged already . . . I'm amazed he saw that so quickly!" Raphtalia said.

"Raph," agreed Raph-chan. S'yne said nothing, but I could tell she was on their side in this. Unfortunately, it was the wrong side.

"Raphtalia, do I look kind to you? Really?" I asked.

"You don't look kind. It's more . . . your heart," she replied. Her explanation only made me feel worse about the whole thing. I did have that side to me though—almost childish— to pay back whatever I got. I knew what this was, anyway—it had been the same in Siltvelt. The modifiers on the shield holy weapon had an effect that made demi-humans and therian-thropes instinctively consider me their ally. A little girl with cat ears moved over to me, tilting her head.

"He has kind eyes," she said.

"Kind eyes like a wild animal?" I asked. I didn't need more annoying kids in my life!

"That must be true, if Cian is saying it! She doesn't like anyone!" said another one of the kids. They all started to crowd toward me. I wanted to fend them off with a stick.

"You don't even know me! Stay back!" I said.

"Look at him. He's trying so hard to play tough!" One of them laughed.

"What was that, you little snot-nosed—" I started in on the kid.

"Mr. Naofumi, please don't get so angry. They are just children," Raphtalia chided me. It looked like even in the past I was going to have to deal with annoying children! I hated this!

"They have a point . . . I do see you trying so hard to be brash and tough when I actually spend time with you. I actually understand what they mean," Melty said. I swore to myself that she would pay for that later!

"Raph?" said Raph-chan.

"Wow, what's this little thing?" one of the kids said.

"It's so cute and fluffy!" said another.

"Raph!" said Raph-chan happily, giving them a charming

twirl. The kids immediately got a bit grabby with their stroking of her, but Raph-chan could take it. This was my chance to establish the cult of Raph-chan in the past so her name would truly go down in history!

"Mr. Naofumi?" Raphtalia said suspiciously. Any more thinking like that and she would definitely realize what I was up to, so I looked over at Mamoru instead.

"These kids lost their parents in the war. I've been taking care of them," he told me. I gave a whistle. So he was charitable too! I couldn't compare with that—actually, my village was pretty much the same thing. These kids would probably get along well with Keel and the others.

"I've seen this lady before. Oh? Are you someone else?" one of the kids said to Raphtalia. A few of them seemed to be mistaking her for someone else.

"Right, about that. I'll need to make those introductions too—" Mamoru started.

"Of course. The one from Q'ten Lo who looks like Raphtalia. I'd very much like to meet with her," I said.

"I know. We'll have to track her down," Mamoru replied.

"You can't just call her here?" I asked.

"Unfortunately, we don't have such a close relationship. Quite a lot happened there too," Mamoru said.

"She still doesn't really trust Mamoru," R'yne explained. "We are trying to be friendly with her, but there seems to be all sorts of reasons holding her back. She's pretty serious about things and seems more stubborn than your own right hand, Naofumi." Even as she talked, the kids were still buzzing around us.

"Kids, we can't talk with you all here. Run along now," Mamoru said.

"We just want to listen . . ." one of them said. Mamoru put his finger to his lips, paying no attention to their complaints. The kid called Cian had a clouded expression on her face. It felt like there was something else going on here, and I didn't like it. More unwanted suspicions. Her expression looked like Keel's when she was ready for a fight.

"Okay. See you later." The kids finally accepted it and left, saying goodbye, all waving eagerly. I gave them a half-hearted wave in return, and then they were gone.

"Sorry if you think we've wasted your time. I'll make sure to introduce you, if you can give me a little longer," Mamoru said.

"No need to worry too much. We just turned up so suddenly. You can't be expected to be ready for us. It looks like we're going to be here for a while anyway," I told him. We really had to find a way to get back to our time—and that wasn't going to be easy. Sooner or later, we were going to find all sorts of information.

"Another reason for coming here is to register our weapons

with the dragon hourglass. That will let us confirm the time before the next wave," I said. The information I was seeing in my field of view was still unclear. "We're here because of S'yne too," I said, looking at R'yne. "You have the sewing kit vassal weapon, right? Can I ask you some questions?"

"Go ahead. What do you want to know? How I met Mamoru? Or about my own world? Maybe about what tastes good in this world?" she replied with a barrage of questions, making it hard for me to find the timing to reply. I also wondered why food was coming up.

"First, about your world. We need to confirm that it's the same one S'yne came from. If you have vassal weapons, you must have holy weapons too. What are they?" I asked.

"Okay, good question. The holy weapons—if you can really call them that, in my world—are the armor holy weapon and the ring holy weapon," she replied.

"Armor and ring?" I confirmed. They didn't sound like weapons. Armor was defensive, and a ring was an accessory. I looked over at S'yne to see her twitch and turn away from me. "Looks like that's a match," I commented.

"Well, well. Not sure I like hearing that my world has been destroyed," R'yne said, frowning, clearly distressed by S'yne not saying otherwise.

"I've heard others from your world say 'well, well' a lot," I commented. "Is that a thing where you come from?"

"I don't think so . . ." R'yne replied. Maybe it was just sub-conscious, a common speech pattern on their world. If they were related, I'd certainly had never seen S'yne pop out wings like that.

"What kind of weapons do armor and a ring make, then?" I asked. I thought for a moment about Itsuki's former underling, who I already called "Armor." That's why he came to mind.

"The ring is a weapon compatible with pretty much any ring you can find, and it mainly specializes in magic. The armor is like the shield, for defense," she said.

"The basics all sound the same," I said.

"After exchanges—by which I mean fighting with various worlds due to various waves—the armor and shield seem to both go into the defense category," R'yne said. "With more research, we might find out more details. That said, after see-ing the Armor Hero out there on a metal-covered rampage, 'defense' might not be the best word for it."

"A rampage?" I asked. Even if he was fully armored, com-pletely protected from monsters or human attacks, I could only imagine him fighting in the same kind of way as me. I won-dered how a guy in armor could go on a rampage.

"I think it's a pretty convenient holy weapon. He can fire off the gauntlets and give foes a good whack too," R'yne said. The armor immediately transformed into a robot in my mind. It sounded like some kind of rocket punch!

"I've never seen it do that," S'yne said, shaking her head. The Armor Hero S'yne knew about probably didn't use the rocket punch then. "They were the same as you, Naofumi," she continued.

"Specializing purely in guarding," I said. S'yne nodded.

"The shield is only for guarding? Why don't you hit things?" Mamoru asked. Everyone from my side of the room looked at him in surprise. All his question did was give me questions for him.

"What are you talking about?" I asked.

"I'm asking why you think the shield is only for guarding. You need to attack a little to keep the enemy focused on you, surely," he said. I raised an eyebrow, wondering what the hell Mamoru was talking about. I recalled the impact I had felt when we fought—maybe that's what he meant.

"Naofumi, why don't we just show them how powerless you are?" Melty said tauntingly. We had Raphtalia, Raph-chan, Melty, Rat, S'yne, and the Shadow here, so what was the best way to explain this to Mamoru and the others . . .

"How about we have the Shadow turn into someone else— say, Takt—and let me whack him," I suggested.

"Oh my! You want to punch me?" the Shadow said.

"Why are you getting emotional now?" I asked him. "I'll look like a real villain if I punch Melty."

"Nope, nope, nope," said the Shadow. I wondered where

that came from. He should transform and let me hit him.

"Hah! Your attacks can't even tickle me, Naofumi!" Melty taunted.

"Oh, you think so? I guess this will be easy to understand, anyway," I admitted.

"Hey, what are you talking about?" Mamoru said. "It sounds like you're about to punch her, Naofumi."

"Just watch," I said. Melty was offering her cheek to me, daring me to hit it. So I proceeded to do so. Mamoru and his allies watched open-mouthed.

"As toothless as ever, Naofumi," Melty taunted. As expected, Melty didn't have a scratch on her. Level would be a factor, but she really was uninjured.

"I'll remember this, Melty!" I said as she continued to taunt me.

"I've still not forgiven you for all the mockery in the past!" she replied.

"I still can't tell if they get along or not . . . That's Mr. Naofumi and Melty, I guess," Raphtalia said.

"I honestly feel bad for the archduke," Rat commiserated. "I'm amazed he has survived this long." I couldn't believe it—someone driven out of their research by that punk Takt was taking pity on me!

"Shut up! Don't look at me with pity in your eyes!" I said. I really didn't need my allies feeling this way about me! I would make them pay for this somehow, that was for sure!

"I'm sorry, Mr. Naofumi, but just who are you fighting with?" Raphtalia asked.

"Anyone who would dare to look at me with pity!" I spat back.

"That's a lot of folks to fight," Melty chimed in. I didn't need her feeling that way, especially not her! I needed everyone to stop looking at me with pity! I was not pitiful!

"Are you seriously telling me that the Shield Hero can't attack in the future?" Mamoru asked.

"Yes, it's as you just saw. Your reaction seems to suggest that things are different for you," I said. Mamoru gave a nod. As I suspected. Those attacks he had performed on me could actually cause damage. "I did feel a bit of an impact. Is it limited to skills?" I asked.

"No. Just a big whack with the shield will cause damage. Nothing compared to the numbers my allies can put out, but still . . ." Mamoru responded.

"Mr. Naofumi, are you maybe just . . . doing it wrong?" Raphtalia asked.

"I definitely can't cause damage," I replied after a pause. That had been proven when I started out with Bitch, attacking that balloon. If I couldn't fight with my hands, I thought, how about with the shield? I'd tried that too, of course. Even that didn't cause any damage. Even recently, I would sometimes whack a monster with the shield, and I'd never seen it count as an attack. No matter how my attack value changed, it never made any difference. Any rare unlock bonuses only increased it by one or two points, nothing more. I'd been without the shield for a while too, meaning it had been a while since I had any chance to work on it.

I felt like rapping on the front of the shield. My predecessor Mamoru was allowed to attack, but I wasn't!

"Should we have told them all of thiz?" the Shadow asked in a quiet voice. I knew what he meant, but it was fine. We had plenty of methods of attack. If they tried to pull something now because they knew I was unable to attack, we'd just show them the error of their ways. Melty had taunted me with an understanding of all these facts.

"Putting this in game terminology, I guess it's like differences in build or status?" Mamoru said.

"Sounds about right. Could just be the shield spirit mucking us about," I replied. Many online games allowed players to distribute their stats however they liked. Under those terms, I was a build specialized for defense, giving up on putting status on attack completely, while Mamoru was a balanced build also capable of attacking. I would ultimately win when it came to pure defense, but in terms of flexibility in battle, Mamoru's build had its advantages too. Putting it honestly, I hadn't chosen the tank role of my own volition and so I was pretty jealous of the setup Mamoru had running. If I could attack even just a little—especially without having to use skills—it would make my life a whole lot easier.

"Do you think there might be differences between now and the future?" Mamoru asked.

"In the future, the Bow Hero can use guns as well," I said. The applicable range might expand over time, from bow to crossbow and then crossbow to guns. Ren's sword could copy a katana too. Motoyasu could copy almost anything with a long handle—in fact, there were some staff and stick weapons he could copy too. When I considered things from that perspective, the shield had a pretty limited range. There were some great shields, of course, and I had made it through up until now, but a little more leeway would have been great. The best I had at the moment was being able to copy certain gloves and gauntlets—and even then, I could still only use them for defense.

"Guns, huh . . ." Mamoru muttered. "We'd better not let the Bow Hero hear that."

"Why not? What's up?" I asked.

"A few things," R'yne admitted. "The Bow Hero and Shield Hero aren't exactly allies in this time period. If the Bow Hero found out he could use guns as well . . ." she said, trailing off. Making peace with a Bow Hero could be hard—I knew that from my struggles with Itsuki. That had been a difficult problem to overcome. He didn't listen and you couldn't talk him down. And just bumping him off wasn't an option either.

"You guys really are besieged on all sides," I said.

"It's hard to stay above water, I'll give you that. The one behind the waves is interfering too," Mamoru said.

"The one who assumes the name of God," Raphtalia said.

"Curse them. Anyone playing at God is going to piss me off," I said. Even knowledge from games had been incorrectly incorporated as a trap, and they were active even this far back in the past! Of course, they were intrinsically linked to the waves, so that probably made sense.

"We just have to keep fighting until those who can oppose the one who assumes the name of God can reach us. That's the same here in our world," Mamoru stated.

"Which leads to my next question. Have you had any interactions at all with these ones who can oppose them? Or have you been building anything, leaving anything for the future?" I tried, just asking generally. Mamoru and the others seemed puzzled about what I was asking, so I took out some paper and drew an image of the creature we had seen on the wall in Fitoria's ruins. "In our time, there are these ruins with a wall that has images of this cat-like therianthrope on them," I explained.

"A cat therianthrope? And this is the creature who can oppose the one who assumes the name of God?" Mamoru asked. It didn't sound like he knew anything, based on that response. There weren't filolials here, which probably meant Fitoria was born further into the future than this. I wondered which hero had made those ruins, then—and if we were destined to search through all of time to find them. Still so many mysteries.

"Whatever this creature is, it seems it came at some point after this but before my own time. Maybe keep that in mind," I suggested.

"Okay, yes. Good information," Mamoru said.

"Anything else you want to ask, future Shield Hero?" R'yne asked.

"Actually, yes—to you. Why are you among Mamoru's allies here? Or are you just helping out as a guest?" I asked. I could imagine her in the same kind of position as Glass or L'Arc, as someone who had visited our world to release unknown weapons and then fell into a collaboration due to that.

"There's nothing that says the heroes aren't allowed to get along, right? But we do seem to be pushed into fighting a lot," R'yne admitted.

"Good point. Things are the same in the future there as well," I said. The one who assumed the name of God had put all sorts of plans into action to make the heroes fight each other—like giving Ren, Itsuki, and Motoyasu incorrect game-based knowledge, boosting up their strength a little, and then making them think they had to beat everyone else.

"In my case, I ended up here after the waves brought my sister to this world. That eventually led me to becoming friends with Mamoru," R'yne explained.

"So you have a sister," I said, unable to stop myself from glancing over at S'yne. Her sister had a pretty crazy attitude and traveled between worlds herself. The sewing kit vassal weapon certainly seemed to have a type.

"Anything else? I want to talk with you more, Naofumi, if I can," R'yne said.

"You really do like to talk," I commented.

"You bet I do!" she replied. I would rather she didn't sound so happy about that. "Say, Naofumi."

"What now?" I asked with some trepidation.

"I bet sex with you doesn't hurt at all," she said.

"Where did that come from?!" I exploded, half in surprise, half in shock, as R'yne suddenly took a turn into dirty town. As if I would know about that!

"I mean, you don't have any attack power, do you? Which suggests to me that you wouldn't be able to make it hurt even if you wanted to. Doesn't that mean it would only feel good?" she hypothesized. She asked so smoothly, so naturally, head tilted, seemingly so pure—almost naive—that it just made me want to throttle her all the more.

"Logically speaking, that makes sense," Rat cut in from the sidelines, amazed at this new discovery.

"Not you too! Enough!" I said. If this hypothesis was proven, I'd become little more than a living sex toy. I was not going to allow that to happen! I never expected my lack of attack power to cause such a lewd question to arise at this juncture in time. This was even worse than them deciding to attack us because they thought I couldn't fight back! I could not allow this idea to spread!

"Hold on, Naofumi. Don't tell me that you're still a . . ." R'yne said cheekily. In that moment, I decided what I would have called her if I didn't know her name: Lewd Woman! She should be thankful that she gave me her name upfront, or she might have gone down in history with that name. R'yne was still pointing at me and looking at Raphtalia and the others. They all nodded, almost in unison, to confirm her unfinished supposition. "Aren't you a serious little boy?" She chuckled.

"Shut it! None of your business!" I replied hotly. With so much else going on, I just didn't have the time—or inclination—for activities of that type. First the Demon Dragon, and now all of this! There was no written rule that I had to sleep around. That was my business!

"Archduke, you really should just give it a try with Raphtalia. Then we'll also find out if it hurts or not," Rat suggested.

"I agree," Melty said. "You're still a bit too clean-cut for me in that regard."

"Holding it in won't do anyone any good," the Shadow said. I didn't ask what "it" was.

"Everyone, if you don't mind . . . can you stop giving Mr. Naofumi any more ideas?" Raphtalia said.

"Raph!" said Raph-chan.

"Nope, not happening!" I said. I could not let this get out. Even if I asked Raphtalia to keep it quiet, who knew who might be listening in when we did the deed? I was also scared of the response from the killer whale sisters once we returned home and they found out I'd put the moves on Raphtalia. Not that I thought they would be angry—I was worried they would think it meant they could get in line.

I noticed S'yne looking over with a little interest on her face too. That was best ignored. All too complex.

"Look what you've done. It just seemed like Mr. Naofumi was opening up about this stuff, and now he's bottling it all up again," Raphtalia said. I didn't like that response either. I wondered if there was no way to move on from this topic. I hadn't even given in to Atla on this!

I looked over at Mamoru, and he quickly glanced away. It didn't look like I would be sharing my pain at being taunted over sex stuff by women with him, then. We were both Shield Heroes, but if he had "experience," then that marked a major difference between us.

"R'yne, you're making him uncomfortable. Maybe don't push too hard," Mamoru suggested.

"You think?" R'yne said. She had a look on her face, like she'd just found a new plaything. That really reminded me of S'yne's sister. If she pushed any harder, I was going to have to push back! *Don't pity me, and don't pick on me!*

"Let's change the subject," Raphtalia suggested. "R'yne, you seemed to grow wings during our scuffle. What was that? Magic?" She didn't have wings at the moment, but they had definitely been there in combat and seemed to have boosted her abilities.

"Ah, my optical wings? That's a special ability belonging to my race," she explained. She focused for a moment and wings formed from light appearing on her back. She even started to float up in the air. Flight would be a convenient power to have. "They demand a lot of stamina, magic, and life energy to maintain, so I can't keep them out for any extended period of time."

"Like demi-humans turning into their therianthrope form," I suggested.

"Pretty much that, yes," she replied. Another power I would never have guessed at.

"When you say 'my race,' does that mean you aren't human?" I asked.

"That's right. In my world, we call ourselves skywings. The humans call us angels though," R'yne said.

"You look human at a glance, but you're actually a demi-human," I said. There sure were a lot of races out there. When I thought about it for a moment, I remembered both Glass and Therese looked pretty close to being human. All they did that was any different was turn transparent or get some jewels on.

"But your friend S'yne is a skywing, surely?" R'yne said.

"She is?" I asked, looking over at her. She shook her head vigorously, indicating that she had no idea about that herself.

"I don't know anything about that," S'yne said.

"I'm pretty sure . . ." R'yne continued, moving over and putting a hand on S'yne's shoulder. Something like life force flowed from R'yne into her. "Yes. The flow of the power is a little weak, but you should be able to use the same abilities as me. I can teach you, if you like," R'yne offered.

"Good idea. I'd very much like S'yne to learn that," I said. To be quite honest about it, the sewing kit vassal weapon was pretty much on its last legs, and S'yne herself was suffering from clearly diminished capacity. She was still making it work with cooking power-ups and raising her level hard, but the limit of those approaches was close, it was clear. Facing all these issues, a way to enhance herself had just dropped into our laps, so she needed to learn it, if she could.

"Why don't you know about yourself, S'yne?" R'yne wondered.

"Was there anyone in your world who could use powers like R'yne?" I asked her. S'yne shook her head at my question. Then pieces started to click into place inside my head. "This is just supposition," I said, "but it seems to fit together. Let's suppose that these optical wings were an inconvenience for the one who assumes the name of God. Maybe that means they sought to wipe your race from history, R'yne." Just like how they tried to wipe out Hengen Muso Style, they would do whatever it took to remove threats to the waves. S'yne has somehow escaped that fate, however, and was now the last of the bloodline. "If we could trace back along her family tree, maybe we could find how some kind of incident occurred that sealed their powers away," I suggested. That kind of thing was part of the story for games all the time. "In the other world, the country that equates to Q'ten Lo had been wiped out, meaning we couldn't use the powers from there," I added. Glass was a good example of this as well. "Whatever the case, S'yne, I want you to study under R'yne and learn whatever you can to help us fight . . . her in the future," I told her. S'yne nodded in agreement at my orders. She seemed willing to give it a try. Finding any method we could to make S'yne stronger was a great idea and more than welcome.

The reason I had paused and then said "her" was because the enemy we faced was S'yne's sister; S'yne's sworn enemy was also her flesh and blood. I decided not to let our new allies know about this ongoing battle between sisters.

"An unknown race from another world . . . this all intrigues me too," Rat said, watching the scene unfold. She specialized in monsters, but I guessed that bled over into this topic too.

I looked at R'yne again. She did look like S'yne—but perhaps more like S'yne's sister, the way she carried herself. Their names were almost identical! She had to be S'yne's ancestor!

A lot of people I had met recently seemed like someone I already knew. There was Fitoria as well. I wondered if that meant something.

"It sounds like you've visited quite a number of places," Mamoru said.

"We do get around," I replied. "What about you guys?"

"I've covered a lot of ground in this world, I'd like to think," he replied. As I thought back over our own exploits, I realized it was true that we'd seen a lot. Not just Melromarc, but also Siltvelt, Q'ten Lo, Faubrey, and then a whole different world with Kizuna and her allies. How did you beat that? Go to the past!

"It zounds like we are on the zame page at lazt," the Shadow said.

"Is that really the line you want to use after practically trying to force me and Raphtalia into the sack?" I said pointedly. We were barely in the same book yet! There was so much more I needed to know!

"Mamoru, about our fight. Which shield did that Tri Barrier skill come from?" I asked. I already knew it was a chain skill leading off from Air Strike Shield. If I could use that myself, it could be pretty handy—but I already had Shooting Star Wall if I needed to defend my allies. Setting this Tri Barrier up had seemed to take a bit of work too.

"I should be asking you about your kit," Mamoru said.

"How did you learn that Chain Shield move?" It looked like there was a lot each Shield Hero was going to be able to teach the other.

"Chain Shield appeared when I added a monster called a White Tiger Clone to my shield. That fight took place in a different world to this one, however," I said.

"Tri Barrier, which more accurately comes from a skill called Combo Barrier, is something I learned by raising my status using the bow holy weapon's power-up method of job levels," Mamoru reported. That sounded similar to how I learned Hate Reaction. Finding the right combination to unlock skills like that could be a real pain.

"I've done quite a lot of that myself, but I've never seen that skill," I replied.

"Even when you use power-ups, Archduke, you never raise your attack, do you?" Rat commented. "Maybe that's the missing condition." Mamoru and I both fell silent at the observation. I felt like hitting the shield again. A little more support in these areas would have been nice! If attack power was a factor, there could be loads of skills I'd never have access to!

"A White Tiger Clone, you said . . ." Mamoru muttered. They didn't have hakuko here, so I wasn't sure how he could learn that one.

"At least you might be able to learn that one. Do you have any shields with skills I could actually use?" I asked.

"Very well. I have a certain shield that I created for a very specific purpose—a little inside joke, if you will—a while back. I'll let you copy that," Mamoru said.

"A joke? Is this going to do me any good?" I asked.

"You'll have to see for yourself," he replied. With that, Mamoru ordered the mutton minister to bring in this inside-joke shield.

What turned up was a painstakingly faithful re-creation of a shield from a game series with a character who wore green, including a trademark green cap—a youth from the bloodline of heroes, a taciturn chap who often ended up pulling a holy sword from a plinth somewhere, perhaps in a forest (after passing through a log). I'd guessed Mamoru was a gamer already, but he was more serious than I thought.

"This isn't just an Iron Shield or something like that, right?" I confirmed with him.

"There's a lot more to this than that, I assure you," he replied. I gingerly lifted the shield and tried copying it.

Weapon copy activated.

Conditions for Otherworld Kingdom Shield unlocked.
Conditions for Otherworld Kingdom Mirror Shield unlocked.

Otherworld Kingdom Shield
<abilities locked> equip bonus: back defense boost (medium)

Otherworld Kingdom Mirror Shield
<abilities locked> equip bonus: light resilience boost (medium), skill "Shine Shield"

I didn't have much good to say about this shield—I meant shields, actually. Copying one weapon seemed to have given me two, but I wasn't sure how that worked either. Maybe it was something to do with the mirror vassal weapon, which didn't seem to have left me. I changed to the Otherworld Kingdom Mirror Shield in order to try it out.

"Huh? That doesn't look like the same shield," Mamoru commented.

"I'm just trying something out," I said. "Shine Shield!" Just like the name said, the shield started to shine . . . and a beam of light extended from it, like a torch. I pointed it at Mamoru, just to see what was going to happen.

"That's pretty dazzling," he said. That looked like the only effect it had. I turned it on the Shadow, perhaps looking for a little payback for his comments earlier.

"He'z right, very dazzling," the Shadow said.

"It reminds me of Keel when she was playing with reflecting

light with that mirror she picked up from a merchant," Raphtalia said, gently casting some magic to adjust brightness.

"So I can't even use it like Ren's Flashing Sword," I commented.

"It might work if you surprise someone with it," Raphtalia said. It seemed like a lame-duck skill. I couldn't imagine any use for this. It was basically a torch!

"If you could at least use a skill power-up . . ." Raphtalia said.

"Then do you think it might finally work like Flashing Sword?" I said with exasperation. This was a downgrade, nothing else. Raphtalia could use light magic, meaning she could dazzle foes with a wave of her hand. Raph-chan could do the same. This was going in with the other joke skills, then. Maybe I could find a use for it if I was locked in a scuffle with an enemy.

"Okay then. We're going to be around for a while, so I hope we can get along," I said.

"I feel the same. We'll help however we can to get you back to your own time," Mamoru said. After that, he gave the permission for our activities inside the country—his country, basically. We achieved an agreement. We would work together to help each other with our respective issues.

Chapter Ten: The Evil Researcher

After finishing our discussion with Mamoru, we stopped by the dragon hourglass to register and then decided to return to the village. I ordered the Shadow to remain in Mamoru's castle and conduct his own autonomous investigation. *A little spying couldn't hurt.*

"Bubba, welcome back," Keel said.

"Naofumi, you're finally back!" Ren said, coming out to greet us with Ruft and Wyndia. Eclair was here too. It looked like something was up.

"Dafu!" Raph-chan II was looking around the village, her fur standing on end.

"We need to tell you something," Eclair said. "Someone entered the village from outside, and it's causing a bit of trouble for Wyndia. She claims to be an ally of the past hero and doesn't seem to be looking for a fight."

"Something else happened while we were gone?" I asked.

"Yes. But she says she isn't our enemy . . ." Ren replied.

"I thought it could be dangerous, so I evacuated the others from the village," Ruft said. He was good at making decisions when they were needed. An excellent response to a potential threat.

"Her movements are so quick. We put Fohl on her to start with, to keep an eye on her, but she took an interest in him too and ended up keeping an eye on him, basically," Ren continued. Why did these problems always have to keep happening, one after another?! I was getting pretty pissed off with everything.

"She said she wouldn't do anything, but she's going to mess up the entire lab!" Wyndia proclaimed.

"What did you say?!" Rat exclaimed immediately upon hearing that comment.

"Okay. Who is this person?" I asked. This whole situation was starting to feel pretty familiar.

"She's a researcher working in this country. An ally of the Shield Hero of this time," Ren reported.

"What? Raphtalia, can you go get Mamoru?" I asked her.

"Very well. I'll be back right away," she replied. She immediately followed my orders and used Scroll of Return to head back to find Mamoru. I wondered if it was too much to ask for a little time to relax. It was just one problem after another.

"Waah! What, what, what are you doing?" There came the shout from a filolial, almost like a scream. "Mo-chan, Melty, Master! Save me!" It sounded a lot like Filo. I was once again reminded how similar all filolials were in terms of personality.

"Hey! What are you playing at?!" Melty dashed over to help the filolial who was in trouble, shouting at the one tormenting her.

"They understand human speech. Quite unique monsters! Should I consider them a new breed, or maybe . . ." said their tormentor. She had long platinum-blonde hair and brown skin. She looked human. A little short in stature. Age . . . that was a tough one. Maybe slightly older than Rishia, maybe close in age to Ren. She was wearing a white lab coat. Her appearance—the atmosphere about her—was very much like the woman standing stunned at my side. This had to be the cause of all the trouble Ren and the others in the village were struggling to deal with. "They are so fluffy!"

"Stop that! She doesn't like it!" Melty said.

"Everyone, just calm down," I commanded. Predicting what was coming next, I used Float Shield to pin the interloper between two shields and turn her attention away from the filolials.

"What's this?" the lab coat woman said. I thought she had noticed me . . . but then she immediately looked away and started looking at the Raph species.

"Raph?" said one of them.

"Oh my, these ones look a lot more docile. That one with the spear was a lot more guarded, while this little cute thing . . . Wow, it's so fluffy," the woman said.

"So she is the problem?" I asked.

"That's right," Ren confirmed.

"Brother! You're back!" Fohl dashed over. "She's a real fast mover. I got too close and she started to give me a full medical inspection . . ."

"Sure, that does sound rough," I placated him. "Still . . ." The feeling coming from her really reminded me of someone else.

"What's this? You seem to be taking an interest in me?" the woman said. Having finished her inspection of the Raph species, this eerily familiar woman finally turned to look at me. "I've heard a little about you from my friends in this village. You're the Shield Hero who isn't Mamoru," she said.

"That's right. And you are?" I asked—but I was pretty sure I knew the answer. This was the Whip Hero and researcher who Mamoru had wanted to introduce us to. I just needed to make sure.

"Little old me? I'm Holn Anthreya. My friends call me Holn," she replied.

"My name is Naofumi Iwatani," I said. Then I looked over at the woman with the same surname as the newcomer.

"From what I've been hearing from my acquaintances here, it seems you have one of my little old relatives here with you," Holn said.

"Indeed," Rat stammered. "My name is Ratotille Anthreya."

"Does that mean I can go ahead and investigate everyone here in the village?" Holn asked.

"Of course not!" I snapped.

"Very well. I'll just have to pick my moments," she replied confidently. I could see why they had been overwhelmed by her.

"Can you lay off a little—" Melty started, warning Holn off, but I signaled for her to stop.

"You'll only make it worse if you keep riling her up. You and everyone else, just take a step back. I'll handle this," I told her.

"I'm not sure that's a good idea," Melty said.

"Don't worry. I can handle this. I'm going to have to talk to her at some point," I said.

"If you say so," Melty agreed. With her in the lead, almost everyone in the village went off on patrol. Anything could happen, after all.

"Ren, Eclair, you too. Wyndia, you help calm down the village monsters," I said.

"Okay," she replied. Everyone moved off.

"Raph," said Raph-chan. Just for safety's sake, I decided to keep her up on my shoulder.

"Let's get down to things, then. Who are you? Mamoru wanted to introduce us, but you weren't around," I said.

"I bet he did. I'm the perfect little old candidate for this kind of situation. If he hadn't brought me into this, then I probably would have moved on from my collaboration with him. Of course, I noticed something was up before that happened and arrived here on my own," she said. She had her own unique tone to her voice, a different kind of arrogance than Rat. It was layered with flickers of confidence. When I thought about it now, I realized I'd never really asked Rat anything about her family. But I knew she was originally from Faubrey, so they were probably quite well off.

"Hey, Rat. Tell me a little about your family," I told her.

"A bloodline of researchers, give or take. We do have distant connections to the heroes," she said. So maybe it was a common surname among researchers in the future. "I was treated as a bit of an outcast among my family, due to the content of my research. Didn't I tell you? The one in the lab coat who was with Takt was a distant relation of mine." So maybe these two were also distant relations—but it was dangerous to just assume anything.

"I've taken a little old look around, seen the facilities you have here, and I have to say that our culture doesn't seem to have developed much in the future," Holn commented. "I would have expected it to be a higher level than this by now."

"Thanks to the actions of the one behind the waves," I said.

"I see. Well, that's certainly a pain. Creating better things just to have them squashed down . . ." Holn lamented, shaking her head.

"There do seem to have been times during which civilization was more advanced," I told her.

"Times change. Just like people themselves. The highest level we are allowed to reach is ultimately being controlled," Holn concluded. I couldn't dispute that. The fact that the Roman Empire had been advanced before the Middle Ages was a famous fact of Earth history.

"Enough getting-to-know-you banter. What do you want?" I asked. I wasn't really sure if we should be showing the research of the future—and the products of that research—to someone like this. There was the possibility that our actions here were going to seriously impact the future.

"I'm a researcher who feels joy in the fulfillment of my little old curiosity. I'm just sniffing out somewhere else that catches my attention—just looking for another fix. If there's anything you want to know, future Shield Hero, maybe we can think about it together?" she offered.

"Okay. I was going to ask Mamoru to basically set that up anyway. It seems that our enemies have attacked us and sent us far back into the past. We need to get back to where we came from. Any ideas about making that happen?" I asked.

"I knew that was what you were going to ask. Of course I did. I'm interested in that as well, so you can bet I'm going to help," Holn replied, already checking the ground at the village boundary line as she spoke. "If you do want to show me more, we should do it in the research lab," she suggested.

"Okay, let's go," I said. I left Melty, Ren, and Fohl on guard and took Holn and Rat with me toward Rat's lab. Once we got inside, we headed over to a large terminal—basically a fantasy computer, a large stone tablet. I'd come here before for things like Raph-species health checks, but it really hit me again how strange this place was.

"The plants comprising this building are very interesting. Is this also technology from the future?" Holn asked.

"These were originally problem plants created by an alchemist at some point in the past. I used the shield to rework them, with help from Rat," I said.

"I see. If I created anything capable of such trouble, of course, I would dispose of it at once," she replied—subtly letting me know that she wasn't the one who had made them. In that moment, I happened to meet the eyes of the mystery creature swimming inside the tank in the lab. It was watching us with really intense curiosity. Not for the first time I wondered exactly what this thing was. I recalled Rat calling it by name, sometimes—Mikey, maybe, or something like that.

Holn proceeded to clatter something into the machine, and a map of our village was displayed. The boundary was also clearly visible—I hadn't looked at it closely before now, but it looked like leaves and branches.

"You can see that this area has arrived from the future," Holn said.

"Sure," I agreed.

"Unfortunately, I didn't bring enough equipment with me to really analyze all this, so I used some of your facilities here. It seems like a network created by plants unique to your village was used to cut through time," she explained.

"Do you mean our enemies used sakura lumina to set a trap for us?" I asked.

"I'm not suggesting so much. Just maybe that they used that outline as their target. Let me give you an example. What if your enemies were to cover the Shield Hero's barrier with a highly viscous substance?" Holn asked.

"It would stick all over the barrier," I said.

"The area covered by that would create the affected range. Then they reverse the protective power emitted by those plants, and it creates the intense technology we have seen used here," she explained. I pondered that for a moment. It seemed Rat's ancestor had a better handle on things than Rat did. Maybe her line wasn't what it used to be.

"Archduke? Can you stop looking at me like that?" Rat asked.

"She does seem very skilled, in her little old way. Her research just leans a little hard into prioritizing monsters. What I can suppose from hearing the history of her research is that it has been considered evil by society, but the content itself is actually all above board," Holn said. She really had Rat pegged already. Rat was a genius, but there was always a bigger genius.

"This looks like a complete upgrade," I commented.

"Do you mean from me to her?" Rat asked.

"You bet I do," I replied. Rat looked pretty upset about that. She did have some pride about her intellect.

"Do you want me to overstep the mark and cause some kind of magical apocalypse?" she asked.

"That's the kind of mistake a rookie would make," I replied. I couldn't help thinking of a bioterror survival game in which evil was always resident. Zombies and stuff like that—seemed right under Rat's umbrella. She had mentioned a magical apocalypse, so maybe the subtitle "Magic Hazard" would work. Rat was right about how careful she was, however, so there likely wasn't anything to worry about—including her actually getting any kind of results. Her motto when handling the bioplants had been to proceed as carefully as possible. My involvement there had definitely helped speed things along. If I had left everything to Rat, who knew how long it might have taken?

"Let's just take a look here, shall we?" Holn said.

"Hold on!" Rat exclaimed. Holn continued to clatter over the interface, and something that looked like Rat's secret file was thrown up onto the screen. She was being hacked! I wondered if I should be laughing about this or not. Holn placed a finger on the stone tablet, and something like a liquid crystal screen popped out from it, displaying some blueprints. It looked like a 3D depiction of something or other. I'd actually seen it before,

I realized, when I came here with Trash. It was a cart monster.

"Whatever are you making something like this for? There are so many limitations with a cart. It hardly seems worth it," Holn said, quickly writing the project off.

"This is still just a monster that can't move for itself, so it's just a prototype. I'll dispose of it once I get it worked out," Rat replied. She probably had to make prototypes for all sorts of difficult-to-create monsters. It made her sound like a bit of a psycho, but I'd known that when I brought her into my team, so it was a little late to quibble about now.

"What do you mean by 'dispose of it,' might I ask?" Holn said, pressing the matter.

"I'm looking at remote experiments for bodies that don't have their own awareness. However, I have others perform a neural connection," Rat said.

"And you get results like that, do you? I guess research requires sacrifices," Holn bemoaned.

"No unnecessary sacrifices required. You can't be such a high level yourself, oh mighty ancestor, if you think work of this level requires sacrifice," Rat shot back.

"Oh my, so aggressive with little old me! How amusing. As an 'evil researcher' myself, I'm going to have to put up a fight!" Holn enthused. I couldn't tell if they were getting along or not, but I could imagine research from the past and future being merged together to create some kind of terrible monster.

"Very well. I accept that you know your stuff," Rat finally said. "But there are some areas I won't back down on, and I'm also going to show you that I'm superior in other ways."

"An excellent reply. I'm a sucker for people who feel that way about things. I really am," Holn said. She seemed to have taken a shining to Rat already.

"Back on topic then," I cut in. "Can we get back to our time?"

"If we can find out what caused something, we can find a way to resolve it. I can see some leads here already. I hope you will allow me to collaborate," Holn said.

"Great. Sounds like we've reached an agreement," I replied.

"Indeed. Can I ask something? I presume this research is leading toward weapon-type monsters, correct?" Holn inquired.

"Actually, no," Rat replied. "Archduke, you mentioned weapon monsters in another world, right?"

"I see. I'm not especially interested in something already completed by someone else, but I guess you could give me an outline," Holn said.

"Okay, well, it was on a different world from this one, and it was a weapon made by a guy called Kyo," I said. I explained to Holn about the weapon that had perverted the power of the Spirit Tortoise.

"That's a bold move, using the power of the guardian beasts as the medium. And using all of that power, that's the only thing he was able to achieve? Pathetic. What a complete waste," Holn declared, shaking her head.

"It sounds like you think you could do better," I said.

"Of course. I know I could. Good materials should naturally lead to a good final product. The best at their job take good materials and make something incredible," Holn said with a wink. I could see what she was getting at. "There's something else I should tell you, future Shield Hero. Among the holy and vassal weapons, there are series that allow for genetic manipulation. If you make use of those, you'll be able to enhance yourselves a whole lot easier," Holn informed me.

"Hey, just a moment there . . ." I started but then realized I had helped modify the bioplants myself. I guess that was pretty much the same thing. They sounded like higher-ranked weapons.

"I've heard you have an affection for that monster on your shoulder. Why don't you make it even more to your tastes? Even stronger?" Holn suggested.

"Make Raph-chan stronger?" I pondered.

"Raph?" Raph-chan asked.

"She is already growing so much on her own," I said. Raph-chan even had a tendency to develop as I desired. Based on Rat's research into a carriage-type monster, I started to imagine her becoming a bus like a cat. I had already gotten to hug the tummy of a big Raph-chan, so next was a Raph-chan vehicle!

I had an image of Raphtalia not being especially happy about that, likely with a sword to my throat. Nope, she really wouldn't like it.

"Raph!" said Raph-chan. Perhaps sensing what I was thinking, Raph-chan climbed down from my shoulder and started walking around on all fours. It looked pretty cute!

"She's doing pretty well with autonomous evolution all on her own. I think we'll get better results without getting involved," I said.

"That's one take on it. Continuing evolution, even after the departure of their creator . . . I'll give that some thought," Holn said.

"I admit, when the other monsters in the village started to get taken over by the Raph species, I was a little worried," I admitted. Just as we were discussing this subject, Raphtalia showed up.

"Mr. Naofumi! I've got Mamoru here with me!" Raphtalia said. That was a close one. She was about to hear my plans to modify Raph-chan. I'm happy I didn't go too deep on that one.

"It looks like you're making yourself at home," Mamoru said.

"You bet. There's all sorts of interesting stuff scattered around here. I can't get enough," she said. Holn and Mamoru sounded very friendly.

"Naofumi, I know you've already talked to her, but this is our researcher here in Siltran," Mamoru said.

"Yes. It seems she sniffed us out," I replied.

"You bet I did. We've just come to an agreement that I'm going to help return them to their own time. That said, as well as understanding the current situation, we also need to investigate all sorts of other stuff too," Holn explained.

"I'm glad things are going smoothly," Mamoru said.

"This whole thing is so much fun. I'd be upset if I wasn't included," Holn said. A big brain was definitely welcome—and then a flash of lightning hit mine.

"If we've been sent into the past, maybe we can get back via Kizuna's world using Raphtalia's katana vassal weapon," I suggested. If we gathered everyone and moved in accordance with the wave summons, it would be a bit of a pain, but we could surely leave this time period. I looked over at Raphtalia, who checked her status and then shook her head.

"It's no good. There's no response," she finally reported.

"In which case, I don't think we can risk it," I said. Then Holn stepped in.

"There are all sorts of reasons why a vassal weapon wouldn't be responding. I can think of a few big ones, but even if you did manage to cross over, you could just be in the past of that world," she pointed out. I grunted. That sounded all too plausible.

"Okay, then. So we need to investigate all we can to get us back home," I said.

"That sounds like our starting point. I look forward to working together," Holn replied.

"Great. Mamoru, sorry for dragging you out here," I apologized.

"I wanted to bring you together, so it's fine. Don't worry about it," he said.

"Descendent. Looks like we're working on this together," Holn said to Rat.

"I guess I don't have a choice. Archduke, I'm going to start working with this ancestor of mine, and we'll see how it goes," Rat said to me.

"I'm counting on you. Let's see what you can really do," I told her. That was how the Whip Hero and Rat's ancestor, Holn, forced her way into the village. My attempt at a snide comment, however, was completely ignored.

That night, I fetched some food from the stores, while everyone in the village headed into what I presumed would be an uneasy evening.

"Bubba, Bubba! Don't we get to go to the castle the other Shield Hero took you to?" Keel asked.

"I'd like to know that too. I'm interested in seeing it," Imiya added, both girls sounding very excited. Those two didn't look at all worried about our situation. They were kids building a secret base . . . and when I considered their ages, "kids" was probably appropriate.

"This is a chance to come into contact with history! We are here in a place any historian can only dream of reaching, Queen Melty," Eclair said.

"All true. My mother would have been as giddy as a school-girl to be here," Melty replied.

"I wonder what is happening in Q'ten Lo during this time . . . The Shield Hero told me that Melromarc isn't even in this world yet?" Ruft said.

"Indeed, it seems that way," Melty responded, the three of them looking out over the unfamiliar mountains as they chatted. I saw those three together a lot. I might not have expected it, but they seemed to be good friends.

"How long do you think that unknown road runs?" asked a filolial to a Raph species.

"Raph," came the reply, both of them expressing interest in the world beyond the village. They didn't seem that bothered either. I guess that was impressive, from one perspective.

Still, I almost wanted to scream at them. The entire village had been set adrift in time! I had to believe they were all acting normally by pressing down all the fear they were feeling.

"Hey, Bubba! Can we leave the village tomorrow? I want to get out there and explore!" Keel enthused.

"Keel, don't make any trouble for the Shield Hero. What you need to say is that you want to be of help to him," Imiya suggested.

"Good choice of words! Thank you Imiya! Bubba! I want to help you out however I can! I can sell stuff and gather information, okay?" she said.

"You guys are pretty resilient, aren't you?" I said, somewhat admiringly. I had been wrong to expect anything close to a rational reaction from this bunch. But having them fall apart wouldn't have helped things much either.

"Everyone, I'm sorry, but I have to speak up. I think you are all going about this the wrong way. Wouldn't it be prudent to at least show a little concern for what may happen to us?" Raphtalia asked, seemingly puzzled herself at this barrage of optimistic questions. I didn't like to hear her say it out loud.

"Huh? What are you talking about, Raphtalia?! Bubba and the others have drilled it into us—we never know what's going to happen with the waves, so we'll never overcome them if we worry about everything that does happen," Keel said brightly.

"You know what . . . I guess you have a point," I said. It had been my intention to raise the villagers to be ready for anything, because anything could literally happen. They had been surprised by the bioplants, but after everything that had happened since then, they had gradually adapted to things. All the trials we had been through so far had trained them for exactly what was happening now.

"If it was just the sword guy and spear guy, I might have been worried, but we have Bubba and Raphtalia and Fohl and

Melty here too! You bet we're going to get back to our time!"
Keel said cheerfully. Everyone within earshot seemed to feel the
same, because they all looked over and nodded. Was she trying
to earn some points with me? The cynical part of me wondered
for a moment. Not Keel though—she didn't have a bone so de-
vious in all of her body. "I think Raphtalia will understand this
next part, because she's visited a different world many times.
We've apparently come to the past, but for us, it's basically like
we're in another world. That's all. And thinking that makes it
easier for us to handle. Now it's our turn, nothing more," Keel
said. She had a point there too. Even better, our levels hadn't
been affected this time, giving us some more leeway.

"That's true. Not much has changed from how we normally do business," I admitted. As I already said when talking to
Mamoru, being summoned to other worlds was already a thing,
so time travel didn't seem like such a quantum leap. Rather than
being confused and concerned, this feeling of almost excitement in the air told me how tough everyone was—and how
they were going to survive.

"Rather than leave everything to you, Bubba, we all want
to do whatever we can to help you out this time," Keel empha-
sized again. There was a saying: "Kids will grow up all on their
own." Seeing Keel right now, I really felt the truth of it. She
was even teaching me a few things with the bravery she was
showing.

"Okay then. It is easier to think of this as just having wandered into another world," I agreed. I recalled what it was like when I first visited Kizuna's world. Just me and Rishia, both level 1 and her the only one who could actively attack, and we had returned alive. Going back even further, I had been summoned and then framed in short order, and yet I'd survived that as well. We weren't at such a disadvantage here. We could make it through this.

I considered for a moment that maybe Keel and the others were tougher than me, mentally.

"Keel is right. Brother, Sister, we must all do our best to return us to our own time," Fohl added. It looked like I wasn't the only one who had been affected by Keel's words.

"You bet," I replied. With that, some unexpectedly peaceful time passed in the village.

"Getting sent into the past, huh," Ren muttered, looking like he was recalling something fondly.

"Was there an event like this in the game you used to play?" I asked him. When they were first summoned, Ren and the other two holy heroes had all operated based on knowledge from videogames they had been addicted to at the time. At a time like this, I kind of hoped such game knowledge would come in handy—but it was difficult to trust it. There was a high likelihood that such game knowledge was a trap, sent here in advance by the one behind the waves.

"Sometimes you played through an event from the past, perhaps, but I don't recall the stages and events all being sent into a period of previous waves," Ren said.

"Fair enough," I replied. If there had been such an event in his game, he probably would have mentioned it before now.

"Maybe I should have followed the backstory for the game a little more closely," Ren muttered. He could say that now, but there were plenty of people playing online games who only cared about leveling up and fighting other people. In the game I played, there had been folks who played along without any understanding of the backstory at all. They just found the best spots or events to grind out experience and didn't bother with the overarching story at all. Ren seemed to know a lot about the main game he had played, but maybe now he had also identified something he had overlooked.

"Don't worry too much about it," I told him. "I'm sure the one behind the waves has scrambled everything up anyway." I really wanted him to lighten up and enjoy life a little more, but having him act completely based on game information would be a mistake too. I had the same issue with Itsuki, both of them thinking in such extremes. It was exhausting. I suspected the strong sense of duty he had now was a rebound from his former lack of emotions—a kind of contradiction, in which having a strong sense of duty pushed him away from taking any responsibility. "Let's not get too into it tonight, anyway. Rest up for tomorrow," I told him.

"You should take your own advice, Mr. Naofumi. But, Sword Hero, in particular, you need to rest and be ready in case anything happens," Raphtalia said. Ren nodded at her words.

"Okay. I'm still not quite in top form. I'll go and get some sleep," he said. He really didn't seem to be in great condition. He had pulled his weight today when it mattered though, I'd give him that.

"Eclair, can you see Ren back to his house please? I'll put Melty in Filo's room, so you can concentrate on Ren," I told her. Then I warned her specifically not to let him start doing practice swings with his sword in his room.

"Understood. Come on, Ren. Resting is also an important part of a warrior's job. Not everyone can be like Hero Iwatani," she said.

"What about me?!" I exclaimed. Everyone around me seemed to have such strange ideas about what I could do.

Then I recalled something. I needed to apply the mirror power-up method to everyone in the village. Raphtalia's katana still worked here, pretty much, so I should be able to do it, and it would provide a reasonable boost.

"It is nice to know you are around again, Naofumi," Ren said, and then Eclair led him away toward his house. As I watched Ren heading away, I almost felt pity for him. How much of myself was I mixing in, I wondered, that the youngest of the four holy heroes seemed the most aged to me in that moment? Having to deal with Motoyasu's rampages for so long would probably do that to any man.

I needed to be careful. If things got too bad, I'd dump everything on Melty and make a run for it.

"Naofumi, do you need something?" Melty asked me.

"No. I wasn't thinking anything in particular," I replied.

"So why did you look at me like that? I had a nasty feeling for a moment there, I have to say," she commented. The people around me were getting far too perceptive. I had to think for a moment about how to dodge this bullet.

"Hey, Melty, you came to visit me for a quick break from your royal duties, but it looks like you'll be taking quite the vacation after all," I said.

"That's true—though I'd hardly call this a vacation. Spending time with you is just so utterly crazy, Naofumi," she said.

"All of this is my fault, huh?" I asked. I was going to get angry if she blamed me for all of this. But I would admit I had plenty of trouble-causing enemies.

"I wouldn't go that far. I'm capable of wandering into plenty of trouble even without you. I've just got a bit too accustomed to peacetime recently," she said. She had been away from the front lines. Nothing really big had happened in the vicinity of Melty or Trash since the defeat of Takt. Then I showed up again and we were all sent back in time; I could see why she would want to complain. "I'm sure my sister is mixed up in all this. I've had enough of her too," Melty said.

"We're on the same page there," I replied. "My side got some good hits in the last few times we met, but she's not giving up," I said. I'd turned her into a great ball of fire, and then she'd been smashed into the ground and whipped like a hundred times before actually being killed. If I was the one coming back to life after all that, I'd probably want to stay away from the sadists who did it to me. But it probably wasn't enough to make that particular bitch reflect on or regret her actions.

"You seem to be suggesting I will be taking a break as queen, but that's not my intention at all. I'm going to be meeting with people from Siltran tomorrow, as village representative, to arrange all sorts of things between us," Melty said. "You continue your work as heroes in order to get us all back to your own time," she commanded. Her face was starting to take on a regal aspect, a real sense of responsibility, far beyond her still young years. I did wish she could take things a little easier . . . but she was being a big help too. Summoned heroes could get involved in public life, but there were finer details they could never really touch or influence. You could make an excellent proposal, just to see it shot down without a second thought. In this world, it was the job of those running each nation to make an environment in which their heroes could move around freely.

"Like I said to Ren—just don't collapse on us, okay?" I told her.

"If this much pressure is going to knock me out, I'll never

make it as queen anyway. I know I need some time to myself when I can grab it. To be honest, I'm most worried about Filo," Melty replied.

"Yeah . . . I can see that," I agreed. I could almost hear her voice calling out for Mel-chan and Master . . . and then Motoyasu shouting her name in pursuit. She would scream so loudly her scream probably would travel back in time.

"I need to do whatever I can for her sake. The bioplants growing in the village and the monster meat we can obtain from hunting are going to keep us alive for the time being. But if we are going to be here a long time, then we'll also need to start thinking about acquiring some money," Melty said.

"Good point," I told her.

"You're good at that kind of thing," Melty continued, almost as though she was checking off some kind of list. "So I've got a proposal. Taking information-gathering into account too, I think we need to start trading." I made a noise to show I was thinking. Trade was one way to naturally gather a lot of information. Luckily for us, I had already directed those in the village to trade as much as they could, and so we had lots of people skilled in the field at our disposal. "Even if we do have information from the future, we can't be sure how it applies to the situation at hand," Melty pointed out. That was true enough too. There were differing opinions on exactly what happened even for things like the Japanese history that I'd been taught in school. Records from the past could be very vague, and so Melty was saying events different from the hero stories she had heard could still very much unfold here. The one behind the waves was involved in all of this too, of course.

"We still need to get stronger, but we also need information and money. Naofumi, I hope you can handle that," she told me.

"You hardly even have to tell me," I replied. I wasn't keen on Melty ordering me around. In the little time I had been away, she had really leaned into this queen thing. As I considered how much she had changed, I recalled what things had been like for us up until the Phoenix battle. That was basically back where we were now—nothing much had changed compared to that.

"Sounds like a busy day tomorrow. A lot of busy days are coming up," I said. We faced problem after problem, but the way we had to tackle them wasn't changing: become stronger and gather information with the final goal of bringing peace to this world.

Just as Melty and I reached this agreement about our upcoming activities . . .

"Bubba! You've got even better at cooking. I knew it!" Keel enthused after cleaning her plate.

"I had to cook a lot while I was away," I said . . . A whole freaking lot.

"I'm so jealous! Next time you go to another world, I want to tag along! But actually, we're in another world right now!

I'm gonna get this done!" Keel shouted. The energy of the village was likely coming, at least in part, from Keel. Thanks to her, then, our first day in the past came to an end with everyone in the village seemingly feeling pretty optimistic about our chances.

Chapter Eleven: Bread Trees and Bread Troubles

It was the next morning.

"Oh boy! I've never seen anything like it!" I was in the middle of my morning routine, feeding the village monsters and getting a little workout in, when I heard Keel's voice ringing out close to the lab. Fohl was standing a short distance from the gaggle of people, pointing at Keel with a troubled expression on his face. He wanted me to go and check it out.

"What's up, Keel?" I said as I approached the hubbub. Keel and others from the village were all getting excited about something with Holn. Rat was part of the throng, too, but had a less-than-pleased look on her face. The villagers really seemed excited about something. I already knew why Fohl was keeping his distance—he didn't like Holn. That only made me lump him in with the filolials though. It was like the natural instinct of a wild animal to keep away from a perceived threat.

"Ah, future Shield Hero. You should take a look at this too. Just a first attempt from little old me," Holn said, pointing at a tree I'd never seen before. I did a double take—it looked like a bioplant, but it was growing something different. Normally, they grew red tomato-like fruit or berries, but this one was growing what looked like bread. .

"Bubba, Bubba, check it out! Isn't that amazing?" Keel yapped. She picked one of the bread berries and carried it over to me. I checked it over to make sure it wasn't poisonous or dangerous in any other way. The poison check came back clear. I split it into two . . . Yep, this looked like normal bread. I gave it a nibble, and it tasted fine too. Bread was the perfect description, apart from where it had come from.

It also had some seeds inside it. They were kind of soft, and looked edible too, but I decided to take them out and keep them. Keel had carried a bread roll over to me, but there were also what looked like baguettes growing on the tree.

"What is this, a bread tree?" I asked. We weren't living in a fairy tale here. Holn gave a laugh that was bordering on sounding like a mad scientist.

"The amount of control over these plants is quite something. So easy to use too. I was just experimenting with this, but even I'm surprised at how well this has turned out," Holn said. I was the one being surprised here. I'd had no idea the bioplants could be used for this kind of thing! It looked like genetically modified food gone too far, to be honest, like eating it might turn your fingers into hot dog buns, even if it was free from poison.

"Hey, hey, Holn! Do you think you could make a crepe tree?" Keel suggested.

"I'm not sure what a crepe even is, for one thing," Holn replied. Keel quickly turned to me.

"Bubba, Bubba! Make some crepes for Holn!" she said.

"From the perspective of intellectual curiosity, I would very much like to learn this recipe from you, future Shield Hero," she said.

"Mamoru knows about crepes, surely," I said.

"He might know about them, but that doesn't mean he can make them," Holn said.

"Archduke, I'm not sure we should be doing things like this," Rat said hesitantly. She had a point. We could return to the future to find bread trees had taken over. This was all very dangerous, so I wanted to keep a tight lid on its operation. Taking all of that into account, I thought if she could make plants like this so easily, it was really going to ease up the food problems in the village. I wondered how best to proceed.

"Hey, Bubba! I want some crepes!" Keel continued over and over about eating some of my crepes.

"Crepes in the morning?" I asked her. Keel liked sweet ones, which were more like a dessert than a meal. The menu I had planned for today was along a totally different trajectory, so changing things to make crepes now would be a real pain. I could probably make some other confectionery, but it seemed like a bad idea to run down our resources. Things like flour could be very limited for the foreseeable future—we would need to find somewhere to get them from in Siltran. They might not even have such things.

If that was the case, we could always have Holn modify more bioplants and boost our food supplies.

"I guess I can make some," I conceded, "but you'll need to work hard to earn them!"

"You bet! I'm going to bring in pots of gold. You'll see!" Keel replied.

"I'm sure you will," I said, and I meant it. Keel actually was one of the better merchants in the village. It had been a while since I'd done any serious merchant work. We'd made some cash during the festival Melty had held. That was based on Filo's pop-star popularity. But when talking about ongoing gains, Keel was probably doing better than me. We also need information right now, so giving Keel and the others a boost might actually be most effective. "Just don't share too many details about us or what we are doing here. We still don't know what could happen," I warned her.

"I'm with you there, Bubba!" she replied. I wondered if she really was with me. I looked over at Imiya at her side. The two of them were good friends, so I hoped Imiya would be able to keep Keel under control a bit. She noticed me looking and gave a slightly embarrassed nod. She guessed what I was asking. Sometimes Imiya really reminded me of Raphtalia back from when I first met her.

"You can worry about making accessories later. For now, do some trading with Keel," I told her.

"Ah, okay. I'm not sure what will sell yet, so I'll do some investigation," Imiya said.

"Crepes! Crepes!" Keel yipped, in full-on dog mode.

"Raph!" The Raph species watched her with happy looks on their faces. The sight was almost soothing.

"If you let little old me get serious about something, these are the results," Holn bragged. "Future Shield Hero. I'm pretty sure you could use these plants to make far more than just this temporary housing, like a castle, for example," Holn said.

"That would be quite something, but what about the foundations and stuff like that?" I asked.

"Yep, that's a good point. If you built a whole castle, nothing else would be able to grow in the vicinity either," she responded. She had already shown she had a habit of just throwing dangerous ideas out there. I could see where Rat got it from—in fact, in a side-by-side comparison, Rat looked like the sane one.

"What's all this morning noise?" Melty said with a sleepy look still on her face. Raphtalia had still been pretty worried about everything last night and had taken a long time to get to sleep, so she was still sleeping now. If this hubbub grew any louder, it would surely bring her out too.

To explain to Melty, I just pointed at the bread tree. She frowned, shaking her head.

"That's a pretty intense piece of botany," she commented.

"Sure is. Raphtalia is going to flip when she wakes up," I said.

"I can imagine," Melty agreed.

"Don't you have these in the future?" Holn confirmed with us.

"Well . . . during the winter, I guess there is the chocolate," Melty said.

"Huh? Chocolate?" I wondered if she meant cocoa beans. "It grows on trees?"

"Yes. Thanks to an event called Valentine's Day that a hero from the past spread," Melty explained. I never expected to hear that here—and we had bigger things to worry about with the waves anyway. "A certain region has trees that grow chocolate. When chocolate season comes, it gets sent out from there around the world."

"Wow, okay," I said. A tree that grew chocolate like fruit. I wondered if that was the end point of this kind of tree, as I looked at the bread tree again. It sounded like something I'd heard . . . somewhere before. Maybe there was an "evil researcher" behind the chocolate trees too.

"I've heard the chocolate farmers have it real hard during harvest season," Melty said. Chocolate farmers! What a job to actually exist. Still, if chocolate-growing trees existed, I guessed someone would have to farm them. It was still a surprise to hear that such a fantastical thing existed. It was like winning a golden ticket. Nice to hear about something hopeful, full of dreams, for once.

Of course, it might have been created by one of the resurrected, but I hoped it been left behind for us by an actual official hero. If it had been created without the use of bioplants, then that was quite something too.

"That all sounds quite interesting," Holn commented. "The issue there being that we don't have one here I can actually see." I certainly didn't have any chocolate, and I also couldn't make any without the right ingredients. "It might be worth conducting some ongoing research into this."

"If you're going to waste your time researching chocolate, please concentrate on getting us back to the future," I told her. I knew she was good, so I really wanted to keep her focused on finding clues for getting us home.

"I understand," she said, but I wondered if she did. In any case, I added crepes to what I was going to make for breakfast.

"Excuse me, Mr. Naofumi? I've heard that we have some strange bioplants in the village?" Raphtalia said. She had heard about the bakery trees and immediately came to ask me about it.

"That's the short of it, but I have nothing to do with it," I told her.

"So it's Holn's work," Raphtalia guessed.

"That's right. She works surprisingly fast," I said.

"And do you think it's safe to leave her unchecked?" Raphtalia asked.

"I understand why you're feeling anxious, but I can't see the harm in it for now," I said.

"It just feels like things are moving away from the village. I know . . ." Raphtalia said, a little sadly. I had always done my best to keep her home safe and secure . . . until maybe around the time I allowed for all those Raph species to be created. "It started around the time you planted all the sakura lumina, for their convenient effects. I was really trying not to let it bother me." This was a dangerous sign. Raphtalia's fundamental awareness was being shaken. I needed her to remain as my stopper, keeping me in check as required. I had to believe she would still do that!

Having finished breakfast, we started planning what to do next.

"Before we start our trading, let's drop in on Mamoru first," I suggested. We were going to start by focusing on selling things inside Siltran and gathering more information. But first I wanted to check Mamoru's stance on this and get his permission to start conducting business. It might inject some new life into the nation, but an influx of new products might also be a cause for concern. Better to have a discussion with him about it first. "We should introduce everyone from the village to him too." I told Raphtalia how Mamoru was taking care of war orphans in the castle. Those kids might make good friends for Keel and the others like her in our village. They all looked pretty happy, but they had to have their concerns. By spending time with people from this world, Keel and the others would get a feel for how things were done here. I wanted to avoid them growing up thinking they could do whatever they liked just because they were underlings of a hero. "So we're headed to Siltran castle! Everyone stick close to me," I told them.

"Okay!" Keel and the others shouted. We used a portal and arrived at the Siltran castle town. I had asked Ren and Fohl to register this location ahead of time, affording us the leeway to transport everyone.

"Oh boy! This is the country of Siltran?" Keel enthused, looking around happily as we walked toward the castle. "It looks pretty basic though, don't you think? Like a country out in the sticks beyond Melromarc," she commented. She couldn't keep her mouth shut sometimes! Imiya had her ears pricked up and was listening to the Siltran people talking around us.

"They don't speak the same language as Melromarc," she commented. That reminded me that many people in the village couldn't speak the languages of other nations.

"We can work around that, surely!" Keel said confidently, thumping her chest. But I was pretty sure things weren't that simple.

"They do have an archaic lilt to their pronunciation," Ruft commented to Melty and me. Being from Q'ten Lo, Ruft shared his language with Siltvelt.

What this meant, of course, was that we were going to need a bilingual villager to come along whenever business was being conducted. I had seen this coming, but it still sounded like a lot of hard work.

"Can you understand the Siltran language, Keel?" I asked her.

"Nope, not a word," she replied smartly. That was no good then. She could be the cutest puppy in the litter and we couldn't use her like that. "I can follow the language in the nations around Melromarc. That's about it."

"They do speak different languages, depending on the region," Imiya said.

"The filolials translate for me, and I've picked up some words here and there. I'm sure it will be fine!" Keel said brightly.

"Some of the other village kids can speak other languages, so I'm sure we'll be able to conduct business," Imiya continued, explaining Keel's overly optimistic take on everything.

"Well, if you say so," I replied. Kids grew up fast, that was true. But I hoped they knew what they were doing. I had to admit I was a little concerned.

We chatted as we continued toward the castle itself. After asking someone where Mamoru was to be found, we arrived in the castle refectory.

"Hey, Naofumi. You're here early. I was just getting some breakfast for myself. Would you like to join me?" Mamoru offered.

"No thanks. We ate before leaving the village," I said. I'd picked a bunch of early risers for my villagers, that was for sure. Mamoru, on the other hand, seemed to take his time with breakfast.

"Okay. What can I help you with so early in the day?" he asked.

"We were thinking of doing some trading in order to gather information and make some money, but I thought we'd better get your permission first," I told him.

"I see. We've been having some distribution difficulties ourselves, so it would be a big help for us too. There are lots of bandits out there who have quietly crossed our borders to plunder us, so you might have to deal with them," Mamoru commented. A small nation being attacked by a larger one was nothing new.

"No problem. If some trouble comes up, you can handle yourselves, right?" I asked my would-be traders.

"You bet!" said Keel, speaking for everyone. They had seen plenty of level gains, so they could fight. I would vouch for that. They had been through the Phoenix battle and taken on Takt's forces, so they also had some big-battle experience too. It would take more than some random monsters or bandits to take them down.

"I've seen a lot of demi-human therianthropes among your people, Naofumi, but not so many of the stronger races," Mamoru said. I thought back over those from the village. The ones who could be considered strong races were likely just Fohl, Sadeena, and Shildina. With the absence of the killer whale sisters, that really only left us with Fohl. Raphtalia was from the bloodline of Q'ten Lo, so she was like a raccoon race, but she was actually something else. Same thing for Ruft.

"I guess you're right. At a glance, we don't really have any strong-looking ones," I agreed. For therianthropes, I'd purchased a lot of the mole-type called lumo, due to them being skilled with their hands. Then the others were just whatever. Imiya and her uncle were representative of them. But her uncle was hardly around, meaning Imiya really held that title.

"They should blend in quickly here then," Mamoru said. From what I had seen of the Siltran people, they didn't seem especially combat-oriented either. From that perspective, they should be easy to trade with too—less aggression to deal with. "You also have those filolials and the Raph species though. Those are rare and will definitely stand out. You might want to give that side of things some thought," Mamoru advised. From what we had learned so far, filolials hadn't appeared in this world yet. Unless I was planning on making a name for myself by completely changing history, it was probably best that we didn't let them stand out too much.

"The Raph species are good at concealment, so I'll have them use that to avoid being noticed," I said. The monsters that had chosen the Raph species route had strength enough to pull a wagon while also being able to use illusion magic to conceal themselves completely. They could turn into a horse or something to hide in plain sight while getting around. If they did get into any trouble, they could work with the filolials to fight it off.

"You have some pretty talented monsters in the future." Mamoru chuckled.

"I guess we do," I said, not sure how to take that comment. Another approach would be to pretend they were monsters who had come from afar to serve under Mamoru. I'd have to tread a little more carefully around that idea, so I decided to approach Mamoru with it later.

"It's that guy from yesterday again! Have you finished talking?" It was the kids who Mamoru took care of. They looked very interested in Keel and the others.

"Bubba, Bubba, who are these kids?" Keel asked me, interested in them.

"They're under the care of Mamoru," I explained.

"Oh wow! Really?" Keel exclaimed.

"That's right," Mamoru confirmed. "They might not be able to understand you, but I hope you can all be friends." Hearing that, Keel looked back at me. I felt the same way. We were going to be here for a while, from the look of it.

"Sounds good to me!" Keel said, then turned to the kids. "My name is Keel! Nice to meet you!" She struck (what she thought was) a cool pose, then turned into full puppy mode to finish off her greeting.

"Wow! She's so cute!" said one child.

"A puppy! A puppy!" exclaimed another. Keel yapped again, frolicking around to communicate with the kids via body language. Her innocent, completely unguarded movements soon broke down the kids' initial hesitation, and they quickly turned smiles on Keel.

She was still rolling around, begging to be stroked and tickled, licking at the hands and faces of the kids who obliged her. She was a dog, a perfect little puppy. Even her attire looked cute when she was a puppy. All of this, this outpouring of cuteness, was probably why she was such a good merchant.

"I'm going to use the techniques Keel and the Raph species imparted to me to get to know these kids too!" Ruft said. He had been quiet up until that point, but now he adopted an expression I had seen him use a lot recently. It was very much like the one used by the Raph species, which I could only really describe as "cunning." He moved over to the kids to talk with them.

"My name is Ruftmila, and this is Keel. I hope we can be friends!" Ruft must have used a language that was spoken in Siltran, because the kids were nodding at his introduction.

"Oh, so fluffy!" one of the kids said, stroking Keel.

"She's so cute!" said another.

"Well? I'm cool, aren't I!" Keel responded happily, seemingly missing that she was being called cute. Some things were still getting lost in translation, but no matter.

"I hope I can be friends with you too," Imiya said, following Keel's example and moving over to talk with them. She was a little stiff in her approach, but she was doing a good job of blending into the group.

"It's a lovely sight to see," Raphtalia commented with a smile as she watched them. Meh, whatever. "One thing though, Keel. I don't think they are calling you cool, not exactly . . ." she said.

"No need to point that out. That's kind of the secret to Keel's popularity," I said. Her being a little silly was part of her charm. One day airheads might rule the world.

"Kids, listen up!" R'yne appeared and clapped her hands to get their attention. "It is breakfast time. You can play with the kids from Naofumi's village later." All the kids chorused their agreement, nodded as one, said goodbye to Keel and the others, and then sat down.

"Food?" Keel said, already sniffing around. She was trying to use her new friends to get fed already. I thought for a moment of a bunch of elementary school kids finding a lost puppy and deciding to raise it in secret.

"Keel, you already ate with us," I reminded her.

"Oh, please! Bubba!" she said. I didn't say anything else. I just prompted her to take another look at the kids. "Okay, Bubba!" she said, realizing what I was telling her. "This is food you guys have to eat!" she said to the kids. They didn't look especially healthy, to be honest. When I combined this with what we'd seen in the town, the overall food situation didn't seem very good here. What with the damage from the waves too, there probably wasn't enough to go around. We certainly shouldn't be taking food out of their mouths.

"She's not going to eat it. Don't worry," Mamoru told them.

"That's right. She's saying they are for you to eat. If you want to feed her, I'll make some dog food you can give her later, okay?" I added.

"Really?" one of them asked. All of their eyes were shining. I thought maybe I was spoiling them a little, but this seemed like another good way to build a friendly relationship with Mamoru.

"Promise!" said another.

"Sure. You play nice with them, Keel," I told her.

"You bet!" she said. I liked the energy, that was for sure.

"Mr. Naofumi, did you notice? You just called food for Keel dog food, didn't you?" Raphtalia said to me. It was Keel we were talking about, so such a slip of the tongue couldn't be helped.

"We can talk once you finish eating," I said to Mamoru.

"Thanks, Naofumi," he replied. It was our fault for coming when they were eating—and learning this new information about the food situation here made a lot of the decisions for us. Food could definitely turn into money here. Proper cooking would probably allow monster meat to be eaten too . . . There was such demand in Siltran that decent food might be worth more than precious metals and jewels at the moment. Medicine was probably high value too.

We waited for Mamoru and the others to finish eating and then settled into a kind of social gathering with Keel and the others. The younger kids were quick to make friends, as expected. I had been a little worried about bullying at first, but Keel and the other villagers made good use of their trading experience to keep the kids happy.

"I have to say, Naofumi, you've really helped to brighten things up around here," Mamoru said.

"I couldn't keep the curiosity of my bunch under control, to be honest. They are planning to travel within your country to stir up some trade and make some money," I explained.

"I'm amazed they made friends with my kids so quickly. They are normally so shy," Mamoru commented.

"My villagers have been through much of the same stuff. That's probably why," I said. Raphtalia, Keel, and most of the others had all lost family to the waves. They understood that same sadness and, as a result, also the pain the others were feeling. They were quick to empathize with them while at the same time not overstimulating them. They were so similar, which was why they were getting along so quickly.

Then the kid who had been concerned with me yesterday—the kid with the cat ears called Cian—was hanging out close to me and Mamoru with a hesitant look on her face. I wondered what was up with her.

"You aren't going to join in?" I asked her.

"I'm happy just watching," she said. I knew the type: the kids who didn't like to take part.

"Okay," I said offhandedly. I wasn't planning on playing the friendly big brother role with her, so I wasn't all that bothered about how I came off.

As we watched Keel and the others, I chatted with Mamoru about which areas he wanted us to visit and what he wanted us to take there. There were all sorts of things he needed, as expected, in order to restore and develop the castle town. We had some serious retail opportunities here, but the issues were the national power and prices in Siltran. We'd just have to consider it a suitable investment and put in the miles. There was also the question of what to do to get home.

As we chatted, Cian was looking at the map with great interest.

"Are you interested in trading?" I asked her.

"Huh? No, why would I be?" she answered with a cold

tone, looking away. That sounded exactly like she was very interested. Mamoru watched over the scene warmly. I wasn't sure if this was something that would be of any benefit to me if I brought it up, but it also didn't seem like a bad idea as I said it.

"I bet it would make them even better friends, Mamoru, if your kids were to go out trading with Keel and the others," I suggested.

"Huh?" Mamoru replied.

"It makes sense, right? You can keep an eye on us to make sure we don't get up to no good, and it will let them learn to fight a little too," I said. Lazy mouths didn't get fed, so the saying went. These were demi-humans we were talking about, so they would grow up fast. Keel might look like a pet puppy in dog mode, but in her demi-human form, she already looked much older than her actual years. Of course, she still didn't have anything on Raphtalia. The only ones that had grown that much were Ruft, who was the same species as Raphtalia anyway, and Fohl from among the slaves, who had already been older.

Simply protecting these kiddies and worrying about them wasn't going to provide any forward progress for them.

"If you're worried about them getting injured or killed by monsters, you could always tag along for a while," I suggested.

"Look at this! One day here and he's leading you by the nose already, Mamoru!" R'yne said, muddying the waters considerably. I wasn't happy about that.

"Mr. Naofumi, you aren't planning something crooked, are you?" Raphtalia asked me.

"No, why would I be?" I replied. My Shield Hero predecessor would make a good advertisement for our trading expedition—that was about as much thought as I was giving it.

"If you all wouldn't mind, I see no reason to turn down such an offer," Mamoru finally said after looking at Cian for a moment. "It will be very stimulating for them, I'm sure."

"That settles it. Have you ever done any trading before?" I asked him.

"The country provided most of what I needed," he admitted. I was quite jealous, having had a completely different experience myself. It looked like we needed to give him a crash course. Preparing supplies and a fighting force correctly could keep even a far bigger opponent at bay.

"Melty from my village will take part in your meetings at the national level, if that would be okay," I said. "Meanwhile, we'll teach you to invigorate trade and get distribution flowing again."

"I won't be able to stay with you for too long, but anything you can teach me would be most welcome," Mamoru replied.

And so our wagon journey around Siltran began, accompanied by Mamoru and the others.

"This is it! We're going to travel all over Siltran and trade, trade, trade!" Keel said excitedly. The kids shouted their general agreement.

"I don't know what's going on, but I'm excited!" said one of them.

"If we work hard, everyone will have an easier life!" another one explained. Keel and the others had an infectious energy, completely unafraid to head out and trade with unfamiliar regions in the past, and Mamoru's kids seemed to be picking up on it.

"Let's go, then," Mamoru said. As he climbed into the wagon, people from the castle town sent him off with crisp salutes.

"Be careful, Hero Mamoru!"

"We hope for success in this new endeavor!"

"Let's restore glory to Siltran!" Listening to their voices, I was impressed again with how much they all trusted him. The rough impression I had gotten from him during the battle might have originated with that trust from the people. The shield's holy weapon power-up method involved trusting others and being trusted by them. In my case, it had started as a vague sort of trust, pushing me to a reasonably high defense, even unconsciously. But once we had become aware of it as a power-up method, it had clearly taken shape as a significant boost. It had also placed the focus on the Siltvelt people and those from Melromarc I had been dealing with, however, and the trust from other quarters wasn't quite so high. In Mamoru's case, he didn't come off as just a saint—he felt like a true hero, someone you instantly wanted to trust.

"That's your mark as a hero," I said.

"What is?" he asked.

"Your charisma," I told him.

"That's not what this is. I just want to protect everyone, and so in turn they believe in me," he said. He made that cornball line work. I had to give him that. He was a natural. So this was the king of heroes whose name went down in history.

"I could never do that," I told him.

"I think you already are, Mr. Naofumi," Raphtalia said, trying to console me. But the difference between us seemed obvious. He would surely earn that Shield Demon King name that he came to be known by.

"The grass always looks greener . . ." Mamoru said. "You've got a bit of a caustic mouth, but Cian has taken a liking to you, so you can't be a bad person."

"Cian?" I looked down at the kid who was clinging close to Mamoru. "This is her taking a liking to me?" She really did look like a cat. She reminded me of the feral ones I used to see sometimes back when I was in Japan. I waved my finger to catch her attention, using only smooth movements. She watched it intently with her eyes. Then I slowly moved my hand forward and stroked her around the neck. She started making happy purring noises, then curled up on Mamoru's lap and went to sleep.

Yeah, so she really was just a cat. We already had a pet

puppy with Keel, and now we had a cat too. At least they were easy to understand.

"I think she really likes you. I'm amazed at how much, to be honest," Mamoru said.

"You are? I always suspected that Mr. Naofumi was good with children," Raphtalia said.

"Really?" I said. I was honestly treating her more like a kitten than a demi-human, and I wasn't really sure it counted as trust. This wasn't the same thing as Mamoru's charisma, that was for sure. If Mamoru was a hero, I was, what, a pet trainer? "The shield power-up method should be the same, but I'm not really feeling it since coming to the past," I said. I checked my status again, and my defense was not really where I expected it to be. I pondered if this was the difference between people believing in the Shield Hero and people believing in Mamoru. Everyone who believed in Mamoru was also receiving the power-up from the shield, which made them better fighters. I wasn't talking about the kids anymore either. "This is my first time meeting another person of the same type of hero as myself, but there are all sorts of differences between us," I commented.

"Indeed," Mamoru agreed. It was a bit rough on me having such a big gap between us. In my case, I was at least still getting the effects of those who believed in the Shield Hero, if not me personally. So while the effects were lower than Mamoru, it was still functioning. I just had to keep going.

"Keel, you start by gathering some customers for us. Your dog-wearing-a-loin-cloth bit should draw a crowd. Then start selling food to the people you can talk to," I told her. Just as I had expected, there was quite the demand for food.

"Okay! Are you going to be doing the cooking, Bubba?" she asked.

"I've chosen things that you villagers should be able to re-create. Focus on learning to make them now so you can sell them yourselves in the future," I said. With the waves and the wars, there was a serious lack of food here in the past. The people of Siltran were not skilled fighters and didn't have the abilities required to kill monsters that could be used for meat. Of course, the nation's soldiers and knights were defeating monsters to maintain the peace, but the resulting meat was not properly prepared. Mamoru knew a little about cooking, but only what he learned back in Japan about light meals. Even if you wanted barbeque, or just a nice thick steak, you still had to dress the meat, cut the tendons, all of that stuff. He had been making do with the shield modifiers and auto-cooking, but all that made was food that was neither delicious nor disgusting, just literally "food." That had worked okay for him on a small scale up until now, but whatever the shield could turn out wasn't going to be enough to fend off starvation for an entire nation.

In order to try and resolve that very issue, we had experi-mentally hooked up some filolials and Raph species to some carts and hit the open road for business purposes. Mamoru had some idea of prices within his nation and some idea of the markets through various merchant connections. The whole operation was a little different from back when I had been trading for myself with Raphtalia and Filo or even when I had left most of the work to Keel and the others—which was all, strictly speaking, in the future. They were also struggling with a lack of horse-like monsters due to the war. We had certainly picked a difficult time to come back to.

"Bubba! Ten more of the skewers!" Keel said, shouting an order. I let her know I was on it. So here we were. Before I realized it, we had become a traveling kitchen, like a medieval food truck. We defeated any monsters we encountered while moving between towns, processed them as required to turn them into food, and then cooked and sold those ingredients at the next town. Many of the people didn't have money, so we accepted trade for other items and made sure they got fed. Things like lumber and stone, which we would have turned down prior to being sent into the past, could be used to help rebuild and so we accepted them now. These materials were sent on their way back to the castle town in order to start the repair work. It was a pleasure to see the recovery proceeding, day by day, right before our eyes. Having the lumos from the village take part in the work was leading to sturdier house construction too.

"You have some most reliable allies, future Shield Hero.

Thank you so much for everything," Mamoru said. In many RPGs, monsters dropped gold when they were defeated, but unfortunately, that wasn't the case here. Ren, Itsuki, and Motoyasu had made some money by taking requests to solve problems within the nation, and Mamoru seemed to have followed a similar approach. Of course, there were also heroes who hit it big in business, and then there was trash like Takt too.

In any case, amid the national havoc that the waves could cause, there were plenty of chances lying around to make money through a little business. All you needed to do was be willing to bend down and pick them up. Our business got off to a good start—that was, until one week after our arrival in the past.

That was when the incident happened.

Chapter Twelve: A Determination to War

It was late at night. I was back in the village, and after preparing the next batch of goods to sell, I was discussing with Melty and the others what steps we should be taking next. I was about to go to bed when Mamoru came and knocked on the door of my house. I answered to find him there with R'yne and his other allies, all of them looking concerned. The villagers seemed to have realized something was up, and many of them had come out of their houses to see what was going on. People from across the village were gathering. Everyone was so sensitive to this kind of development.

"Naofumi, we need to talk. It's an emergency," Mamoru said. I gave a sigh and headed to the village square to hear what Mamoru had to say.

"What is it?" I asked.

"A coalition of our enemies, including Piensa, has advanced into Siltran," he explained. "We don't want you and yours to get involved, Naofumi, so please prepare to evacuate this area."

"This certainly is sudden. Why do we need to move though?" I asked.

"We really don't want to drag you into this," Mamoru replied. It reminded me of something he had said when we first met, about patrolling his borders in this region. After bumping into Ren, they had quickly engaged him in battle, which highlighted how tense they had been.

"You're not trying to get us to abandon the village so you can take our tech, are you?" I asked with an arched eyebrow. Raphtalia and S'yne shook their heads at my continued distrust.

"What's going on? I just nodded off . . ." Melty said sleepily, coming out from Filo's room.

"Mamoru wants us to evacuate the village. Other nations are attacking. This place could become a battlefield," I told her. At my reply, Melty snapped awake and stood alert at my side. I was glad she could switch on so quickly.

"I've heard talk at the Siltran castle, but I didn't expect them to attack like this," Melty said.

"Why does this Piensa and their coalition have it in for you guys?" I asked.

"They likely take issue with the fact Siltran won't bow down to them, but there seem to be other reasons as well. They have the past Bow Hero with them, for one thing, and they also seem to want to turn the remains of a country founded by a past hero—holy land—into their territory," Melty explained, spreading a map and pointing. Piensa itself was actually a little distance away. They weren't a direct neighbor, but it looked like they were aggressively expanding at the moment. The issue was that Siltran, the nation we were currently in, was in the perfect spot to act as a staging area for Piensa to attack their real target.

"The holy land . . ." I muttered, thinking back.

"You remember that too, Naofumi," Melty said. It was the ruins Fitoria had taken us to during the whole Melty-kidnapping thing by the Church of the Three Heroes. That place hadn't seemed all that special to me.

"It seems, in this time, that the place is believed to be land the one who will rule this whole world must hold. If Piensa can take it . . ."

"They will have a foundation for world domination," I replied. It all sounded a little too good to be true.

"There are other legends about the place too. They believe powerful weapons, magic, anything you want can be found there—some real fairy-tale stuff. No one back in our time would give it any serious thought," Melty huffed. That was why they called it the holy land then, but if they were going to start fighting a war on such a baseless story, I kind of wished they would just send the hero in to fight.

It wasn't hard to see it all as a pretense to invade.

"The crazy king of Piensa doesn't think we should be fighting the waves," Holn said, appearing to offer some additional information. "He believes his own nation should first unite the world and receive the blessings of the holy land in order to overcome the waves." So we'd been dropped in a bad spot. I was starting to worry that maybe this wasn't the place that became Siltvelt after all.

I'd heard some information during our trading, of course. Siltran's issues with distribution were all coming from Piensa too. Piensa was also the home of the Bow Hero, which they seemed to be using as an excuse to just do whatever the hell they wanted.

"Sounds like there are issues with the Bow Hero in whatever time you go to," I remarked. Be it Itsuki or this hero from the past, the Bow Heroes seemed to love doing things that they really shouldn't. I felt like finding the guy and giving him a good talking to.

"He has accepted that the best way to combat the waves is through the stability offered by the unification of the nations," Mamoru explained. That sounded a lot like Melromarc back in our time. The defeat of Faubrey created an atmosphere of swearing off pointless fighting, not only among neighboring nations, but on a global scale. Meanwhile, after we were unable to achieve the same shared feeling in Kizuna's world, the threat of war still lingered there. L'Arc had been busy trying to resolve those issues . . . and now he was on another world, learning how to make accessories. I wondered if maybe that was the real reason he went. He was trying to escape those annoying negotiations. He had dumped everything squarely onto Glass, which only made me more suspicious.

"Even if the goal is to overcome the waves, that's no excuse for unnecessary invasions. That's why I decided to oppose

Piensa rather than just bow to their demands. Everyone else here is the same," Mamoru said. His allies did all look very determined.

War could only lead to tragedy. If a large nation got serious, they would just roll over any smaller ones. It looked like the idea of the heroes working together to take on the waves wasn't a thing in this time either. Talking worked against opponents who weren't strong enough to have their way with you. Those powerful enough to force you to obey didn't care what you had to say about it. The only way to reach the discussion table was to make them think they would have a tough time taking you down by force. That meant, in the end, it still just came down to strength.

War could be merciless too. All sorts of terrible things could happen. Trash and Melty had been dealing with those kinds of problems. With her understanding of the issues, Melty didn't speak out against what Mamoru said.

That said, from our point of view—historically speaking—Piensa had been wiped out, and by Siltvelt no less. Destroyed by the Shield Hero who opposed them, it looked like. Melty took that moment to elbow me in the ribs and then whispered in my ear.

"The Church of the Three Heroes, the religion we followed in Melromarc, originally splintered off from the Church of the Four Holies. They adopted a religion that hated the Shield

Hero, growing larger as a result. Maybe whatever happened in this time was the trigger for that hatred," Melty suggested. A connection to the Church of the Three Heroes from this incident was lost in the darkness of history. The foundation of the Melromarc Church of the Three Heroes had to be a religion from the world of the spear and sword, after all. They had likely adopted the bow more quickly after absorbing the remnants of Piensa. I didn't really care for the history lesson.

"I understand what you came to say. That said . . ." I looked over at Keel and the others, who were watching with concern on their faces.

"Bubba! We'll fight too!" she yipped. She was as full of energy as always—her trademark. Just like Filo would have done, she was helping to keep the others optimistic.

"If you order it, Shield Hero, then we will fight," Imiya said. She and the other lumos took up their weapons in a display of solidarity, ready to fight. They were skilled with their hands, which was perhaps why they favored daggers and bows as weapons. Claws too . . . or maybe those counted as gloves. They were good at earth magic too, from the look of it. Personality-wise, they weren't really made for fighting, however, and they were a quieter element of the village. "We won't lose anything again," Imiya said strongly. Her village had been destroyed by slavers. That was another reason why she had gotten along with Keel so quickly.

"What kind of scale are we looking at for the enemy?" Ruft asked calmly.

"Just in terms of numbers, mastery, and levels, many times higher than us," R'yne said. It sounded like a big gap in fighting strength. "Their forces are comprised of humans, demi-humans, and therianthropes who are all completely specialized for warfare. That's the kind of force we face coming to completely destroy this small nation. They move quickly too. If Holn and I weren't allied with Mamoru, this nation would be a smoking ruin by now."

"The Shield Hero can't do anything without allies, after all. If I lose all my allies, then I'm finished," Mamoru muttered. The same went for me, of course. He had to understand that.

"We'll be facing the fighting core of the coalition led by Piensa, their dragon battalion," Mamoru continued. "If I make an appearance then, under the pretense that heroes should not be used in warfare, the Bow Hero should make an appearance too."

"What about their main force?" I asked.

"They are likely planning to move methodically in behind the battalion," Mamoru said. I wasn't sure if that was an efficient approach or an inefficient one.

"So they're leaving everything to his other forces? A true warrior engages in battle themselves!" Eclair said disparagingly.

"He probably wants to keep damage to a minimum while

making it sound like he was there in the fighting." The king probably did get his blade wet, just as rear support, mopping up whatever the hero and fighting core left behind.

"Brother! Do you plan to run?" Fohl asked. He seemed ready to fight as well. His fists were tightly bunched.

"You want to fight, Fohl?" I asked him.

"Of course. Abandoning the village would be a betrayal of Atla's wishes!" he declared.

"I understand that," I replied, "but if the only other choice is getting embroiled in this pointless fighting, abandoning this base and running for it is definitely one option. Fohl . . . are you here to protect some buildings? Or some people?" I asked him. If he wanted to protect a place, it might already be too late—the entire village had been kicked into the past, after all. If he wanted to protect people—our people—then the place wasn't all that important.

"You are not wrong, Brother. I understand your point. But should we really run away from this?" he countered.

"I wouldn't recommend trying it," Holn advised.

"I would very much like to avoid abandoning this place," Rat agreed.

"Why?" I asked them.

"First, this is the only land we have that physically came here from the future. If it gets trampled by open warfare, we might lose some vital hints as to how we were sent here or how to get back home," Rat said.

"Furthermore, if Piensa advances and takes this region, it will take time to retake it and that will delay our research further. Everything here is definitely worth protecting," Holn added.

"If the technology we have here falls into enemy hands," Rat continued, "they are only going to become bolder." If they took future technology and could work out how to use it, they would, of course. If we started changing the past, we had no idea what would happen in the future, which meant it was hard to decide whether we should stay or go. Wanting to maintain the current situation was definitely Rat's opinion, and Holn sounded like she was in agreement.

"How long will it take for them to reach us?" I asked.

"At the earliest, the attack will begin tomorrow," Mamoru replied. One choice, then, was to destroy everything in the village and flee before that happened. But I didn't like the sound of that.

"Dragons . . ." said Wyndia, muttering the name of the enemy we would face before I could say anything.

"You want to try talking with them?" I asked her, putting a hand on her shoulder.

"If possible, I would. But if they believe in the cause they are fighting for, though, I'm not sure what I'll be able to do," she said.

"The dragons aren't going to listen to you, missy," Holn said, shooting down Wyndia's idea.

"How can you be so sure?" she replied, a little hotly.

"Because we are talking about the further development of a type of modified dragon that little old me originated," she explained.

"What?" Wyndia said.

"I forgot to mention this, didn't I?! I'm formerly a researcher based right over there in little old Piensa. When I decided I didn't agree with the thinking of the Bow Hero, I defected," Holn explained brightly. So she started out belonging to a large nation and then ended up with the Shield Hero. I shook my head—she was Rat's ancestor, no doubt about that.

"What thinking of his didn't you agree with?" I asked.

"The current Bow Hero is very interested in raising monsters and using them in combat. That's why the dragon battalion has grown into such a powerful threat. But he's also highly discriminatory—he doesn't care for any other monsters that might work as allies, apart from dragons," Holn explained. Dragons were certainly far more powerful than other monsters at the same level. If you could afford it, they made for an efficient fighting force. They just weren't cost-efficient. "He seems to want to reduce the monster population of the entire world to just dragons," she said. The dragons in this world, including here in the past, had the capacity to mate with any other monster. Holn explained that the Bow Hero had turned all the monsters in his army into dragons.

"Survival of the fittest is one thing, but proclaiming dragons as the king of monsters is to throw countless other possibilities down the drain. My innate curiosity won't allow any such foolishness. That's why I'm going to turn a balloon into the ultimate monster," Holn exclaimed. I wasn't sure I liked that much either. The ultimate balloon was not something I was interested in encountering. I couldn't help wondering if maybe it was Holn's research that had resulted in the monsters in our world remaining unorganized. Over in Kizuna's world, they had quite an organized structure, with the Demon Dragon at the top.

"A Bow Hero who will only accept dragons as powerful monsters . . ." I muttered, looking over at Wyndia. Then I stroked the caterpilland that had become a Raph species and looked back at Holn and the others. In our village, there was no competition for the top spot between dragons, filolials, or the Raph species. They sometimes bickered about what to change into when performing a class-up—with most of them wanting to become Raph species. Maybe there was something there that appealed to them. Even the monsters Ren and Itsuki raised had started to show that trend. That had Rat very interested.

"Do they have a Dragon Emperor?" I asked.

"My own investigations have only gotten me so far. I can't be sure about that," Holn replied. In which case, we should assume that they did.

"What do you think, Wyndia?" Ren inquired, looking over at her after sharing a glance with Eclair.

"Shouldn't you ask our Shield Hero first?" she asked.

"I want to hear from you first, before Naofumi," Ren replied, his face deadly serious. "I turned my blade on your father, Wyndia. That's why I've made a vow to never kill dragons without good cause."

"I don't care about your silly vows!" Wyndia snapped.

"I know. It's almost selfish of me. But those are the feelings I took into my battle with Takt's Dragon Emperor," he said.

"Gaelion killed that one, so I heard!" she replied. That was true. Ren had fought Takt's Dragon Emperor, but he hadn't landed the killing blow. This all made more sense when it came to his general attitude—his actions had traumatized him.

"But I still fought. Things are different this time though. Wyndia . . . in order to protect everyone here, is it okay for me to face this dragon battalion? I want you to decide," Ren said. Then he turned his sword into the Ascalon, the weapon he had copied from the one we found lying in the filolial sanctuary. Wyndia looked around the village and then met the eyes of the caterpilland that had become a Raph species.

"What if I say I don't want you to?" she answered.

"I'll think of another way. Negotiation, something else," he replied. Wyndia gave it some more thought.

"I don't think they are special just because they are dragons, not anymore," she finally said. "I don't want to lose the village . . . to lose anyone else. Please, Ren. Fight."

"Okay, Wyndia. I will use my sword to protect you and everyone else here. That shall be my atonement!" he proclaimed. I liked his energy, but we hadn't actually made the decision to fight yet.

"Bubba! So we're going to fight?" Keel yapped, staring me down when I didn't reply. "You said it yourself, Bubba! We have to choose for ourselves! And we have to protect the village and everyone in it!"

"Keel . . ." Raphtalia said, sounding very moved by this. The dog had gotten one over on me. I was indeed always telling Keel and the others to make their own decisions. That's why I'd let them choose their own class-ups.

"That's all very well," I said, "but that doesn't mean you should just fight everyone who comes along. You understand that too, right?" I told them.

"Of course! No killing the Bow Hero, right?" Keel replied.

"That's one thing, for sure," I said back. This might be the past, but the nature of the waves was likely the same. Killing a holy weapon hero would only place greater strain on the remaining ones. That wasn't even the worst of it—if all the holy weapon heroes were wiped out during a wave, then that world was finished, apparently. This was coming from S'yne and the forces of her sister—people whose world had actually been destroyed—and so it sounded like legit information. Even if we were enemies, killing a holy weapon hero would be the height of foolishness.

That said . . . it might be faster to just kill a hero who wouldn't listen to reason.

In that respect, they had done pretty well in summoning me. Ren and Itsuki had come around and listened to reason now too.

When I thought that all of this was probably a trap set up by the one behind the waves, the one who assumed the name of God, it did make me sick though.

"But it would be a mistake for you to lead the charge into battle, Keel," I told her.

"What?! If we don't fight to protect this place, what's the point?" she replied.

"We've got other moves we can make first. You'll see," I told her. There was no reason to throw Keel and the others meaninglessly into battle.

"Zounds like you need me," said the Shadow, popping into view and bowing to Melty and Ruft before heading over to me. "I zensed trouble and have been out zcouting. Hero Iwatani, what theze people from Siltran have told you appearz to be the truth," the Shadow reported. He had confirmed that a large force was approaching the borders of Siltran. "I wanted to inform you az quickly az pozzible, but they move very quickly, zo it wazn't eazy."

"Are you sure Mamoru isn't counting on our aid in order to pick a fight with other nations?" I asked him, lowering my voice to almost a whisper. We couldn't ignore the possibility that he was playing the victim to make use of us—or make a run for it, leaving us carrying the can.

"Az far az my invextigationz have revealed, he iz in the clear. The reazon for thiz attack iz more likely to be becauze of your aid, Hero Iwatani. You've been helping them recover zo quickly. That iz not zomething their enemiez can eazily over-look." So helping them recover through trade had made their enemies move more quickly. It sounded like those looking to capture Siltran would prefer a soft target—and they were going to try and roll right over us now.

I pondered this news. I was still worried that making the wrong move here could change the entire future . . . we were yet to confirm the effects of any such changes, however. It was definitely a thing that time in this world didn't really affect me, since I had been summoned here from another world to this world's Melromarc in the future. So we had to choose between abandoning the village and delaying—or completely losing—our chances of returning to the future. Or we could fight and risk changing history itself. Quite the plot twist. It was a tough choice to make. Whichever one we chose, I was sure it would change history anyway. I would just have to hope that any ripple created in the past would be smoothed over by history's power to correct itself in the length of time prior to us reaching the present we had departed from. That said . . .

"Just hitting them head-on isn't the only solution here," I commented. We had seen our fair share of warfare, but very little of it involved face-to-face battle. There was the conflict in Q'ten Lo, for example. We had made good use of Ruft's ridiculous policies to take the castle without spilling any blood. The battle with Faubrey had been won thanks to the strategy from Trash. It really hurt that he wasn't here, to be honest.

"I think we can come up with some more interesting plans than that. Right, Queen Melty?" Ruft said, giving her a look that suggested the two of them had something to share.

"Huh?" Melty didn't seem to be in on the secret.

"If you think back over the countless strategies Trash has proposed, I'm sure something you can use will come to mind," Ruft said.

"You remember all of those plans?" I asked him.

"Huh? Yes, I mean . . . it was fun watching him explain them all," Ruft said, a little abashed. Just like Raphtalia was so good with remembering names, Ruft seemed to have a good memory too. He had learned the Melromarc language in short order. He was a smart kid.

"Shield Hero," Ruft said to me, keeping his voice low. "We

might have a problem if Siltran wins a complete victory here. Queen Melty told me that Piensa isn't meant to be wiped out yet."

"That's true," I said. We might have a problem if Piensa was wiped out at this point in time.

"In which case, I'll make sure not to hit them too hard," Ruft replied. Then he increased the volume of his voice again and started talking with Mamoru. "Are we to presume that the battle between Siltran and Piensa is going to proceed through a number of stages?" he asked.

"That's right," Mamoru replied.

"To recap: first, there will be the attack by the dragon battalion. Second, there will be the battle between the heroes. Third, the arrival of their main force. After that, to the victor go the spoils. The boundary between the dragon battalion attack and battle between the heroes is a vague one though, isn't it?" Ruft continued.

"The hero is also being used to legitimize what they are doing," Mamoru said.

"In terms of other things they might already be doing . . . do you think they have active operations within Siltran already, for the purposes of distraction and confusion?" Ruft asked. Mamoru nodded.

"We've received reports of suspicious raids by bandits on our villages. Some of our allies have been dispatched to take care of it," he said.

"So they have a thorough plan in place. The cowardice on display reminds me of someone else," R'yne said. I wondered if she was talking about a resurrected, like Takt. The enemy had the Bow Hero among their forces, so it was possible.

"Hey. Do you know where the Bow Hero is?" Ruft asked the Shadow.

"I don't know the exact location, but I have a rough idea," he replied.

"Why don't we have your Shield Hero meet with the Bow Hero before anything else happens, then?" Ruft suggested. By putting the Bow Hero on the spot, maybe we could nip things in the bud before it all became about the pretext for this conflict.

"They are the ones attacking us. If the heroes meet while we still have no intent to attack, even as they talk, the dragon battalion will be advancing. Which side will that put in the right once the fighting is all done?" Ruft asked. It was cunning, I'd give him that. A way to gain some leverage even if we lost. Very much the kind of thing Trash would think up. I wasn't sure how happy I should be at these signs of growth in Ruft.

"What about the dragon battalion though? Won't they zmash uz under that plan?" the Shadow asked.

"If we're going to use one of my father's plans . . . we want something to confuse and confound the enemy. They have the numbers, so why not have the Sword Hero and Fohl run a raid on them?" Melty suggested. An operation using a small number, hit and run.

"Seeing the Sword Hero in action will surely throw them into chaos, but their trump card—the Bow Hero—will have already met with your Shield Hero," Ruft said.

"If we can create a rift between Piensa and the Bow Hero, that will be big," I said.

"Indeed," Melty agreed. "The powerful dragon battalion is going to be a problem too though. I hate to ask, but maybe you could thin them out and weaken them a little. That will make the negotiations go more smoothly. That said, we need you to fight in such a way that they won't realize you are the Sword Hero right away. It's a pretty tall order."

"I think you are getting a little ahead of yourselves," Mamoru said, cutting in from the side.

"These are all just proposals. You're the leader of this nation, so you ultimately decide if we go ahead or not. We're just thinking of the best steps we can possibly take," Melty explained. I wasn't sure about having Melty and the other kids thinking up strategies for war, but they were relying on tactics they had picked up from Trash, meaning we could probably expect decent results.

"If we do use this strategy, should Raphtalia, S'yne, and I set up an ambush somewhere?" I asked.

"If we are going to be talking with the Bow Hero . . . it would be a help to have Raphtalia along," Mamoru said.

"Me?" she asked.

"Yes. I think that will get a better result. She should make a good deterrent," Mamoru said. It sounded like his plan was to make them think she was the one from Q'ten Lo in this time.

I wondered again, for a moment, if sakura stones of destiny existed in this time. Those were a cluster of weapons that were effective against heroes, and activating the Sakura Sphere of Influence was an easy way to quickly weaken an enemy. Our purpose wasn't to defeat them, however; it was to create a situation in which it was just difficult to wage war.

"If we announce that there are multiple heroes in Siltran, that might make it harder for them to invade, but it also might provoke further retaliation," I mused. The latter of those things was exactly what had happened in Kizuna's world. It might not be a bad move overall, but I also wasn't sure it would really function as a deterrent. We would also be unsure what the ones pushing for this conflict might do. If possible, I just wanted to cut out those radical factions and buy us some time to get back home. It might appear selfish, from one perspective, but I really wanted the people from this time to sort out their own problems.

So while the hero from the enemy nation and Mamoru were meeting and chatting, we would cause enough damage—without relying on the power of the heroes too much—to drive the enemy away.

"The problem being the number of enemies we will face . . ." I pondered aloud. I had heard "ten times" being bandied around. Even if a hero was worth a thousand regular fighters, the numbers still didn't match up. It would be a real hassle if they got inside Siltran too.

"How are you guys set up in terms of large-scale magic?" I asked.

"I hate to say it, but poorly," Mamoru admitted. I hadn't seen any units with the potential to fire off some large-scale ritual magic. One facet of warfare in this world was the exchange of ritual magic, so I had been told. There was always the possibility that, while we were dealing with the dragon battalion in front of us, a rain of ritual magic would pour in from behind. We had some Collective Attack Magic at our disposal, but there were limits to that. It wasn't going to be very effective against a force carefully raised by the Bow Hero—and any attacks from them would probably hurt even a hero and cause serious problems for Keel and the others. They had the numbers, and we only had empty spots in our forces. Even if we did have a response, I didn't really want to use Keel and the others in battle. If Mamoru and his allies came to rely on us too heavily, they could easily be defeated once we returned to the future, messing everything up for all of us. We lacked decisive firepower . . . . We just needed more boots on the ground.

"These are pretty tough conditions to deal with . . ." I said. Then a proposal based in my game knowledge came to mind. "Hey, I have an idea. If we are lacking in numbers, how about we just inflate them a little? Ren, do you remember when Motoyasu and I fought over Raphtalia? Do you remember how I damaged him?" I asked, looking over at Ren. It all felt like a long time ago now—a battle that took place after my first experience with the waves. Having no means of attacking myself, I had hidden a balloon in my cloak and used that to bite Motoyasu, which caused damage instead.

"Huh? Yes, I do recall . . ." he said.

"I've heard about that," Melty chimed in. "What are you planning?"

"Like I said, we inflate our numbers. I need to move on this quickly. Our enemies are going to be advancing too," I said. This might not be definitive, but we could definitely expect some results. Even if we had to change our strategy afterward, this could still hurt our foes—or at least hold them in place. Then we could try a different approach or spring a trap on them. "What I'm planning should be useful no matter what you decide in the end, but I need time to set everything up. I'm going to have to get started."

"Understood," Melty said. "We'll be counting on you, but we'll play our own part too."

"Raphtalia, you go with Mamoru and buy us some time," I said. "After that, I'll take a fast mover, and Raph-chan too." Chick, Raph-chan, and Raph-chan II all came forward. The filolial sat down in front of me and the two Raph-chans jumped onto my shoulders.

"Shield Hero, can I go with you?" Ruft asked. "I can help out instead of Raphtalia."

"Just don't fall off!" I said.

"No problem! Queen Melty, I'll leave things here with you," Ruft said. He could use illusion magic, just like Raphtalia, and had the same properties as the Raph species. All of that would be vital for this operation.

"Mamoru, when you and your team encounter the Bow Hero, try and drag out the conversation as much as possible," I told him. "I'm going to get moving. I can see the surprise on their faces already—and I don't even know what they look like!" I said and gave an evil chuckle.

"I'm sorry, Mr. Naofumi . . . Are you sure this is a good idea?" Raphtalia asked, looking across at me with concern on her face.

"I'm fine. We're facing enemies who think wars are won by striking first. We're just going to turn the same kind of cowardly tactics against them to teach them a lesson," I said. If this was a game, then you could say I was about to do some serious trolling.

"Naofumi, are you sure you should be taking part in this fighting at all?" Mamoru asked, just to confirm things with me.

"I don't think I have a say in this anymore. Everyone else has decided to fight. Tell me, if you wanted everyone in Siltran to abandon their nation and survive, but they all decided to stand their ground and fight, what would you do even if you were sure how things would turn out?" I asked him. At my words, Mamoru gave a start, eyes wide, his body shaking. That was certainly an overreaction.

"Mamoru. . ." R'yne said, supporting him with concern in her eyes.

"If you're going to help, we have no reason to turn you down. Thank you," Mamoru said, giving me a deep and low bow.

For the sake of this operation, I'd be acting as a decoy, so I should disguise myself too. I could use magic to conceal myself as long as I had Raph-chan and Ruft along with me. As I still had the mirror vassal weapon along with my shield, there was something else I could do. I tossed a hand mirror to Ren.

"Ren, if you take that with you, then I'll be able to follow your actions to a certain degree. When I give the signal, I want you to incant support magic enhanced by your weapons. The reinforcements will know when the time comes," I said. This was an application of the Movement Mirror skill that used a mirror as its medium. Now that the shield was my main weapon again, most of the mirror skills were no longer functioning. But I could still get some visual and audio through a prepre-pared mirror. Ren had an aptitude for water and support magic. Motoyasu was fire and healing magic, and Itsuki was wind and earth. I couldn't raise magic level using the shield, so I placed my expectations on Ren, who could do so.

"Okay, sure," said Ren.

"One last thing." I turned to look at S'yne, who was looking quietly at me. "S'yne, you can move to me at any time. There's no sign of your sister causing trouble here either. Can I ask you to handle the Piensa soldiers that are causing trouble inside Siltran?" I asked her.

"Sure. Leave it to me," S'yne replied.

"If you sense that I'm in danger, you can pop out, but you have to pretend to be R'yne," I told her.

"Okay," she replied. The cooperative relationship between Mamoru and R'yne was widely known. If S'yne and I started a bit of a rampage, we would easily be mistaken for those two, based on our weapons. That would make it easy for us to act.

"Right, everyone. I'm leaving," I said. I hopped onto Chick's back, along with Raph-chan and Ruft, and then indicated that we should get moving. Chick gave a triumphant squawk and dashed off. We spent the rest of the night preparing for our raid.

Chapter Thirteen: Online Trolling

It was the following morning and the sun was almost completely over the horizon.

"Check it out. It looks like Mamoru was telling the truth," I said. We had reached a small hill with an excellent view out over the surrounding terrain, and I looked toward the front lines. A veritable horde of dragons was seething forward across the ground and through the air. There were some massive dragons among them too. It looked like the latest dinosaur park gone wrong again. This many of them was stomach-turning, to be honest. I was also immediately starting to see the advantages of a dragon battalion. It even made me want to increase the number of dragons among my forces.

There came some more dragon roars and a responding shout from a lone figure. Ren, swinging his sword alone against the dragons—without even using any skills—looked like the protagonist of his own heroic story. He certainly didn't look like the guy who had been convalescing in the village after collapsing from too much stress. Eclair also appeared. She seemed to be warning him about pushing himself too hard. Then Fohl and Keel pushed forward themselves, providing some support for Ren to ensure he didn't overextend himself. They weren't having the easiest time of it though; I could tell. When I asked them about it afterward, they explained that something was definitely different when compared to fighting normal monsters. In any case, everyone from the village—starting with Fohl—was receiving hero blessings from Ren and me so they could put up a good fight. The fighting was being led by Fohl, Keel, the other villagers, and the Siltran volunteers. Those volunteers were comprised of the few races they had who were skilled at combat. Both Ren and Fohl were fighting using only techniques and magic, without any skills, in order to hide the fact that they were heroes. Part of the plan was to lure the enemy into position for me, after all.

I wasn't on the battlefield myself, so I didn't know where Mamoru and his party were fighting. I turned to look behind the enemy forces . . . and there they were. A three-fold force comprised of humans, demi-humans, and therianthropes. They were watching everything unfold under the pretense of support from the rear. This was a new type of enemy for us. It was a composition we hadn't seen before, even in battle with Siltvelt. It felt more like the Melromarc army that had fought with us against Faubrey.

Even at a distance, it was easy to see the difference in the size of the two forces. Our enemies saw nothing other than a small, weak nation feebly trying to fight back.

"Shield Hero," said Ruft. Chick and Raph-chan made noises too.

"Yes, good point. We'd better get moving," I agreed. The Shine Shield had proven more useful than I expected. It had made the perfect lure, attracting even more of my targets than I had expected. That was enough time and numbers now. It was time to go on the counterattack.

Ruft intoned some illumination magic, so I matched my breathing with his and raised the shield. It was a chance to use a combination skill.

"As the source of your power, I implore you! Let the true way be revealed once more! Create light to illuminate us! Drifa Illumination!"

"Into a combination skill! Prism Light Shield!" I shouted. While giving off ridiculously brilliant light, almost divine in its brilliance, we charged into the dragon battalion and the forces behind them. A cacophony of roars and growls greeted us. The forces in the rear had countless wild monsters with them too. You really could find wild monsters anywhere. I kept Chick running at a speed that wouldn't wear her down completely. I pushed into the mountains and used Hate Reaction on all the monsters we encountered in order to gather them together and threw in some liberal Shine Shield to make sure they all saw us. I even used Liberation Aura on any monsters that looked like they wouldn't be able to keep up, which increased their speed as we ran. I had wondered what to do if the monsters started fighting with each other, but an intense Hate Reaction was a wonderful thing. The simple-minded monsters fixed their sights completely on me, with no in-fighting at all. The shield already had intrinsic properties to attract monsters, and I had to make use of every advantage I had.

"What's going on here?!"

"A horde of monsters?!"

"Is that the Shield Hero?!"

"Impossible! He's already engaged with the Bow Hero!"

"What is the Shield Hero doing here?!" The enemies in front of us had a lot to say about the massive makeshift horde of monsters I had put together, and I felt cracks of chaos starting to run through the Piensa chain of command.

"MPK using a train . . . bringing in more monsters to make up the numbers. This is my first time actually seeing it in action," I breathed. MPK was an online game term that stood for "monster player kill." It was exactly what it sounded like—a form of trolling that involved using monsters to kill other players. It was used in games that didn't allow direct PK—player killing—as a way of killing players you didn't like. Of course, as a form of trolling, it was, strictly speaking, against the rules. But I wasn't in a game right now and so I saw this as a legit tactic. If this was "cheating," so was raising up a crazy dragon battalion and using it to hammer down other nations. This would be a fine punishment for the Bow Hero and his dragon supremacist way of thinking. The dragon battalion he had raised so carefully and had ultimate confidence in was defeated by a raid launched by wild monsters . . . Okay, maybe "defeated" was going too far. But it certainly struck a resounding blow. It was time to rake these untrained dragons over the coals a little.

"You always surprise us, Hero Iwatani," Eclair exclaimed.

"Ren, stop standing and staring! We need to incant before the Shield Hero hits their lines or this will all be wasted!" Wyndia called to Ren as she sensed my approach, even as she helped with the magic at the rear.

"Okay, I'm on it!" Ren took the signal and started to incant magic. Everyone was smiling at my arrival as they formed up the magic. Ren led the incanting support magic.

"I, the Sword Hero, command the heavens and earth! Transect the way of the universe and rejoin it again to expel the pus from within! Dragon Vein! Bring together my magic and the power of the heroes! As the source of your power, the Sword Hero implores you! Let the true way be revealed once more! Bring them power! All Liberation Bless Power X!" The magic Ren had just incanted was different from the aura that increased all status. Instead, it just increased specific statuses like power and speed. I specialized in healing and support, meaning he couldn't quite match me overall. But at the moment, Ren could actually use support magic that offered a higher boost to attack power than mine did. Having received the benefits of his support, the monster army I was dragging along behind me all started to speed up, coming up after me even more intensely.

Of course, I had a full wall of Shooting Star Shields deployed around me, so even if any attacks reached me and my small party, they weren't going to break through. Chick gave a squawk, informing me that Ren's magic had been applied to us as well. She spread her wings and speeded up. We were almost transformed into nothing but a pure bolt of light that was piercing into the dragon battalion and Piensa army. Just when it looked like we would cut right through the enemy, a singular shaft of high-speed lightning—

Ruft and the two Raph-chans all activated their illusion magic, and we vanished completely. In the same moment, I released both the Hate Reaction and the Prism Light Shield. For those around us, it would have looked like we simply turned into light and vanished.

A horde of fresh growls was thrown up into the air as the monsters—losing their original target—quickly turned on the dragon battalion and Piensa army located all around them. Our enemies were quickly thrown into complete chaos.

"What's going on? These monsters are so fast and strong!"

"Even the dragons can't hold them off!"

"What are you doing? Fall back into ranks! Match the Siltran attack with support for our dragons!"

"The fighting has devolved too far already! Do we need attack magic, healing, or support? I can't tell!"

"You fool! We can't let the dragons provided to us by the glorious hero be killed like this!" The chain of command was collapsing already. The cries of the men were drowning out any attempts to restore order. With Mamoru and his group tying up the Bow Hero, there was only one other person who could turn this situation around. As the Piensa army continued to fall apart around us, we dashed among them, still hidden, searching for the one in command.

Ruft and I were in agreement that he would be found some distance from the battle but close enough to see what was going on. Their commander would keep to the safest possible location while enjoying the ambitions of open warfare. I still had some hope that it would be the king of Piensa himself, but he probably wasn't quite that stupid.

"Stand firm! Don't fall for the cowardly tricks of the Siltran! They are using wild monsters, nothing more! Do you really believe that our invincible dragons can't put them down? You rabble! Believe in the glorious hero and defeat the Siltran army and their petty tricks!" A guy who looked like some kind of fancy wizard was shouting pointless platitudes at the other men as my monster train rolled over them. He looked like the boss—or he would do for now. "I can't believe the Shield Hero in Siltran, Mamoru, would use such a tactic as this . . . No, it must be proof that we finally have him cornered! This is his final spurt of pointless resistance! Pile on! I know him, I know him!"

"Oh! You are the magician who defeated the upstart king of Siltran, so I guess you know what you're talking about!" one soldier conveniently shouted, almost for my benefit. So this was the guy! This was the traitor Mamoru had mentioned!

"Drop our lines back. Allow the dragon battalion to fight more easily!" the magician shouted.

"Hold on. I'm not about to let you put an end to our fun so easily. More chaos, please," I quipped, grabbing the turncoat by the shoulder and turning off the invisibility. I still had Ruft and the Raph-chans making me look like Mamoru, of course.

"What! How can you be here, Shield Hero?! You are engaged with the Bow Hero even as we speak. I am sure of it!" the magician raged.

"You, of all people, should understand that one never reveals how the trick is performed!" I replied. It was a pretty good comeback, for me. I hoped a lot of people heard it.

"Let go of me, charlatan! Your tiny nation is going to be squished today!" the magician raged.

"Remove your hands from our strategist!" a soldier shouted, coming with other subordinates to protect their leader. At the same time came a guttural roar from what looked like a bodyguard dragon that the leader had held back for protection. Of course, they thought I was Mamoru—and so was able to attack for myself—and obviously hadn't totally underestimated what might happen during the battle. If I activated Shooting

Star Shield again, I would knock the magician away and he would escape. That seemed to leave me with only one choice: take all the incoming attacks head-on and cause some damage using counterattacks.

"Air Strike Shield! Second Shield! Dritte Shield! Chain Shield!" I deployed my shields and then transformed them, catching all the magic and arrows flying in toward us. The incoming attackers weaved between my shields, pouring in to attack me. I also started to feel a little pain—no more than a tickle, but there was definitely contact. It was a sign that maybe the Bow Hero could train his goons after all. The shield gave a solid response and the countereffect was triggered. I had the Spirit Tortoise Carapace Shield equipped, and the countereffects of C Magic Snatch and C Magic Shot quickly scattered out among all of those who had attacked me. My tactics were greeted with pleasing cries from the attackers and shouts about their magic being drained away.

"I've got a little bonus for you too! Take this!" I tossed out the enhanced snake balloons that had been biting onto me. It was just another little piece of fun I had cooked up.

"What's this? Snake balloons?! Owww, that hurts! Stop it!" Further chaos ensued, and I reveled in their shouts and cries. That said, it was an annoyance that I couldn't cause any truly incapacitating injuries. Using these methods only reminded me of when I'd first had to resort to such tactics, and I honestly didn't like that feeling.

"Shield Hero!" Ruft was still using his illusion magic. He split himself into multiple copies, then snatched an axe from one of the enemies and smashed it with considerable force back into him. He was fighting a lot like Raphtalia and unleashing some powerful attacks. In his therianthrope form, he looked pretty brawny while he did it too. It was starting to feel like Raphtalia would be the technical character and Ruftmila the power one.

"Raph!" said Raph-chan.

"Dafu!" said Raph-chan II. The two cuties were also working together to send Piensa soldiers flying. Raph-chan II was swinging her Beast Lance around as her weapon. She had really been favoring that one recently. Meanwhile, with a mighty neigh, Chick sent incoming Piensa soldiers tumbling away with a powerful kick. She was pretending to be a horse at the moment and so had probably decided it best that she didn't squawk like a bird. Melty had told me that Chick was quite unlike Filo in that she was actually a pretty smart filolial. I wasn't sure I saw much of that in how she generally carried herself, but being a filolial, she was at least good at voice work, I guessed. Her neigh was pretty convincing.

The bodyguard dragon gave another roar as it closed in, swinging its arms as it targeted me. Black fire welled up from my front shield, and then the Demon Dragon asserted herself inside my field of vision.

"Look at this," the Demon Dragon said, her voice ringing inside my head. "A dragon who would dare to fight us!" This was a new trick! I thought all she could do was provide support for incanting magic. "I'm a copy of my original personality. One of my best features!" the Demon Dragon said, and the voice faded away. I really didn't like this. It was starting to feel like she might have embedded her actual mind inside mine!

Even as the dragon narrowed its beady eyes and prepared to strike me, it suddenly jerked back with a grunt. There was a look of terror appearing on its lizard features. It seemed to have felt the presence of the Demon Dragon inside me.

"We can't have you recovering just yet. More chaos, that's what this battle needs!" I shouted. We didn't want to win the battle outright, but we needed to break the will of the Piensa soldiers. I didn't want this turning into a full-blown war while we were still around.

"You scum, you aren't Mamoru—" the magician shouted.

"Let's not spill those beans yet," I replied, covering his mouth and taking him hostage. It hadn't taken him that long to work it out, but it still made sense for me to act as Mamoru's double for now.

Mamoru himself gave me the impression that he was very serious about things, but in a different way from Kizuna. Apart from that, I didn't really know much about him. That made it hard to put on a convincing performance. From the way the magician was reacting to everything I'd done so far, he didn't seem like the type to use these kinds of tactics. That said, I had used skills—something only heroes had access to—and so I could tell our enemies had really been thrown into confusion.

"You coward! Is this something the Shield Hero would do?!"

"So barbaric! No true hero would act this way! You dirty the battlefield with your cowardice!" The infantry around me didn't like this turn of events, but I only scoffed. They could invade purely to fulfill their own ambitions, but what I was doing was cowardice! Talk about a double standard—especially when they had been happy to let the dragon battalion do all the work. But when they shouted names at me like "demon," I felt that this was still preferable to fighting back in my time.

"I think we're done here. This guy seems to be the commander, so he'll make a nice gift to take back with us. Ruft! Raph-chan, one, two!" I shouted.

"Okay!" Ruft hammered the shaft of his stolen axe into the abdomen of the traitor, causing him to grunt and collapse. I was impressed with how Ruft had handled himself. It still wasn't that long since he had arrived in the village, and I didn't recall him ever saying he had been in combat when he was in Q'ten Lo. He was growing up as fast as Raphtalia had and was proving himself incredible at adapting to his surroundings.

"Master Strategist!" one of the enemy shouted.

"Don't let them get away!" another chimed in. "The master would choose death over a return to Siltran. We must honor that loyalty!" Worried that our captive would be taken alive and spill his secrets, the men seemed to have decided to just take us all out. I couldn't really tell if that was smart or not.

"Not on my watch." S'yne appeared in an instant, her scissors at the ready, deploying threads all around us and binding up the closest soldiers.

"Now the Sewing Set Hero from another world has appeared too!" a soldier exclaimed.

"It is the Shield Hero! We have to let the Bow Hero know at once!" another shouted.

"Think he can make it in time?" I asked as S'yne wrapped the traitor up in her threads to make him easier to handle. It felt like a good time to depart.

"Let's move!" Riding on Chick, we quickly disengaged. "Now! Start the next phase!" I commanded. Ruft sent up the flare that marked the signal. As soon as he did so, a flurry of skills—a veritable explosion—erupted from the front lines.

"Dragon Wipe Sword . . . into Comet Sword X! Hundred Swords X!" Ren launched an imbued skill that gave his sword blade a blackish-purple hue and then followed that with two other skills. He sent countless blades raining down onto his foes. It was clearly an attack designed specifically to damage dragons, and the results were suitably decimating. The dragon battalion erupted into roars and growls as its member dragons were cut down one after the other. "I understand that you aren't in the wrong here. This is all the world of people . . . the ones who got you involved in this terrible conflict in the first place. But I will fight for the sake of those I must protect!" Ren really sounded like a hero for a moment there. I wondered if he was getting a little high on the whole situation.

"To protect everyone! Atla, lend me your strength!" Fohl started to unleash his own barrage of skills, slamming them into massive dragons one after the other. "Dragon Wipe Fist X! Air Strike Rush V! Second Rush V! Dritte Rush V! Moonlight Kick V! And then . . . Boldest Boulder-Busting Body Blow V!" First, he charged in like a dragon himself, thrusting his fist into the throat of the beast. As it reared back, he used that opening to strike its exposed belly; this flowed into a succession of swift blows. After Fohl unleashed four powerful kicks, the dragon recovered itself and moved in to try and smash him down. Fohl proceeded to summersault the beast, lifting it into the air from where he used its downward trajectory to unleash a final smash into the ground. The dragon crashing into the ground matched perfectly with his killing blow, taking the massive dragon out with a devastating impact. I'd heard him calling for aid from Atla, but I was pretty sure she had nothing to do with his combo. In fact, she'd likely only call him out on everything she thought he'd done wrong.

The gemstone on my shield was flashing in much the same way it did when taunting Raphtalia. That settled it. Atla was still as hard on Fohl as she had ever been in life. I was glad he couldn't hear her, anyway. He was fighting like a monster out there—and a monster full of life, at that.

"Fohl, that was so cool! We need to show off what we can do too!" Keel said, accompanied by the other villagers. He was yipping around in dog mode, keeping the attention of the monsters I had brought in with me focused on the Piensa army. A dog rushing across the battlefield . . . it sounded like something from a Spielberg movie. But the dog in question was a crepe-loving money-maker with a questionable taste in attire. The dragons and monsters all seemed to have decided Keel would be easy pickings and charged toward her.

"A dog! A dog!" one soldier exclaimed in surprise.

"We can't let a dog beat us!" said another.

"Think you can take me down, do you?" Keel yipped back. "Sorry, but you're too slow to catch me!" Whatever Keel was, the other villagers and I had trained her. She weaved easily through the incoming attacks and then through the legs of the Piensa army, off and away to freedom. When one enemy still continued after her, Keel skillfully kicked him away. With a howl, the wolfman flew backward and crashed into his allies.

"That's no ordinary mutt!" one shouted.

"Bye-bye now!" With more woofs, Keel raced away. I was

impressed. Keel kept things loose, never getting too tense. That was definitely one of her strengths.

"What's going on? They are using the same strange techniques . . . the same skills as the glorious hero!" a soldier shouted.

"Don't tell me . . . this is the holy weapon hero who came from another world and his party of hangers-on? But why are they working with the Shield Hero?!" another exclaimed. I was pleased with the chaos all across the battlefield.

"I've heard that the Sewing Kit Hero is working with them," said a general-looking type as I sneaked past, still concealed.

"The cowardly Shield Hero and Whip Hero! What means did they use to summon heroes from other worlds?!" another one shouted. As I slipped onward, I wondered why Mamoru's charisma and the authority of the Shield Hero didn't seem to work on these guys. I guessed we could just chalk it up to warfare.

"Everyone! We are holding the enemy back here! Melty, Wyndia, with me!" Imiya said, taking the lead. The other girls shouted their agreement as they all started to weave some co-operative magic. "Land bereft by the chaos of war! Flow of the Dragon Vein caught up in this sea of conflict! We ask you to spit out that tainted, foul blood! Dragon Vein! Hear our petition and grant it! As the source of your power, we implore you! Let the true way be revealed once more! Open the way before us! Collective Ritual Magic! Continental Cleft!" With a suitable cracking sound, the ground between the Siltran and the dragon battalion forces split apart, spreading wide to the left and right. Back to making bird squawks, Chick—with me and everyone else in my small group still aboard—leapt into the air and crossed over to the safe side of the new crevice. The monsters we left behind, those unable to fly for themselves, turned and fixated completely on the Piensa forces, including the dragons. Faced with the unexpected assault from my horde of monsters, our support magic, my capture of their commander, and the appearance of heroes from another world, the Piensa army was completely overwhelmed. Their command structure was shot to pieces and they were forced to retreat. Even the dragons seemed to realize they were at a disadvantage. Those that remained scattered and fled the field.

"Hey! Bubba and the gang!" Keel dashed over to me. "Welcome back! You were amazing out there!"

"I think I pulled my weight. I hope you see now that there is more than one way to win a battle," I told her.

"Yep, sure do! Who's this guy, anyway?" Keel said, looking at the magician, who I was still roughly holding onto. In the same moment, Ren and the others were moving over as well, keeping an eye on the Piensa forces as they did so.

"A magician who looked like he was in command over there apparently started out here in Siltran. I thought he might make a nice gift for our hosts," I explained, pretty pleased with myself. Keel and the others all looked impressed. It had gone well, even if I said so myself.

"Naofumi, I do think we may have gone a little far," Melty commented. I turned to look back at the Piensa forces, watching them flee as they barely managed to fend off the monsters that I had unleashed on them. They had been more than just a big flock of weaklings, but I wasn't sure how I felt about our actions. I guess I chalked it all up to strategy. It didn't look like they had suffered too many fatalities, apart from the dragons, and there was nothing wrong with whittling down the number of wild monsters.

"All part of the strategy," I mused, looking down into the pretty deep crevice that had been created. Warfare in alternate worlds was quite a crazy thing. I wondered if there was combat in modern Japan that involved changing terrain on such a scale. Digging trenches, traps using bombs, and those things were possible, but probably nothing on this scale. "That settles the fighting for now, anyway. The Piensa army had been defeated. I doubt they will get any ideas about attacking again too soon," I commented. "Melty, you know what to do next."

"I'm on it! We'll seize the narrative at once and spread word around the world about how monsters and new collaborators raced to the aid of Siltran and sent the Piensa army and their dragon battalion packing!" Melty said. This kind of battle wasn't won on the field. We were facing the kind of enemy who would easily make excuses about how cowardly enemy tactics led to their defeat, turning us into the embodiment of evil and turning the world against us. In that case, we needed to strike first and use the rumor mill to our advantage. "Whatever gets spread around now can only help us out! The real battle—the information battle—only starts once the fighting has been won!"

"I will aid you in thiz," the Shadow said, also keen to help. All of this should really put a crimp on any Piensa plans to wage war anytime soon. They wouldn't be invading the Sanctuary anytime soon. I didn't know if they had ever managed that feat or not in the "official" history either.

"I was thinking, Naofumi, that maybe you just sowed the seeds of all the Shield Demon stuff for the future," Melty said. That question was like a knife in my heart—like I might be the one responsible for all the grime I suffered attached to the Shield Hero name. "Bringing in a horde of monsters to defeat an enemy force sounds a lot like a Shield Demon King to me." Melty chose to press the point, perhaps seeing that I wasn't really enjoying the situation. I had long become numb to such names, however. If they wanted a Demon King, I'd give them the cackling king of all evil.

"Did you see the terrified faces of those weaklings as they fled from me?" I laughed. "Wasn't it wonderful?" I laid it on nice and thick.

"You want something like that, do you?" Melty said. She knew I was joking and chuckled along with me. It was nice to have allies who got my sense of humor. "What about Mamoru and Raphtalia? How did I do?" I asked, looking in the direction Mamoru and his party had gone. They were in the forest some distance from the battlefield. I saw smoke rising from the trees. That looked worrying.

We headed in the direction of the smoke.

By the time we drew close to where the smoke was rising, the forest was quiet—perhaps because the fighting had finished. We arrived at the scene to find scratches gouged out of the ground that spoke of the battle that had happened there.

"Mr. Naofumi!" Raphtalia noticed our arrival and came over, accompanied by Mamoru and the others. It didn't look like the Bow Hero was around.

"How did things go here?" I asked.

"It worked well. Their Bow Hero was shocked to hear the Shield Hero was on the battlefield when Mamoru was right here," Raphtalia reported. It sounded like our raid had been a success.

"And? What was the Bow Hero like? Something like It-suki?" I asked.

"Well, he listened to us, and it seemed like he might coop-erate with us depending upon the circumstances. But he also spoke of prioritizing his own goals," Raphtalia replied.

"That sounds about right. That's the Bow Hero," I replied.

"He was like the Sword Hero used to be, but maybe with a bit of a broader perspective on things. I don't think he's going to be a good fit with us," Raphtalia explained. So another hero with a pain-in-the-ass personality. "Unlike the vanguards of the waves, he gave the impression of taking being a hero pretty seriously. He fought in good unison with his allies, which made me think it would be hard to overwhelm him with pure force." He was one of the four heroes, and a legit one at that. I wished Mamoru had been able to get through to him.

"Mamoru tried to negotiate with him," Raphtalia continued, almost reading my thoughts, "but there's something about all of this . . . something behind it that we're not seeing yet." There was something lurking there that even Raphtalia could see. There were numerous possibilities, so I couldn't whittle anything down yet. But if they were stubbornly going to try and use warfare in order to get things done, we could only respond as required. Since we had encountered them here first, that placed righteousness on our side. Now we just needed to strike first before they had time to come back with any complaints. This kind of information warfare was a specialty of Trash and others in his league. Melty and Ruft had absorbed it so thoroughly from spending time at the king's side that I was almost worried for what they might get up to in the future. "He

THE RISING OF THE SHIELD HERO 20   321

did break out into a bit of a cold sweat when he saw my face,"
Raphtalia added.

"Did you show him your hero-hurting sakura stone of destiny?" I said mockingly.

"I knew you would enjoy this, but yes . . . in order to prevent them from realizing I was using a vassal weapon, I used
the sakura stone of destiny katana from the start of the battle,"
she said with a sigh. "They seemed to know it put them at a
disadvantage." So they had some knowledge of being on the
back foot against enemies from Q'ten Lo. That sounded like
something worth asking Mamoru about. "When they heard
that you and the others had defeated the Piensa army, Mr. Naofumi, they beat a hasty retreat. But the Bow Hero seemed to
show some concern for Mamoru prior to departing."

"Concern for him, huh?" I said. It sounded like all this
wasn't exactly what the Bow Hero wanted either. Maybe he was
a hero who had graduated a little from the I'll-do-everything-
however-I-like phase. There had to be some reason he still
stood against us. Here we were in the past, and the heroes were
still all fighting each other. What a pain. "Whatever the reason,
things have worked out pretty much how we wanted them to,"
I concluded. If we had brought an end to their march without having to kill the Bow Hero, that meant victory for us. We
might end up having to fight him again in the future, but this
was more than good enough for now—even if I still couldn't

shake off the feeling I was shaping the future antagonistic relationship between the Shield and Bow Heroes. I wondered if maybe he had really just wanted to help us out. Then Mamoru finished talking to his allies and came over.

"It all worked out as planned, Naofumi. Thank you for drawing the Bow Hero away. It sounds like they won't be bothering us again for a while," Mamoru said.

"Not that we really understand anything that side is thinking," I said. "Oh, Mamoru, I did pick up a little something for you." I told him about capturing the bossy strategist from among the enemy forces. He had apparently started out here in Siltran. Traitors needed to be suitably punished. At that moment, he was trussed up back in the Siltran main camp. Even if Piensa made overtures to get him back, there didn't seem to be any reason to listen to them. "You can get him to spill his guts, and then . . . well, spill his guts, if you like," I told him.

"Mr. Naofumi, you have the most evil grin on your face," Raphtalia said.

"You bet I do. Betrayal should carry a heavy price. In any case, we want to stop them from even thinking about attacking again for the length of time we are here," I replied.

"Yes, of course. Thank you so much for all of your help. You seem very capable at this kind of thing—it makes me think the future must be a hard place," Mamoru said.

"It has its moments," I replied. I was the Shield Hero who

had been framed almost as soon as I arrived, cast out without allies or coin, and who couldn't even attack for himself. At least Mamoru had some ability to attack; he couldn't understand what I had been through. I wouldn't still be here if I wasn't pretty tough. It would take more than being sent into the past to make me complain now.

"This means you've protected my little old research subject. Maintenance of order is nothing to sniff at," Holn said.

"My village is more than just a subject for your research," I pointed out.

"You've been a massive help, Naofumi," R'yne chipped in. "Pretty rare for us to get out an attack with so little damage taken. Just hearing about you plowing into the enemy with a horde of monsters gets me all worked up over here! I'm amazed that worked against a bunch of dragons. Mamoru is the Shield Hero too. Maybe he should try copying it? Hey, Mamoru? Are you listening?" She was as breezy and casual as ever. She really did love to talk. I wish she'd take a note from S'yne's book—but I had my suspicions that S'yne was actually something of a talker herself. Her sister definitely was. I wondered if even a trait like that was passed down by blood. A terrifying thought. Mamoru's face looked tense too.

When I thought about the situation, it sounded like someone who could well be an ancestor of Raphtalia's was also stirring up trouble with the heroes in this time period. I was suddenly nervous about meeting with them. If we ended up in a scrap, at least we had the sakura stone of destiny weapons to fight back with. Raw strength wasn't going to count for much against us.

"Okay. We're heading back. We can hold meetings or whatever later. Melty and Ruft can handle that stuff," I said.

"Why are you leaving now? We need to report our damages and then hold a celebration for this victory," Mamoru said. He still seemed full of energy.

"Hey, guys . . . I've been up all night getting ready to pull off this attack. I'm getting sleepy. The sun is up now anyway. Any kind of celebration can be held after it gets dark," I said. Sure, I could stave off sleep for a pretty long time, and the protection of the shield could help keep me going. But my exhaustion was really building up. I needed some sack time. "I've been preparing all sorts of dishes for you too. Look forward to it," I told him. His castle was a bit poor on the provisions, but Holn had modified more of the bioplants and our food shortages were easing as a result. The village was doing okay, but everyone ate so much I was starting to worry about our production capabilities. That said, failing to provide a huge feast after a big operation like this would significantly damage morale.

Mamoru looked at me and then at Raphtalia.

"This is how we've done things so far," I told him.

"Okay then. We'll mop things up and handle all the details here," Mamoru replied.

"See you later." With that, we retreated. Keel and the other villagers had managed to get some sleep while we were preparing for the fighting, and so they stuck around to help out. The remains of the monsters I had led into battle and the dragons were carried away, processed as required, and delivered to the village. Once I finished my nap, I came out to find a veritable pile of monsters and wasn't really sure what to do with them. Then I put the cooks who hadn't done any fighting to work.

Epilogue: Different Constellations

We had so many people to accommodate now. We invited Mamoru, his soldiers, and his other collaborators to come to the village for a large victory party. It was being held outside—more on the scale of a festival, to be honest.

"Wow! That tastes great!"

"What a strange plant. Is this edible too?"

"A tree that grows bread! Whatever will they think of next?"

Everyone seemed pretty impressed with the produce of our village and enjoyed the meat dishes—including some flavorful dragon—the village cooks and I prepared. It seemed celebrations in the past weren't much different from those in the future, however; all the small-animal-type demi-humans and therianthropes running around created a bit of a different atmosphere. They also all had that look in their eyes that was unique to those who had come from regions that lacked food. Seeing people with a lingering hint of desperation in their eyes (the eat-now-or-I-might-not-survive look) tucking into this veritable feast gave me mixed feelings.

"Bring more in and get it cooked as quick as you can. Don't worry too much about the taste. Just suck it in!" I said. All the food I had prepared in advance had been consumed in a flash, and now we were making barbeque from some newly defeated monsters. Roasting them whole might have seemed like one possible idea, but that was actually a pretty difficult, time-consuming process, and the resulting meat didn't taste very good anyway. Get it wrong and you could end up eating meat that was still raw.

Still, running a party like this was great experience for the village cooks. Monster meat needed to be completely drained and the sinews cut before one could even consider eating it. The meat that hadn't been prepared properly or that didn't taste that nice could be used to feed our own monsters. Or it could be processed into fertilizer. It could also be used for shield compounding, so there was no waste—everything got used.

"Interesting. I had some knowledge of the skeletal structure and musculature, and I've performed some precursory examinations myself, but I've never done such a thorough dissection before. This is a great opportunity for me, so let me help out," Holn said. She was very passionate about her research, I'd give her that.

"Oh? You don't know the best places to cut them, ancestor? For this monster—" Rat was showing off, putting on her teacher face.

"Here, here, and here," I finished for her. "If you cut it here, it can't walk."

"You have a good eye for observing monsters, Archduke.

If you could swing a weapon in battle, I think you'd clean up quite nicely," Rat observed.

"Maybe. Monsters will use magic to recover themselves even while you fight though, so you can't count on just knowledge like this," I said. They could often pull off unexpected movements too. Just another one of the rules you had to live with in an alternative world where healing magic was a thing. Healing magic went as far down the tree as you could imagine, right down to bizarre but useful stuff like healing tooth cavities. I took a moment to wonder how that worked—maybe gathering calcium from around the rest of the body. I wasn't quite skilled enough with magic to understand something that complex. "There are ways you can defeat monsters to make them taste better. Would you like to know more?" I asked.

"You bet!" Holn replied. Her intellectual curiosity was clearly tingling. I didn't see the harm in sharing this information.

"A hunter would tell you this too, but the secret is to finish your prey off without causing any undue stress. Any stress at the moment of death makes the meat taste worse. One blow, pop! You want to finish them quick," I said.

"That sounds pretty fundamental to me," Holn said.

"But the basics are important! It might be something unique to this world, or alternate worlds, or whatever, but I've also noticed that the monster seeming to accept its death makes it taste better too," I said. A monster that put up a good struggle and went down fighting didn't seem to degrade in flavor as much. Maybe it was a sentiment on their part of not wasting their death. Just like the quality of the blood provided by the Demon Dragon had been so high, the monster's consciousness might have an effect on the quality of their meat. That was an aspect unthinkable back in Japan. The produce that we got from the monsters we kept as livestock, such as eggs and milk, might also fall into this category.

"I've heard some talk of a similar nature," Holn admitted. "So there might be some truth to the idea that monster meat obtained from a close battle tastes better."

"My research also suggests that defeating a monster while imbuing it with some life force will keep the flesh almost in a living state for a short while, making it easier to dress and process," I said. Maintaining a "live" state meant the blood would not seep into the flesh, meaning it could be drained completely and would taste and smell even better. Aging the meat still tasted the best, but it was a start.

"That's because the cells are activated by the life force," Rat theorized.

"Sounds right to me. We already know that not only in cooking, but when producing anything, using life force can improve the quality of it," I said.

"Such wide applications. So much room for research," Holn said.

"Please, try to stay focused on how to get us home," I said.

"I know, I know," she replied. I wasn't sure that she did. Her reply felt too glib for my liking. Holn did seem to be in a very good mood though, maybe because we had struck such a blow to the dragon battalion. I got the impression that she didn't like dragons much. Something there nagged at me, but I wasn't going to pull too hard on that thread.

"There's one final trick, but it's only available to heroes. You can place the corpses of poor-quality monsters into the weapon, turn them into meat, and once the quality is normalized again, you can cover the rest with your cookery skills," I explained.

"Wow. Such a cunning ploy, and only available to heroes! It's not even a way to defeat them that makes them taste better—it's a cheeky way to enhance them after you've defeated them," Holn said.

"Just the kind of cunning I'd expect from you, Archduke. How much of today's cooking relied on such methods?" Rat inquired.

"Enough! If it tastes good, that's all that matters!" I replied.

"Okay then. Little old me is going to get back to my little old research," Holn said. She started off back toward the lab like it was the most natural thing in the world. Rat started after her with suspicion in her eyes. "You want something?" Holn asked.

"I've seen you looking at my Mikey," Rat replied. "Don't try any funny business, okay?"

"That's for him to decide for himself, isn't it?" Holn responded. "You seem to have put a lot of work into him, but just what is that thing? I can't back down until you let me know."

"Mikey is my precious research sample! He's clumsy but lovable and can't come out from his tank due to a terrible accident, but one day I'll let him emerge again!" Rat said. It almost looked like the two of them were fighting, but they seemed to be getting along, so I decided to leave them to their own devices. I'd let Wyndia know to report to me if either of our two resident crackpots tried anything too risky.

"This is the band of traders Naofumi leads. He is a collaborator with Shield Hero Mamoru. I hope we can all get along," said Ruft, making introductions to some of the soldiers.

"Dafu," said Raph-chan II. Ruft was different than Raphtalia in that he was politically minded and also had some understanding of trade, which was a big help. Our village had popped up from the future onto the border between two nations, which meant soldiers defending that border were likely to drop by often. We might not be in a bad spot, if this was peacetime—at least in terms of being able to obtain things from other nations. The soldiers Ruft was talking to only had good things to say.

"This is all such a big help."

"I've heard the talk, but I'm so glad Hero Mamoru has found such powerful allies."

"Now the people of our nation will surely survive into the future."

"We have to come together and fight off the waves!" The Siltran soldiers had sublime looks on their faces. I wasn't completely confident in the capabilities of demi-human therianthropes, but this had definitely boosted their morale.

"Bubba, Bubba! If we don't cook more meat, everything is going to be gone in an instant! Hey, Fohl, you help out too! You can cook, right?" Keel yapped.

"Hold on! I'm not as good as Brother!" Fohl objected.

"But Bubba said the kind of flavors you like suit the taste buds of the people in this nation, so I bet you can make something delicious!" Keel said.

"You can do it!" I offered from the sidelines.

"Bah! Why do I have to cook for you all? Atla, is this also for the good of the village? I think I'm starting to lose my way. Should I continue to take Brother as my target?" Fohl asked, mainly to himself.

"Fohl seems to be struggling with something," Keel said. She was sharp. The issue was that... Well, she was the issue.

We continued to process the bodies of the monsters, making sure nothing was wasted.

Mamoru and his allies had also brought his kids along to

enjoy the victory celebration, and they were all eating their fill too.

"Mamoru, we need to do something to thank Naofumi for this," R'yne said.

"Indeed. What can we give them though?" Mamoru replied. Siltran was struggling with recovery from all these attacks, after all. They weren't going to be able to give me much.

"What about this Sanctuary that Piensa is after? Could we go and take a look around?" I asked.

"There's not much there, to be honest . . . but if you want to go, I can arrange it for you soon. But that's not really a reward." Mamoru made a noise that let me know he was thinking. "We don't have money, food, or resources. The best I can do is issue rights within our nation or passes for travel to other nations . . . and rank, I suppose."

"I don't need rank," I quickly stated. This was the past, so rank might come in useful if we were going to be here a long time. But with Mamoru helping us out, I didn't really feel the need for that. Maybe getting Melty a temporary position would make negotiations easier, but that was about the only use I could think for it. And again, with Mamoru helping us, it didn't really feel needed.

"I didn't think so. Then maybe helping Holn to work out how to get you home?" Mamoru suggested.

"She's working on that well enough already. You're doing

plenty. No need to worry about it too much," I said. Maintaining a sense of debt toward us might make future negotiations easier too. Having something to hold over them could be important, but we needed Mamoru to feel things were resolved too. "In which case, can you share any monster materials that you and the other Siltran forces have collected with us?" I asked. "I'm sure you know what I'm after." The heroes could obtain new weapons from various materials coming from all around the world. Receiving such materials from one in authority could be more than enough of a reward.

"Very well. I will make the arrangements," Mamoru agreed.

"We could always hit the hot springs together. No better way to get to know someone than in the buff," said R'yne. I was starting to worry that she was getting a bit sexual with me.

"I can show you to a secret spot I found. That could be nice," Mamoru said.

"That could be a good way to ensure you have good intentions," I said, still keeping my cards close. Since I'd come here, it felt like I was bathing in hot springs even more than I had at home—like on the Cal Mira islands.

As I pondered these things, a strange look came over Mamoru's face.

"Filolials, huh?" He was looking over at a bunch of the birds as they stuffed their beaks with food. They didn't exist in this time from the sound of it, so maybe that was from where his interest stemmed. From his perspective, we were from the future. So we had access to futuristic technology. If we could share some of that with him, he might make new gear for facing off with the waves. I had to hope that Holn and Rat would work together and come up with something to compete with the bizarre inventions S'yne's sister's forces kept coming up with—something to really knock their socks off. Something a bit more exciting than that useful but boring bread tree!

"Mamoru. . ." R'yne was observing my conversation with Mamoru with a look of concern on her face that definitely caught my attention. Cian breathed his name as well, looking between him and me.

"You know now is the time to be happy everyone is still alive, right?" I said.

"That's right. Well said. Cian, I want you to eat your fill and grow up big and strong too," Mamoru told the girl.

"Okay! I'm going to get strong too and protect everyone from nasty wars!" Cian said with a look filled with conviction. It sounded like the villagers had started to influence her too.

As we chatted, I saw Ren eating with Wyndia and Eclair. The three of them seemed to spend a lot of time together now. I also got the impression that the two girls could be a little hard on Ren, but maybe that was just me. I found a point to depart the conversation with Mamoru and moved over to this other group.

"Please, stop trying to take care of me all the time!" Wyndia was just saying to Ren, looking quite upset about it. Ren stammered some kind of apology. "No need to play the guardian with me! I can make my way through life alone, and right now this is the place I belong! It's the same for you, right, Ren?" It sounded like Wyndia was entering her rebellious phase—or maybe she was just pissed at Ren always trying to smother her. "That said . . . I know I said this before, but . . . thank you."

"No problem," Ren managed.

"I took a moment to think about it again, and I realized what has happened to us here really is quite insane. I wonder how my father would have reacted to all this," Eclair pondered.

"He was the original ruler of the territory that Naofumi now holds, wasn't he?" Ren asked.

"That's right. I want to become the same kind of ruler as he was, a wonderful man, trusted and loved by the people. But . . . I'm honestly not sure what I should be doing in this time," Eclair admitted. Even before coming to the past, she had just been living in the village, operating with Ren. She was a guard for Melty as well, but she clearly wanted to achieve more than that. At least she was continuing with her Hengen Muso Style training. "I've said it before, haven't I? I've seen the way Hero Iwatani and Queen Melty have worked to restore their territory . . . and I'm ashamed of myself for not being close to being able to do the same thing."

"I know your best is good enough, Eclair. You can do it. I'll help you," Ren said firmly.

"If you help, Ren, we'll just end up with a bunch of fanatics who want a piece of the Sword Hero," Eclair bemoaned.

"You could say the same thing about Naofumi. What's wrong with me, then?" Ren replied.

"This is a hard one," she said, thinking. "Would it be wrong for me to use you like that, Ren? I mean, everyone uses everyone else to some extent at the top, don't they? Hero Iwatani, Queen Melty, the former queen, the king . . . all of them have used each other. But I'm not sure I'm at that level . . ." Eclair crossed her arms and really started to think. She was a serious, straight-laced woman, but also more a warrior than a ruler. It was hard for her to understand that mindset. "Observing Hero Iwatani and the king—King Trash—I understand that sometimes you have to make decisions that cost you things that are important to you. I'm just not sure where to draw that line myself," she continued.

"Those are exactly the times that you have me, Wyndia, Naofumi, and Queen Melty around for, right? You can discuss anything with us, anytime you need to," Ren said.

"Yes, good point . . . In that case, Ren, I need to discuss something with you," Eclair said.

"Sure. What is it?" he replied.

"Ruftmila, Raphtalia's cousin, only really joined us fairly

recently and yet I'm starting to feel like he's beating me in all sorts of ways. In this last battle, look at everything he achieved . . . and it will only be the same in future battles, I'm sure. Can you tell me how to achieve the same kind of growth myself?" she asked. Ren gave a visible gulp. Eclair had really gone for the throat with her first question! Eclair had numerous points of contact with Ruft, and the two of them were close in terms of position. That might have given her an awareness of him as her rival. Furthermore, if that was the case, then it was true that Eclair was losing to Ruft at the moment. The combat side of things would need a stricter comparison, but if Ruft managed to learn life force, then Eclair was going to have trouble defeating him at anything. I had to have Ren tell her later that having a rival around could actually be a good way to grow stronger. Ruft was going to continue to make his own impressive progress, day after day, and she would have to try and keep up with that.

It made me wonder if I was really doing a good job of leading myself. It felt like the only real instructions I was giving were about trading. I did say things that I hoped would boost morale, and I had used my experience in a guild for an online game to create an environment favoring the villagers. In Q'ten Lo, Raphtalia had taken on the role of Heavenly Emperor. But all of this didn't really feel like being a "ruler."

I looked over at Mamoru. I could tell with a single glance at the soldiers gathered in the village that all the expectations of Siltran were focused on him. They had been willing to stand firm even in the face of the dragon battalion. Even if they weren't the most highly suited demi-humans or therianthropes for combat, they had a willingness to go into battle. The same thing could be said about those in my village, even if they weren't the strongest species either—Keel and the others would still fight without backing down. The fear of loss, losing those they loved or losing their homes, had been carved into the psyche of these slaves. We were both Shield Heroes, of course, meaning the trust people placed in us was also very important. Maybe I should tell Eclair not to study swinging her sword, but rather how to be a good ruler.

"I think maybe," Wyndia suggested, "that the way you and Ruft watch Trash and Melty work, Eclair, is probably all a bit different. Eclair, you just let the operations Trash proposed kind of wash over you, but Ruft was watching everything closely."

"I see what you are saying," Eclair admitted. "Honestly, though . . . I couldn't possibly remember all of those operations like that. Do you think I have to?"

"You're the ruler, right?" I told her. "So you can leave that stuff to someone who can handle it." I had to say that Eclair seemed more like a L'Arc type to me—throwing everything to skilled subordinates and then bearing the brunt when a tough decision had to be made. I wondered why so many people around me, like Rishia and Ethnobalt, were so keen to overextend themselves and push themselves to tackle challenges that seemed far beyond their skill sets. Looking at Eclair, I could kind of understand how Melty felt.

Having these thoughts, I looked over at Raphtalia and Melty, noticing them a little distance away and looking up at the sky. It reminded me of when we had to sleep outside during the Melty kidnapping thing. That was a long time ago now. Filo had been there, but she wasn't here now.

We needed to get back to our own time, and quickly. If we took too long, the stress of dealing with Motoyasu was likely to bring poor Filo to her knees—like a certain Sword Hero before her.

"What's up? Can you see something up there?" I asked Raphtalia.

"Oh, Mr. Naofumi. I was just looking at the stars with Melty," Raphtalia explained.

"Okay. Did you see anything useful?" I asked.

"Actually, there are numerous famous constellations missing. There are others that I recognize, but I guess this is something that can happen too, isn't it?" Raphtalia said. I looked up into the sky with them. I'd done the same thing in the hot springs on the Cal Mira islands, but I couldn't remember any of the constellations from back then.

This was the world prior to the fusing . . . so it probably made sense that certain familiar constellations from the future wouldn't be present now. That would suggest that entire universes were being merged together—but I guessed they all came as a package deal. It probably made some kind of bizarre sense to say we were talking about entire worlds being merged together.

"It feels like we've crossed a lot more distance than just hopping to another alternate world," I commented.

"I know. I never thought we would come into the past . . . The world really is full of so many mysterious things," Raphtalia agreed.

"I hope Filo is doing okay," Melty muttered, looking up at the stars.

"We just have to hope she can give Motoyasu the slip," I replied. Seeing Melty still worrying about Filo, even at a time like this, I was moved by how deep their friendship was.

"I thought I was going to be able to leave these trips to bizarre places to you and the others, Naofumi. I can't believe I got caught up in this," Melty said.

"It wasn't exactly my choice to come here either. It was an enemy attack," I reminded her.

"I know that. Complaining about it isn't going to change anything either. You've fallen into enemy traps before, Naofumi, and you've survived. We need to learn from your example! Let's pick up some incredible lost technology from the past and return to the future even better than before!" Melty said optimistically.

THE RISING OF THE SHIELD HERO 20

"Well said. We need to be just like Mr. Naofumi and return to our time as quickly as we possibly can," Raphtalia said. I wasn't sure about them trying to be like me, but they had the right idea for getting through this.

"You're right, girls. We still don't even really have any clues about how to get back yet, but we need to make whoever did this to us pay for it," I said. Just like the magician we had caught today, we'd make them pay.

"I should have known that's where your mind would go, Naofumi," Melty said, shaking her head.

"Not to quote the Demon Dragon, but that's one of my best features, right?" I joked.

"You think your bloodthirsty desire for revenge is a good thing?" Melty shot back.

"I guess you girls get to decide, in the end," I replied.

"Things have worked out so far, so I can't deny the effect it has had," Melty admitted. "Let's just keep working toward getting home."

"Never giving up is very important, I will give you that. You can count on me," Raphtalia said, neatly sidestepping the whole bloodthirsty bit. We might have been kicked into a new type of alternate world—right back into the past—but with the unfamiliar stars twinkling overhead, the three of us vowed more strongly than ever that we were going to make it back home.

The Rising of the Shield Hero Vol. 20
(TATE NO YUUSHA NO NARIAGARI Vol.20)
© Aneko Yusagi 2018
First published in Japan in 2018 by KADOKAWA CORPORATION, Tokyo.
English translation rights arranged with KADOKAWA CORPORATION, Tokyo.

ISBN: 978-1-64273-105-7

Written by Aneko Yusagi
Character Design Minami Seira
English Edition Published by One Peace Books 2021

Printed in Canada
2 3 4 5 6 7 8 9 10

One Peace Books
43-32 22nd Street STE 204 Long Island City New York 11101
www.onepeacebooks.com